Trouble Brewing

Spruce Grove Cozy Mysteries, Volume 5

B. Allison Miller

Published by Barbara Allison Miller, 2022.

This is a work of fiction. Similarities to real people, places, or events are entirely coincidental.

TROUBLE BREWING

First edition. November 25, 2022.

Copyright © 2022 B. Allison Miller.

ISBN: 979-8215195673

Written by B. Allison Miller.

"I am a firm believer in the people. If given the truth, they can be depended upon to meet any national crisis. The great point is to bring them the real facts, and beer."
— *Abraham Lincoln*

ONE

A Friday Evening in Late August

"Why don't we park your car at the back," my fiancé David Moore suggested from his seat beside me. I pulled my SUV into the muddy dirt field reserved as a parking lot for the county farm show. I waited as a teenage boy wearing a high visibility vest and waving a glow stick directed me to an available parking spot. "If we're in the back, we'll be out quickest when we leave," David said. I shrugged and rolled down my driver's side window and addressed the young parking attendant.

"Oh hi, Sherman! I didn't know you were working the event," I said to the boy as I recognized him. Sherman is the quarterback of the Spruce Grove Spartan's high school football team. Sherman is quite talented, and everyone expects that he'll be recruited by one of the Big Ten teams before he graduates high school in the spring. "Is it okay if I park back there?" I pointed to the darkest corner of the lot. In the passenger seat behind me, my friend Joe Binder cranked the window down.

"I guess so," Sherman replied, he peered into the car and saw his assistant football coach, Joe, in the seat behind me. "Hey, Coach!"

"Hey, Sherman. I hope you aren't working too late tonight. There's a big game tomorrow," Joe said. "The Montgomery Mustangs were nine and one last season."

"Don't worry, Coach," Sherman said with enthusiasm, "I'm off in thirty minutes, and I'm ready for the Mustangs."

"Good man!" Joe said.

"You better not stay out too late either, Coach," Sherman joked, then the tall, friendly, football player waved me forward with the glow stick.

I pulled my old SUV to the back of the lot, parked, and turned off the engine eager to get out and walk around the Spruce County fairgrounds. Somewhere there was a funnel cake calling my name. My intention was to eat junk food all night, visit the livestock pens, and go home to crash from a sugar-induced coma. I love the Spruce County Farm Show!

"Where to first?" I asked as I stepped out of the car. David, Joe, and his wife, Cassie, joined me as I dodged mud puddles and walked down the slick wet turf toward the farm show's attractions. The recent heavy summer rains left everything more than a little waterlogged. I could already hear the sounds of the barkers. I saw the lights of the tilt-a-whirl, and smelled the hot grease that sizzled frying all the delicious confections that I hoped to eat that evening.

David looked down at the Farm Show program that he'd printed from the County website earlier. "It looks like the craft beer contest is happening right now. I suggest we check it out. We may even discover a future favorite."

"The beer brewer's contest is a new event at the farm show this year," Cassie—who happens to be my best friend—replied. "I don't mind telling you, there are a few residents opposed to the contest. The vote at the county planning meeting was sixty percent for the contest and forty percent against it this year."

"Yeah, I seem to recall that there was a lot of concern about having alcohol at the farm show. In the past, the hardest beverage you could get at the county farm show was the coffee served in the 4-H tent," Joe added. "Some residents think having alcohol here changes the character of the event. They believe beer makes this a less wholesome gathering or something."

"Huh," David said with a chuckle as he reached for my hand so he could hold it while we walked together. "It's hard to believe a community of farmers would be so opposed to beer. After all, there's a long history of brewing in this part of the country. Even Ben Franklin himself liked to indulge on occasion." I was too busy checking out the food stalls we passed to partake in the conversation. I smelled

TROUBLE BREWING

something sweet in the air—churros. My tummy rumbled in anticipation of receiving a treat.

"At any rate, there's bound to be a few upset people here tonight," Cassie said. Our little quartet made its way down the midway. Cassie added, "I heard that Wilma Platt started a Spruce Grove Temperance Society for the farm show. So far, there are only a handful of members."

"*Temperance Society?*" David asked with another hearty chuckle, "Are you serious? What year is it?"

"I am serious," replied Cassie. "Wilma is serious too. I overheard her speaking to Father George at Magic Beans. Wilma plans to stage a loud protest at the competition tonight."

"What did Father George say about Wilma's plan?" I asked having finally tuned into the conversation. Father George is my priest—or he would be if I wasn't a fallen-away Catholic—that's something I am working on. Ever since my engagement to David, my mother has urged me to rejoin the church in the hope that Father George will preside over our wedding vows.

"Actually, Father George told Wilma that he wasn't opposed to indulging in a cold beer on a hot day," Cassie replied with a smile. "Did you hear that Scooter Wells entered the competition?"

"Scooter? I can't even imagine Scooter brewing beer. He's so straightlaced and nerdy," Joe said with a laugh.

Scotty "Scooter" Wells is the Assistant Principal at Spruce Grove High School. He's also a former schoolmate of ours. Scotty graduated after Joe, Cassie, and me. The slight, nerdy, young man made a habit of following Cassie around like a lost puppy during our senior year. To my knowledge, Scooter has never gotten over his crush on Cassie—even though Joe and Cassie married years ago and have a daughter. Joe still finds the crush amusing—he's not threatened by Scooter's affection for Cassie at all. Joe is a big, popular, handsome, ex-football player. Cassie, a former cheerleader and high school librarian, is too kind to say anything dismissive to Scooter, but I find the man creepy.

"Actually, Joe," David interjected, "there is a lot of science in brewing. You might joke about Scotty's nerdy nature, but it won't surprise me if he comes up with an interesting beer. Scotty majored in Chemistry in college before he went on to get a Master's degree that helped him land the Assistant Principal's position. The farm show program says Scotty's beer is a pilsner called Queen Casandra."

"What?" Cassie asked with a gasp.

"Oh my gosh, you were the muse for Scooter's beer!" I exclaimed with a laugh. Poor Cassie. It appeared that my bestie would never escape Scooter Wells' affection.

"That has to be a typo," Cassie replied as she reached for David's program. She took the paper in her hand, scanned it, and shook her head. "Okay, it's not a typo. I don't understand Scooter sometimes. Why would he do that?"

Joe spoke, "That guy has a lot of nerve. I mean, I'm not threatened by Scooter, but doesn't he realize how creepy and inappropriate it is to pursue my wife?"

"Well," David interjected again, "in Greek mythology, Cassandra's story is interesting. She was a prophet who only told the truth, but no one ever believed her. It was her fate."

"Meaning?" I asked as I squeezed my brainy fiancé's hand. David's brain is like an encyclopedia. I knew there was a point to the tale.

David shrugged. "Isn't it possible Scotty didn't name the beer after Cassie? He could have been aiming for something else. You know—you drink too much beer, and you might say things that no one will believe."

"Nice try," Joe said to David as we made our way to the craft beer tent. "I'm sure Scooter thinks that naming his beer after Cassie will make her sit up and take notice of him."

"You don't have to worry, Joe. I'm afraid I am quite smitten with my husband." Cassie stood on her tippy-toes and kissed Joe's cheek.

TROUBLE BREWING

We arrived at the large, white, canvass tent that housed the brewing competition. My feet felt soaked because I'd insisted on wearing sneakers instead of sensible hiking boots like my friends. I am a tree farmer, and I wear work boots five days a week for work. I try to wear comfy shoes whenever I am not working. Unfortunately, because of the mud, my sneakers went from comfy to cold and squishy in about five minutes. I squish-walked down the aisleway in the tent behind my friends.

"The farm show is no place for alcohol!" shouted Wilma Platt as she waved a sign—nearly hitting me in the head with it. Instinctively, I raised my hands to push the sign out of my way. The sign had large black letters against a white background, "Keep the Farm Show Dry!" From what I could see, Wilma was the only protester at the event.

"Careful, Wilma," I said as I passed her. "You could hurt someone with that sign."

Wilma pulled the hood of her yellow raincoat over her tight, silver updo and grunted, "Watch yourself, girlie." She pointed the wooden cane that she held in her other hand at me.

By arriving to the farm show late, we'd managed to miss the preliminary competition which weeded out all but four brewers. I felt grateful that I didn't have to witness the entire competition.

My friends and I joined a small crowd of observers—there were only thirty or so people in the crowd under the tent. Despite the small size of the crowd and the damp breezes of the summer evening, the air under the tent felt clammy and smelled of hops. The damp, smelly atmosphere made me feel a bit nauseous. I hoped the awards ceremony would end quickly, and I could stand outside in the fresh air and find a nice pastry or French fries to settle my queasy stomach.

The remaining four brewing contestants assembled on stage. To my surprise, Scooter Wells was one of the four. Nearby, a table contained four identical looking trophies that resembled golden beer mugs on pedestals. I imagined that the front plates on the awards specified whether they were for first, second, or third prize.

A loudspeaker crackled to life and one of the judges, Norman Hammer—the owner of Spruce Grove's local hardware store—spoke.

"We are ready to announce the winners of the first annual craft brewing competition. First, I want to say, that all the brewers who competed today should be proud of their efforts. We had ten independent brewers competing, and I don't mind telling you, we judges had a very difficult time narrowing down the top beers. I hope that you all plan to enter the competition again next year.

"Seated before us, we have the top four finalists. As you may or may not know, we will award three trophies as well as a framed honorable mention certificate. The top prize is the Golden Pint Trophy and a check for five hundred dollars. Second prize is the Silver Pint Trophy and one hundred dollars, and the third prize is the Bronze Pint Trophy and fifty dollars. Now, without further delay, I will announce our winners.

"The honorable mention goes to the Lawbreaker Lager submitted by Zach Grimes." Norman handed a certificate to Zach—a big, middle-aged man with a round face and short-cropped graying hair. I didn't know Zach well, but I had heard rumors about him—rumors about a criminal past. From what happened next, I guess Wilma heard the rumors too.

"Zach Grimes is a criminal! Don't let criminals compete in the farm show! He lost his rights when he broke the law!" Wilma shouted as she stomped and waved her sign. She managed to drown out the applause that Zach earned.

I saw Zach's face grow red. It was no secret that Zach was recently released from prison. He served three years for fraud, but I didn't know the details of his conviction because I was living in New York when Zach was arrested.

TROUBLE BREWING

To Norman's credit, he didn't let Wilma's outburst prevent him from presenting the rest of the awards. He cleared his throat to regain everyone's attention. "Next, the bronze trophy goes to our very own Assistant Principal, Scott Wells. His refreshing, Czech-style Pilsner is Queen Casandra—a delightful little blonde."

Cassie blushed, Joe and I laughed, and once again, Wilma's angry shouts interrupted the applauding crowd. She shook her sign and yelled, "Shame on you, Scotty Wells! You are a professional educator! Think of the impressionable children! You shouldn't keep your post if you want to brew beer!"

Scooter shook his head at Wilma's comment but smiled when Norman handed him a large, shiny trophy and the check.

"I have to say," Norman continued, "the competition for the gold and silver awards was tough. Both beers were excellent examples of their styles. I don't mind telling you that the other judges and I had to go back and sample them a few times before we chose our winner."

"Boo!" Wilma called out.

I scanned the crowd and saw that most of the observers seemed to be angry with the head of the tiny Temperance Society. Many of them stared darts at the silver-haired woman holding the sign. Wilma didn't seem to mind the negative attention she was getting.

"As I was saying," Norman continued after he cleared his throat, "if I seem a bit wobbly, you can blame extra samples of the delicious beers for that." The judge stopped speaking so that the audience could laugh at his corny joke. We obliged.

"The silver trophy goes to an interesting chamomile whit beer named Sunnyside Wheat. The brewer is none other than our resident yogi, Poppy Flint. I tell you what; if I had known that yoga and meditation included beer, I might have joined your class months ago. Namaste, Poppy." Norman handed the silver medal trophy to the petite, young, flower child. Poppy was the proprietor of the *Namast-Stay* Yoga Studio in downtown Spruce Grove.

"It's never too late to start yoga," Poppy replied to Norman with a wink. She pushed her long, thick, wavy red hair back from her face, and smiled at the Norman. Her disobedient waves fell over her face again.

"Boo!" Called Wilma, "Poppy, your third eye is blind! You should have listened to me!"

I shook my head. Wilma was going too far with her insults and slurs. I wondered where the security guards were. My second oldest friend, Brian Gold, often provided security for local events when he wasn't on patrol for the Spruce Grove Police Department. I didn't see Brian anywhere.

"And last but not least—if you can't do the math, shame on you—our final award—the gold trophy—goes to Jack Indigo for his Scream and Shout Stout. Jack also wins a check for five hundred dollars. I hope he uses it to continue making delicious beer. Congratulations! Let's hear it again for all our contestants!"

The crowd clapped.

Jack stood to receive his trophy and an envelope that, presumably held his check. It was hard not to notice the colorful tattoos that adorned both of Jack's arms. He even had a tattoo that ran up from beneath the collar of his t-shirt and wrapped around his neck.

"Jack! I always say that the greater number of tattoos a man has, the lower his IQ!" Screeched Wilma as she waved her protest sign.

Jack frizzled at the verbal attack but shook Norman's outstretched hand all the same.

"Wow," said Joe, "Do you think Wilma thought of those insults beforehand or did she come up with them off the cuff?"

"Maybe she's been sampling the beers," Cassie joked.

"She's lucky no one has carted her off," I replied, still looking for Brian. "Who is providing the security tonight?"

"Not Brian, if that's what you're wondering," Joe said as if he was reading my mind. "He's been putting in too many hours at the station lately. He can't do security for a while."

TROUBLE BREWING

"Oh," I replied.

"Thank you all for attending this spectacular event. And thank you to our contestants," Norman said into his loudspeaker. "And a reminder, the herding dog competition will begin in ring three in fifteen minutes. The mud bog starts in the arena in ten minutes. Have a good night! Enjoy the rest of the farm show."

"The herding dog competition sounds fun," Cassie said as the four of us began to walk away from the tent. "I love watching those dogs. They're so intelligent."

"Hey, Cassie! Wait up!" The unmistakable foghorn voice of Scooter Wells met our ears.

I turned and saw Scooter approaching us. He carried a trophy, and his face was pink with the effort of jogging while carrying his prize.

"Hey Scotty," Cassie greeted the man. "Congratulations on your win."

"Thanks, Cassie," Scooter said with a wide grin. "This is the first trophy I've ever won! I wish I could give you a sample of Casandra, but we aren't permitted to provide beer to the crowd. Unfortunately, the permit for the competition specifies that only the judges can taste the beer. They hope to get a full license to sell samples next year. If you want, you can stop by my place sometime and taste your namesake."

"Uh…" Cassie looked and sounded like she was taken aback by Scooter's suggestion.

For the record, this wasn't the first time that Scooter asked Cassie to join him at one of his homes. The assistant principal invited Cassie to his vacation cabin in the woods the previous winter. I couldn't decide if Scooter was clueless or if he was conniving with his invitations.

"Namesake, huh?" Joe stepped forward towards Scooter. "You named a beer after my wife?"

"Uh, well, my beer is a blond—a pilsner—and when I was trying to come up with a name for the competition…well… Cassie is the first blonde I could think of," Scooter said. His face flushed and he clutched his trophy to his chest.

"Funny, it sounds like we have that in common. Cassie is the first blonde I think of too. Only, she's my wife," Joe countered. He wrapped an arm around Cassie's waist. Was he jealous of Scooter?

"Maybe you should say you named the beer after that Greek prophet—Cassandra," I suggested, trying to be helpful. David grinned at me. He appreciated it when I remembered his stories.

"Yeah. Maybe," Scooter replied. "Hey, are the four of you going to hang out for a bit? I came here alone, but I'd sure like to check out the rest of the farm show."

"Sure, the more the merrier," David answered for the rest of us. "We were going to go watch the herding dogs."

"Great!" Said Scooter. "I need to drop this off at my car." He held the trophy up. "It's heavier than it looks. Give me five minutes?"

"Okay," I replied. I shrugged my shoulders when both Cassie and Joe gave me the stink eye. But what could I do? David had already invited Scooter to tag along with us. It would be rude to ditch him.

"I'll be right back!" Scooter said before he dashed off with his trophy.

"David!" Cassie scolded after Scooter was out of earshot. "I can't believe you invited Scooter to join us."

"He seems harmless," David said. "And he won a trophy and has no one here for him. That's kind of sad."

Joe shook his head, "There's a reason for that, David. Scooter's a little creep. Did you hear him? He confirmed that Cassie was the inspiration for his beer."

"I don't see the problem with that. It's a lot like you inviting Brian Gold to go out with us," David mused, catching me by surprise. It was true that Brian joined our little group during most outings. It was also true that Brian and I used to be an item, but Brian, Joe, Cassie, and I, are lifelong friends. David came to Spruce Grove later. We were all grown up and living our lives when we met David. Besides, I thought Brian and David had set aside their differences months before.

"What I am saying is, I never mind it when Brian tags along; what harm is there in inviting Scotty to join us?" David added, "It's not as though he and Cassie were ever in a relationship."

"That's true," Cassie relented, "and Scooter is such a loner. Maybe we should offer to fix him up with someone."

"Who?" I asked as I tried to ignore my fiancé's burn. I couldn't think of anyone who went to school with us who wanted to date Scooter Wells. Scooter had a reputation for being odd. Besides, I imagined he would insist on dating someone as great as Cassie. Where were we going to find another woman as wonderful as my bestie?

We all quieted and waited for Scotty Wells to return. The problem was. He didn't come back.

Five minutes passed and then six. Scooter was a no-show. My stomach was grumbling—it wanted a churro. "How much longer do we have to wait for Scooter?" I asked with impatience.

"He's obviously not coming," Joe replied.

"I bet Scooter ran into someone he knows, and he had to tell him about his beer and show off the trophy," Cassie added.

"Should we go?" I asked, hoping for a yes.

"Should we text him and let him know we are going to the arena?" Asked David.

"No. Scooter knows we are going to the herding dog demo. He knows where he can find us," Joe said.

"Great! If we leave now, I can buy a churro before the herding dogs get started," I said with enthusiasm.

"You and your appetite!" Cassie replied with a laugh. "Although, I could sure go for a slice of that County Farm Show pizza. Let's go!"

TWO

Cassie and Joe separated from David and me at the churro stand. Cassie wanted pizza so she and Joe set out to find a slice while David paid for my crispy, cinnamon treat. The rich, doughy pastry hit the spot. I swear the treat melted on my tongue.

"This is so good!" I exclaimed. I held the wax paper-wrapped, warm, fried dough, dusted with cinnamon, and took another bite. "You should try it." I held the stick out to David. There was only a small piece left. I'd skipped lunch that day so that I could load up on carbs and grease at the farm show that night.

"Pass. I still have eight pounds to lose before the wedding," David patted his midsection. I didn't see a problem with his weight. Yes, David gained a few pounds in the last couple of months. I didn't mind. David is comfy and snuggly, exactly the way I like him. Anyway, I imagine it is difficult to find healthy things to eat when you spend as much time in airports as David does. He helps run a small nonprofit and travels a lot. I wasn't going pick on him about his weight.

"What do you mean you need to lose eight pounds before the wedding? We haven't even set a wedding date yet," I said before taking another big bite of my churro and finishing it.

"I know we haven't chosen a date. But we should do that soon. Don't you agree?"

I shrugged. We got engaged almost exactly a year ago to the day. People started asking us when and where we were getting married. I wasn't in a hurry to exchange vows. This would be my second marriage—thanks to a nasty divorce. It would be David's second marriage too—he is a widower.

"I don't see what the big deal is. I don't understand why we have to have a big wedding. Honestly, you should take up my dad's offer, and borrow his ladder." I chuckled at the idea. My dad is aware that weddings turn my type-A personality mother into a momzilla—she wreaks havoc on everyone in her path. Dad drops hints that David and I should elope. Offering us his ladder is part of my father's elopement joke.

"You want to elope?" David asked. He sounded surprised that I'd mentioned it. We'd joked about eloping a few times. We hadn't seriously considered slipping off and getting married without our friends and families present.

I shrugged again. "It would make things a heck of a lot easier. Remember how my mother acted when my brother Danny got married?"

"I do remember, but I kind of like the idea of watching you walk down the aisle," David replied. I saw his shoulders sink and his face turned a bit green. "Wow, what is that smell?"

I sniffed the air. I am a country girl and farm show smells aren't overwhelming to me. I don't like the vomit odors near the carnival rides, but animal scents don't usually offend me. "That, David, is the smell of pigs!" I practically squealed. "Let's go see them!"

"You want to see pigs?" David's face looked skeptical.

"Yes, I do. There might be a sow with piglets. You won't believe how cute and soft they are. And they are so smart—like dogs." I grabbed his hand and pulled him in the direction of the pig odor.

"Not all dogs are smart, Char," David reminded me.

"Is that a slam against my dog?" I asked.

Clouseau is my family's rescue Cavachon dog—half Cavalier King Charles Spaniel and half Bichon Frise. The little dogs were bred to be cute little companion animals. Clouseau might not be the brightest bulb in the box, but he's a sweet, friendly dog, and that's all I ever ask of him.

"Not at all. I love Clouseau," David replied.

"Good, because Clouseau had a hard start at life—growing up in a puppy mill. He can't help it if he's a bit behind the curve."

TROUBLE BREWING

"I know that. I don't have to touch the pigs if I don't want to..." David protested, "right?"

I laughed. I know my fiancé. There is no way that the big, ole softy would be able to resist the delight of new, baby pigs.

"Trust me!" I exclaimed.

We arrived at the pig exhibit a few minutes later. The pens were quiet—aside from the occasional snort. There weren't any other people around. Blue and red ribbons hung from the steel rails of the pens indicating which pigs were prize-winners.

"Hmm. Everyone must have gone to the herding dog exhibition or the mud bog," I said to David as I dropped his hand and quickened my pace leaving him a few feet behind me.

"What exactly is a mud bog?" He called out to me. "Remember, this is my first County Farm Show."

"Oh! The mud bog is good, dirty fun. The contestants have these vehicles—usually SUVs on lift kits," I replied as I edged closer to the pigpen so I could see the pigs inside. "And well, the drivers race the SUVs through a giant pit of mud, and the winner is..."

I stopped speaking because before me, lying face down in the pigpen was a woman—and not just any woman. I recognized the steely silver hair wrapped into a tight bun and the yellow raincoat she wore.

"Wilma?" I said with a gasp.

"Wilma won the mud bog?" David's confused voice responded to my unfinished sentence.

"No!" I climbed the steel fence and jumped inside the pigpen. When I landed, my sneakers skidded in the slick mud. I lost my balance, fell bottom-side down, and slid on my butt toward the woman. The pigs scattered in all directions, but Wilma remained still.

"Char, I don't think you are allowed in the pens. Are you okay?" David leaned against the rail and looked down at me.

I fought my way through the deep, wet mud that squelched in protest to my movement. I approached Wilma. Her face was completely submerged in the muck. I rolled her a bit so that she was on her side and her face was out of the mud. Her eyes were closed and her mouth was open. I placed my fingers against her neck. I hoped to find a pulse but I knew that I wouldn't.

"I'm fine, but I think Wilma is dead."

"What?" David asked, shocked at the news.

"Can you help me up? And dial nine-one-one?" I pleaded.

The first responders arrived in less than twenty minutes. That is a quick arrival when you consider that the farm showgrounds are on the outskirts of Spruce County. The police and paramedics must have raced to the scene at top speed. By the time my Uncle Mark Wright, the Chief of Police arrived, David had already rescued me from the slick, sucking mud. My fiancé helped me to a dryer spot outside of the pigpen. We left poor Wilma's lifeless body where I found it. I was covered from head to toe in sticky mud and lord knows what else. I knew I must have smelled as bad as I looked.

"Here's a blanket, Char," Brian Gold handed me a thin, dark gray blanket with one hand as he pinched his nose with the other. The police officer was wearing civilian clothes, but he wore a SGPD baseball-style cap on his head. I imagined Brian was called in for the investigation. Joe had already told me that Brian was taking some time off because he'd been working a lot of hours.

Brian was a newly-minted crime scene investigator—Spruce Grove's only one. I was not sure why he was needed at the scene. To me, it looked like Wilma had gotten into the pigpen and had fallen. A younger person might have walked away from the embarrassing incident with nothing more than a bruised ego. Wilma was over 80 if my math was correct. She would have struggled to escape the quagmire.

"I thought you weren't working tonight," I said. I gratefully accepted the blanket from Brian, and David helped me drape it over my shoulders.

TROUBLE BREWING

"Nah. I wasn't on the schedule, but I got the call. We're a bit short-staffed at the station these days," Brian said as he pushed the cap back on his head. "How did you end up like this?"

"I wanted to see the pigs," I said with a grimace. "I suppose Wilma had the same idea. I saw her in the mud, and when I realized that she wasn't moving, I jumped in."

Brian nodded as he listened to me.

"I guess I slipped—the mud is slick and thick—and I fell into the muck. It was hard to get back up once I was down in the stuff. I imagine Wilma fell in and couldn't get out. Anyway, she was already gone when I found her. She must have drowned in the muck. What a horrible way to die!"

I felt David wrap his arm around my shoulder and pull me closer to comfort me despite how bad I must have smelled.

"Right. Well, if you two could stay here a few minutes in case we have any other questions. I'll let you know when you can leave and get cleaned up," Brian's mouth turned down in a frown then he turned to face the pigpen.

"Are you okay?" David asked.

"I don't know. This is awful. Poor Wilma!"

"Char! David!" Cassie came jogging towards us followed by Joe. When they reached us, Cassie bent at the waist with her hands on her knees and gasped for breath. I guess she'd been running for a while. When she finally looked up, she said, "We were looking all over for you. Then we saw the police and..." She put a finger up indicating that she needed a second, and she took a deep breath. I already knew what she was about to say.

"You naturally assumed we were in trouble?" I asked.

Wilma Platt is not the first dead person I've found. It wouldn't be unreasonable for Cassie to worry that I was somehow involved in the chaos around us that night.

"Not exactly," Cassie's blue eyes searched the scene. "But I worried when you didn't meet up with us for the herding dog event. First Scotty disappeared, and then the two of you. I was beginning to think that you were abducted by aliens."

Joe shook his head at his wife's comment. "What happened here?"

"I wanted to see the pigs. When we got here, I found Wilma Platt face-down in the mud. She was dead," I explained again.

Joe's eyebrows raised. "What was she doing over here?"

"I have no idea. Maybe Wilma wanted to see the pigs too—who can resist piglets? I think she fell in and couldn't get out," I replied. David gave me a little squeeze.

"That sounds awful and odd," Cassie said. "How did she get in there? The pen's rails are high. The gate is closed and there is a lock on it. Was the gate open when you arrived?"

"Um. I don't know. I hadn't planned to go inside the pigpen. I climbed in when I saw Wilma in the mud," I said. "I thought she needed my help, but I was too late."

"The pen had to be locked when we got here," David added, "we haven't touched anything, except Wilma—to check her pulse. And no one else was here when we arrived."

Cassie still looked doubtful as she cast her eyes toward the pigpen. Wilma's body remained in the mud, but mercifully, someone had covered her with a blanket. "But her body is close to the center of the pen. How did she get there? Even if she fell in, she'd be closer to the rails, wouldn't she?"

We all considered this for a moment. Then Cassie spoke again.

"Wilma was eighty-one years old. Yes, she was in relatively good shape, but she used a cane most days. I can't imagine her climbing the fence to get inside the pen. That fence has to be at least four feet tall."

"I agree," David replied. "There is something not quite right about this."

TROUBLE BREWING

I shook my head. Of course, it wasn't right! The poor woman drowned in the muck, and no one seemed to notice. Her death was a travesty!

"Do you think someone pushed her?" Cassie asked as she plopped down next to me. She didn't seem to care about the mud and the smell. Before I could reply, Brian Gold reappeared.

"Char, I know you must want to go home and hose off. The Chief said it's okay if you want to leave. He can interview you tomorrow at the station," Brian told me. "He will call you."

"Oh, thank goodness," I replied. "A hot shower and a cup of peppermint tea would help a lot."

I turned and looked at my friends, "But, to tell you the truth, I don't want to be alone. Would any of you be willing to come home and hang out with me at the cottage?"

"Of course," Cassie volunteered. "Joe's parents have Max. They're dropping her off at our place around noon tomorrow. We can keep you company for a while."

"You know I'll be there," David replied.

I set my eyes on my former beau. I thought I saw his face flush a bit when he realized that I wanted him to come with us. It was a long shot, but I didn't want to leave Brian out. I wanted all my friends around me.

"Sorry, Char. I wish I could. We've got interviews to conduct here before everyone goes home. We need to find the murder weapon too," Brian replied. Then I saw his sea-blue eyes grow a bit larger and he bit down on his lower lip. He didn't mean to let the murder weapon part slip out.

"Murder weapon?" I asked, hoping for more information.

Brian shook his head dismissively. "Go home, Char. You know I can't tell you anything about an open case."

"I hate to say it, but Wilma was not out to make friends today," Joe said as he sat down next to his wife on my plush, green sofa. "You saw and heard how she behaved at the craft beer competition. Wilma was merciless. The things she said about the winners were pretty mean. Any one of those competitors could have killed her."

"Really?" David asked.

He, my dog Clouseau, and I shared the loveseat that I'd recently purchased at a rummage sale. Clouseau was sound asleep on David's lap and was snoring and yipping in his sleep—catching dream bunnies I guessed.

I had a shower as soon as I arrived home, and I was cozily clothed in my fluffy bathrobe with a towel wrapped turban-style around my long, wet hair. I knew that my hair would be a mess of rowdy curls in the morning, but I didn't want to think about it.

David continued speaking.

"I don't see it. Wilma was ill-behaved for sure, but would someone push an old woman into a pigpen and leave her there to die because of a few harsh comments? That seems like an overreaction to me. Can you see that happening?" He paused for us to consider his argument. "Also, I have a hard time believing she climbed that fence. The woman wasn't exactly frail, but she used a cane for balance. The gate must have been open. Maybe she went inside and fell. Someone must have locked up without seeing her."

"Do you think someone could lock up the pigpen and leave without seeing Wilma?" I asked. "If Wilma had gone into the pen and fallen, she would have called out for help."

I hated to think that someone pushed Wilma into the pen to harm her, but from where I was sitting, it sure looked like that is what happened.

Cassie shook her head. "I hate to say it, but I agree with Joe and Char. Wilma was awful. Those things she said about Jack, Scotty, Poppy, and Zach were so unkind. Wilma took their most vulnerable characteristics and shared them with the entire crowd. Wilma publicly shamed them."

I felt my eyebrow rise a bit. Cassie was right. One of the contestants at the craft beer competition might have had a grudge against Wilma Platt. The question was, was the grudge reason enough to kill her?

What had Wilma said about the contestants? She'd accused Zach of being a criminal. She shamed Scotty for being and educator who made beer. As for Poppy, Wilma said that her third eye was blind—whatever that meant. And Wilma insulted Jack's intelligence.

Cassie sat up straighter. "I don't know much about the others, but what Wilma said about Zach Grimes being a criminal, had to have stung. I know Zach is trying his best to reform himself. Did I tell you that he applied for a job at our bookstore? I didn't hire him because Zach didn't have the kind of experience that I was looking for—a background in literature and retail sales. I told Zach that a sales position at Page Two wasn't quite the right fit for his skill set. He seemed to handle the rejection well. I don't think it is easy for someone to get out of prison and start over."

"But he served his sentence. What good would it do to call him out in public the way that Wilma did? She must have had some kind of motivation to shame Zach and the others," David countered. He kept his voice neutral—David is good at being a moderate sounding board.

"Well, as for Zach…" Joe started but then didn't finish his thought. I grimaced. Apparently, for once I knew more about what was going on than David.

"What am I missing?" David asked.

Cassie drew a deep breath and exhaled. "Zach served three years in prison—that's true—but that's because the prosecutor wasn't able to prove the rest of the case. A lot of people think that Zach did more than launder money."

"What else was he accused of?" David asked. He leaned forward, interested.

Joe, Cassie, and I exchanged a cautious look. It was almost as if none of us wanted to be the one to answer David's question. Finally, I spoke.

"I heard this story third hand—I was still in New York at the time of Zach's arrest. It was alleged that Zach Grimes was cooking the books and helping launder money for some unsavory characters," I replied.

Cassie nodded her head. "A sort of syndicate," she added, "Zach might have covered up more serious crimes for the bad guys."

"A syndicate? Here? In Spruce Grove?" David's voice was doubtful.

"Zach lived here, but the group he was linked to was from New Jersey," Joe said. "I heard that he cut some kind of deal with the Feds and that is why Zach's sentence was so short."

"Huh," was all that my fiancé managed to say. He scratched his chin, and his eyes grew distant.

I knew that the wheels in his giant brain were spinning. I imagined he would return home and do a deep search on the internet to learn more about Zach's criminal past.

"Are you feeling any better?" Cassie asked me as she put her hand to her mouth to stifle a yawn. It was already past midnight. Joe stretched and cracked his neck. We were all exhausted.

"I am better, thank you. I shouldn't keep you any longer. I know you have to open Magic Beans in the morning, and Joe has a preseason football game to coach at one," I said.

"Yes, and we have to wrangle Max. She wants to go to the football game too. Our daughter has decided that she wants to try out for the quarterback position when she gets to high school," Cassie added, standing. "I can't imagine she'll last past half-time tomorrow. Her grandparents feed her all the sugar and junk food that she wants and then let her run around like a whirling dervish. I bet Max will be a handful tomorrow. Anyway, I have Ted filling in for me at the coffee shop."

"Try to get a good night's sleep," Joe said to me as he stood and planted a kiss on my cheek.

"I will," I replied, "thanks again, both of you."

Cassie and Joe left quietly leaving Clouseau, David, and me alone in my cozy living room.

"Are you okay?" David asked me for the one-thousandth time.

"I will be. I was thinking on our drive home; Wilma Platt was all alone. I don't think she ever married or had children. I don't know of any other Platt family members living in Spruce Grove. It feels like there is no one here to grieve for her. It's really sad." I took a sip of my now-tepid tea, "It makes me wonder if loneliness was why Wilma was such an angry woman."

"You never know," David replied. "It's late. You should try to get some sleep."

"You're right," I said. "I am sleepy."

"Will you be okay alone here tonight?"

"I'm not alone, I have Clouseau," I said. Hearing his name, my dog's little ear lifted. "I imagine you won't be getting much sleep tonight. If I know you, you'll be looking up Zach Grimes on the internet when you get home. You'll probably look up all the other beer makers too."

David shook his head and smiled. "Actually, no. I need to get some sleep. Joe invited me to watch the game from the sidelines tomorrow and meet some of the players after the game. There are a couple of kids on the team who need scholarships for college but most likely won't be scouted. I thought I might see if I could help."

"That's a great idea, David!" I replied.

"I know that there a lot of parents in Spruce Grove who want to send their kids to college, but struggle with tuition," David said.

"I love how generous you are with the community. Some people choose to turn their backs or pretend they can't help, but you always step up. You are a good man, David Moore." I kissed his cheek.

"I know what it's like to struggle. I had to earn scholarships and work my way through college doing construction during summer break. If I can help someone get an education, I'd like to." He tweaked my cheek. "Are you sure you'll be okay alone... err with Clouseau?"

I yawned as I nodded, "Yes. I'll be okay. I'm practically fighting to keep my eyes open," I replied.

"That's it then. My cue to go." David stood and I walked with him to my front door to say goodnight to him.

"Sleep tight," David said as he pulled me in for a hug.

"You too. And have a nice time at the game tomorrow. I promised Cassie that I would check in on Ted when I am finished at the farm tomorrow. Cassie doesn't want to leave Ted on his own on a busy Saturday."

"I'm sure Cassie and Joe would understand if you don't feel like helping out," David said as he reached for the doorknob.

"No, I'll be fine. Working will help me keep my mind off Wilma Platt," I replied with a shiver remembering that poor woman's face. I gave David a sweet kiss goodnight, and I locked the door once he'd left—a habit that I was still getting used to. I never used to lock the door. Spruce Grove always seemed like a safe place.

"Okay, Clouseau, it's bedtime!" My fluffy little dog raced up the stairs and dove onto my bed. I swear he was lying on the extra pillow, snoring before I slid under the covers.

THREE

The following morning, I worked on my family's tree farm. It was Saturday, and my extended family usually gathered for a big brunch most Saturdays, we chose to cancel the meal and fend for ourselves. My Uncle Mark and Brian were busy investigating Wilma Platt's death. I knew David was probably sleeping in after a night of internet research and then going straight to Spruce Grove High School to help with the football game preparations. I ate a bowl of cold cereal in my tiny kitchen while Clouseau crunched his kibble. Then, we headed to the tree farm to work for a few hours.

The O'Hara clan has owned and operated O'Hara's Christmas Tree Farm for three generations. I recently took on the role of Assistant Manager alongside my father, Gary O'Hara. My mother, Patty O'Hara, keeps the books and runs the office. Our dog Clouseau keeps me company while I am working. My dog occasionally cocks his leg to water the trees. One day, when my parents retire, I will take over the entire operation of the farm. I hope David will join me at work when he finishes traveling the world for his nonprofit organization, Moore Reach.

I finished checking the trees for deer damage and was happy to find that the herd of whitetail deer I saw the day before had better things to munch on than the bark of our Christmas tree crop. It was nearly noon when I finished, so I hustled back to my cottage to shower and change into work attire for my shift at Magic Beans. Clouseau settled in his bed and promptly fell asleep. I set a dog biscuit at his bedside before I left the cottage to drive into town.

Magic Beans is one of my favorite haunts in Spruce Grove. When I was penniless and newly divorced, my best friend, Cassie Binder, hired me to work at the quaint coffee shop. My friend's generosity helped me recover from my sadness and to pay off some of my debts. I had a lot of debt due to a cheating, lying ex-husband. Another benefit of working at Magic Beans? I met David. He was my most loyal customer. I was a horrible barista. Despite my inability to craft a delicious coffee drink, David returned to the shop every day and ordered a latte from me so we could talk and get to know each other better.

I opened the coffee shop's door around one in the afternoon and saw Ted working behind the counter. A quick look around the place revealed that there weren't any caffeine addicts fueling up. Aside from Ted and me, the shop was empty. I wasn't surprised. It was a bit late for a Saturday afternoon lunch, and the much-anticipated Mustangs versus the Spartans preseason football game was probably underway. I guessed that everyone in town wanted to see the game. What can I say? Spruce Grove isn't exactly a mecca for arts and entertainment. The first game of the season is about as good as it gets around here.

"Hi, Ted," I said as I entered the shop. The young ginger barista smiled at me.

"Hey, Char," Ted said, "I probably should have called you. We've had three customers in the last half-hour. It's pretty dead here. You could have stayed home."

I stepped up to the counter and looked longingly at the display case. A spinach croissant remained after the morning rush, and I hadn't had lunch yet. My tummy loudly grumbled at the prospect of food. The rumbling was so loud that poor Ted heard it. I imagine he noticed me eyeing the croissant as well.

"How about a peppermint tea and a spinach croissant?" Ted asked politely. In the past, Ted and I worked together often, so he knows my usual lunch order.

"Yes, to the croissant, but I think I'll have black coffee instead of tea today," I replied.

"Living dangerously, I see," Ted joked as he pulled the croissant from the case and set it on a plate for toasting.

"How are your classes going?" I asked as I rounded the counter and poured myself a large coffee from the carafe marked Jamaican

TROUBLE BREWING

Blue Mountain—a premium, mildly sweet, rich brew that's responsibly sourced and, of course, fare-trade-certified. Ted is a part-time barista. He is also attending summer courses at the local community college.

"Good, thanks. I got an A on my accounting test," Ted replied as he pulled the warmed croissant from the toaster oven, "Saying that makes me feel like a little kid with a report card."

"Not at all. Good job, and congratulations on your A," I said as he handed me my lunch, "I wish I'd taken more business classes when I was in college, but I was dead set on becoming a stage actress."

I guffawed at my comment. I wanted to be an actress so much that I didn't take my other studies as seriously as I should. I graduated with a 3.4 GPA and a BFA. I married the infamous X soon after graduation. X and I moved to New York for work and auditions for plays. I auditioned for several off, off, off, off-Broadway plays, but I spent most of my time waiting tables in a greasy spoon. I never got my big break, and X continually lied about his success as a financial planner. We were doomed from the start.

"It looks like you're doing okay now," Ted replied kindly, "Working outdoors must be great."

"It is—except when it's raining or snowing or when the temperature is below freezing," I replied, "I'm also learning how to keep the books, pay the bills, and collect past due payments. I spend a good chunk of my time working indoors too."

I took a bite of my croissant. The flaky, buttery pastry melted in my mouth, and crumbs from the delicacy floated to the otherwise clean floor.

"I like doing bookkeeping," Ted offered. He poured himself a coffee, and we walked to an empty table. Since there were no customers at the moment, it seemed like a good chance for Ted to take a break and for us to catch up. I might have been a horrible barista, but I liked my coworkers at Magic Beans. Sometimes, I missed working with Cassie, Joe, Ted, and the other coffee shop employees.

"I find crunching numbers and finding bookkeeping errors relaxing," Ted admitted.

"Really? I find those things extremely agitating," I admitted, "I hate tracking down my data entry errors—I make so many of those. After you finish your degree, you should interview for my office manager position. My mother plans to retire in a few years, but she could use a push out the door."

"Maybe I will," Ted replied, "although I would like to try for a job in the big city before I get old."

His face scrunched a bit, and he spoke again. "I heard you were at the farm show last night."

"I was," I confirmed. I wondered what Ted had heard. "Speaking of which, did Brian Gold stop by at noon today as usual?"

"I didn't see Officer Gold today," Ted replied, "Is it true that someone was murdered at the farm show last night?"

I thought about what I should say. I wasn't sure how much information was on the news or social media. I hadn't seen TV or listened to the radio since Friday morning. I hadn't logged on to the internet yet that day. As a recently-lapsed, part-time blogger, I hadn't even considered writing a blog post about Wilma's unfortunate death. I knew, however, that there were plenty of bloggers who might use her death as a way to gain more subscribers.

"Um, yes, someone died last night," I finally answered.

"I heard that it was Wilma Platt. I also heard she was ragging on the brewing contestants," Ted offered.

"Yes, she did sling some insults last night," I answered. I hoped my response was vague enough that I neither confirmed nor denied Wilma's murder. I was trying to keep my nose out of police business—something I knew my Uncle Mark and David would appreciate.

"I also heard that you found her body," Ted said.

"Oh. Geez, word spreads fast around here!"

TROUBLE BREWING

"So, it's true?" Ted asked.

"Yes, I'm afraid so," I admitted, "but I don't know if someone murdered Ms. Platt or if she had a horrible accident. Finding her body was awful."

"People are already saying she was murdered," Ted told me, "I read online that someone beat her to death."

"Where did you see that? Do you remember what site?" I asked, suddenly furious.

Ted shrugged. "I did an internet search when I heard about Ms. Platt's death. I visited many websites. I don't recall exactly where I saw the article."

"What else did the article say?" I couldn't help my curiosity. I hadn't heard anything from Brian Gold, and my Uncle Mark hadn't called me yet to set up a time for an interview.

"It said that the police were looking for the murder weapon," Ted answered. He was interrupted by the jingling of the bells above the door to Magic Beans. A customer had entered the shop.

Instinctively, I shoved the remainder of the croissant in my mouth and stood, ready to get coffee or food for the customer. Mouth full, I looked towards the door and met eyes with Scooter Wells.

"Scotty," I mumbled as I darted to the door. I was surprised at how alarmed I was to see him. My group had lost track of the Assistant Principal the previous night. I swallowed the food in my mouth. "What happened to you last night? You disappeared."

"Hi, Char. I am so sorry about that," Scooter apologized as he headed to the counter, "Could I get a large cappuccino with an extra shot of espresso?"

I eyed Ted. He was better prepared than me to make Scooter's drink. I was a terrible barista before I resigned to work on the tree farm. Who knows how bad my barista skills were after so many months?

"I'll get that," Ted offered as he hustled behind the counter, "Can I get you anything else?"

"A shot of bourbon?" Scooter joked without smiling. Everyone knows that Magic Beans doesn't have a liquor license.

"Is something wrong?" I hazarded a guess.

"Actually, yes," Scooter confirmed. He ran his fingers worriedly through his short hair.

"Do you want to talk about it?" I asked, again, surprising myself. I realized I was dying to know if Scooter had seen anything or heard about Wilma Platt. He'd disappeared right before I'd found Wilma's body.

"Honestly, that would be great," Scooter replied as Ted handed him his drink, and Scooter gave Ted his credit card, "I have a lot on my mind."

Once Scooter finished paying for his drink, we walked to the table that Ted and I had just abandoned and sat.

"First of all, congratulations on winning last night," I began.

"It was only third prize, but it is a start," Scooter said flatly.

"So, by the tone of your voice, I guess the brewing contest isn't what you want to talk about," I replied, "Something else is bothering you."

"It is, and it isn't," Scooter said before he took a sip of his drink.

"Okay. Mysterious."

"Sorry. Last night, after I left the four of you, I took my trophy back to my car. I left it in the backseat. On my way back, I ran into someone. We started talking, and the next thing I knew, we had agreed to go out for a drink. I left the farm show and forgot I was supposed to meet you. I apologize for that."

"Oh," I said as his words finally clicked, "you mean that you met a woman?"

Scooter's face flushed. "Yes. I apologize for not texting or calling you, but I was taken a bit by surprise. It's not often that women ask me out."

"I'm sure that's not true," I lied politely. I was sure that Scooter never got asked out. Scooter is nice enough, I suppose, but he's odd.

"No, really. It is unusual. We decided to meet at that sports bar near Crystal Creek. I drove my car, and she drove hers. Anyway, one thing led to another, and we talked until right before the bar closed."

"Wow. It sounds like the two of you hit it off," I said.

"Um. Sort of," Scooter offered a half smile. The smile disappeared as quickly as it appeared.

"You don't seem very happy about it. Did you do something regrettable?" I asked. I hoped he would spare me from the details. There are just some things that I don't want or need to know about Scooter Wells.

"No! No, nothing like that," Scooter protested with a laugh, "We just talked, and anyway, I'm a gentleman, Charlotte."

I exhaled, relieved that I wouldn't have to hear a Scooter Well's tale of conquest. Hallelujah!

"So why are you so glum?"

"I left the bar and drove straight home. It was late, or early, two o'clock in the morning. I went home and fell asleep. I slept in late this morning. I was exhausted after last night. I got up around eleven, showered, and got ready to go to the game. When I got into my car, I realized it was missing."

"What was missing?" I asked, confused.

"My trophy. Someone stole my Bronze Medal," Scooter's face fell, "I know it sounds dumb. The trophy is cheap metal and plastic—not bronze—but it was the only trophy I've ever won. Well, I got a trophy for playing tuba in the high school marching band competition, but everyone in the band got one of those." Scooter's shoulders drooped, "I guess I must have left the backdoor of my car unlocked."

"Oh, Scotty! I am so sorry." I reached out and lay my hand on his. I truly felt sorry for him, "Who would do such a terrible thing?"

"I have no idea," Scooter replied.

"Do you think someone stole the trophy while you visited the bar or after you reached home?" I asked.

Scooter took a deep breath and exhaled. "I don't know. It could have happened anywhere. I left the trophy in the back seat of my car when I was at the farm show, and I didn't look for it until this morning. I planned to put the trophy in my office at school. I was excited about meeting up with... my friend last night that I didn't even check to see if the trophy was still in my car. Why would I?"

"Was anything else missing from your car?" I asked.

"No. I checked. My old CDs are still in their case, my Spruce Grove Spartan's Band jacket is still on the passenger seat, and even my bag of quarters for the carwash was in the glove box. The thief went after my trophy."

"I am sorry. It does sound like the trophy was what the thief was after." Suddenly, I had an idea.

"Scotty, I am sure the trophy meant a lot to you. If you'd like, I can place a notice on my blog site asking people to keep an eye out for it."

Putting up a missing/reward-type post on my blog could help Scooter locate his trophy and maybe even cure my writer's block. I hadn't posted much content on Around the Town in weeks.

"No," Scooter replied, "I'm sure there are people in Spruce Grove who would think it was hilarious. *Poor little Scooter Wells had his trophy stolen.* Thanks, but I'll write off the trophy as lost forever."

"If you're sure," I didn't know what else to say.

"I am. Charlotte, I know I'm a bit of a laughingstock in this town. I don't want to feed the wolves."

Suddenly, I felt horrible for Scooter—mostly because he was right. There were people in town who would laugh about his loss. I wouldn't laugh about Scooter's trophy, but I was guilty. I've said some unkind things about Scooter in the past. Also, Scotty was aware that we called him Scooter behind his back. I felt awful. Maybe it was time to make amends.

Scotty abruptly stood. "Thanks for the talk, Charlotte. You are a surprisingly good listener. I never would have guessed that. In high school, you always seemed a bit dramatic and self-absorbed. I guess I was wrong about you."

Right. Maybe I would post something on Around the Town after all.

"Where are you off to?" I asked as I walked with Scotty to the door.

"I guess I should make an appearance at the football game," Scotty replied.

"And what about your friend? Do you think you'll see her again?" I have to admit that I was curious to find out who the mystery woman was.

"I'm sure I will," Scotty replied as he opened the door, "she's local. I'm bound to run into her around town."

Scotty's answer was non-committal, and it left me wondering if I'd misunderstood the undertones of our conversation. Perhaps Scotty wasn't romantically interested in the woman he met for drinks.

"What were you doing at the pigpens last night, Charlotte? Everyone else was at the herding dog competition or the mud bog race."

My Uncle Mark was seated at his desk across from me. I was sitting in my usual spot—his guest chair in his office at the Spruce Grove Police Department. The door was closed. I finished hanging out in the all-but-dead coffee shop and walked to the station to see if my uncle was ready to take my statement about Wilma Platt's unfortunate demise.

"I like the baby pigs," I replied as I shrugged my shoulders. "David, Cassie, Joe, and I had just left the craft beer contest. I was hungry after the event, so David and I agreed to hunt for churros while Cassie and Joe looked for pizza. Oh! Scotty Wells was there too. He had just won third prize in the beer competition. He asked to hang out with us at the herding dog competition."

"Scooter Wells? I didn't know you were friends," my uncle looked at me cynically.

"Well, we weren't friends—yet. I don't think you should call him Scooter, Uncle Mark."

"Is that so?" My uncle leaned in.

"Yes, I'll get to that. Give me a second. I'm building a framework here," I implored.

"Alrighty. Go on," my uncle said with an amused chuckle.

"As I was saying, I wanted a churro, Cassie wanted pizza, and Scotty wanted to hang out with us because, let's face it, we're the cool kids."

Again, my uncle chuckled.

"Scotty asked us to wait for him—he wanted to stash his trophy in his car. We waited about seven minutes, and then we decided that Scotty wasn't returning, and we left to find our food with plans to meet at the herding competition after that."

"Seven minutes? That's very specific," My uncle remarked.

"We were waiting for Scotty, Uncle Mark. We could only wait so long for him. There was food to gather and dogs to see. Anyway, Scotty knew where he could find us. Once I had my churro, I asked David if we could head to the herding dog arena after we visited the pigpens. David knows I love piglets, and he agreed to go there with me."

"I see. Go on." Mark formed a temple under his chin with his fingers.

"Right. We arrived at the pigpens, and no one was around. That's when I saw someone face-down in the mud. I was concerned. I jumped in to check on the individual. It was Wilma, and she was dead. David helped me out of the mud, and we phoned you. That's a synopsis of what happened."

"Okay. Did you see Wilma last night before you found her in the pigpen?"

TROUBLE BREWING

"I did. And I am sure you've already heard that Wilma made her presence known at the beer competition. She was angrily protesting and slinging slurs at the contestants."

Uncle Mark nodded.

"Do you remember what Wilma said?" Uncle Mark asked. I was sure other witnesses had already filled in my uncle on Wilma's tirade, but I humored him. I told Mark the cruel things that Wilma said.

"We—that is, Cassie, Joe, and I—think that Wilma was probably killed by one of the contestants in retaliation for her rude remarks," I offered. "I heard that someone beat her to death."

"Is that so?" My uncle asked. He seemed determined to keep quiet about what he knew.

"Yes." I crossed my arms over my chest.

"You said there was no one else at the pigpens?" My uncle asked after a beat.

"That's right, and what I found odd was the pens were padlocked, and Wilma was well within the pen when she died. How did she get in there?"

"That's a good question, Charlotte. Do you have any theories about that?" Uncle Mark asked me.

"Well, Wilma had to get into that pen some way. Either she climbed the fence or she walked inside. I think it is more likely that Wilma entered through the gate. She used a cane to get around. I can't see her climbing into the pen. But the gate was padlocked. Did she have a key?"

My uncle didn't answer my question. He asked me another question instead. "But why would Wilma want to see the pigs?"

"I think someone lured Wilma there. It seems like she was at the farm show to protest the beer contest—not to enjoy the exhibits. Maybe I am wrong. Maybe Wilma wanted to see the pigs, and the killer got lucky and found her there. Have you seen piglets, Uncle Mark?

They are freaking adorable! Those snuffling noses and the curly tails make piglets so cute."

"Yes, Charlotte, I have seen piglets, but what I am saying is..." Mark didn't get an opportunity to finish his statement. Suddenly, the door flung open, and Brian Gold appeared in the doorway. A large ziplocked bag containing what looked like a mud-covered trophy dangled from his left hand.

"Oh, sorry, I didn't know you had a guest, Chief," Brian apologized, stepping back a bit.

"No, it's fine. Charlotte was about to leave," Uncle Mark told him.

"I was?" I asked.

"Thanks for stopping by, niece." Mark patted me on the head and stood from his chair. He nodded to me to tell me; our interview had ended.

"Brian, why don't you take that to the lab, and I'll meet you there?" Uncle Mark said as he walked out of the room. He left me alone with Brian. My uncle is generally a man of few words, but he knew I'd want to speak to Brian Gold, and he left. My uncle's room-reading abilities are just one of the things that make him such a good cop.

"Right, Chief," Brian answered. He turned away but changed his mind and spun around to face me. I stood from the visitor's chair. "Char, you know that you shouldn't say anything about this." He lifted the evidence bag, "This is potential crime scene evidence. We don't plan to issue a press statement yet. So, this is hush-hush for now, okay?"

I gazed at the muddy evidence in the bag. I was almost mesmerized by it because the trophy seemed significant. I finally spoke. "Brian, I think there's something you need to know."

"Oh?" Brian asked. "It isn't about you and David, is it? Because I don't have time to play relationship counselor right now, Char."

"No, this isn't about David and me; it is about that trophy. I think I know who it belongs to."

TROUBLE BREWING

I told Brian about my conversation with Scotty Wells at Magic Beans. The trophy must belong to Scotty.

"We'll see, I guess. There were three trophies handed out at the craft brewing contest. The trophies were all the same—aside from the name plates—according to Norman Hammer," Brian replied. "The plate is missing from the trophy. Right now, I don't know who the trophy belongs to."

"You're right, we have to keep our minds open," I replied, "Scotty lost his trophy, but that one might not be his."

FOUR

After I left the police station, I drove to David's place. I opened the door to David's house and stepped inside. I heard two male voices talking, catching me off-guard. David must have had a guest in his home—something that is relatively rare despite the large size of his house. David is a friendly man, but he values his privacy.

I followed the voices to David's home office and found David sitting at his desk with Joe Binder standing next to him. Both men were staring at the large, center computer monitor.

"Hi," I said. I offered a friendly wave from the doorway, "How was the game? Who won?"

"It was great," David said, beaming. "I'm surprised you don't already know who won. Didn't you see the human parade on Main Street?"

"Uh, no? What are you talking about?" I asked.

I wandered into the room and sat on a cozy armchair near the fireplace.

"The Spartans won seventeen to three," Joe informed me, "and our marching band captured the Mustangs mascot—Mumford the Mustang. They paraded him down Main Street while playing the Spartan's fight song."

Joe and David both busted out laughing at the memory.

"Oh my gosh! Please tell me Mumford is a human in costume not an actual horse," I pleaded. "The marching band wearing their giant hats and playing loud instruments could be terrifying to a horse."

I hated anything to do with animal cruelty—the main reason that I became a vegetarian.

"No. Mumford is human, Char," Joe replied. "He's a kid wearing a ridiculous furry blue and white horse costume. No one harmed any animals in the parade."

"Still, parading a kid down Main Street isn't very nice either," I said, defending my original statement.

"He was fine, Char," David replied, "A bit embarrassed maybe, but the band didn't hurt him. I promise. The crowd just pulled off his horse head and put a funny sign on his back—the sign said *Broken*."

Joe and David chuckled at his comment.

"You know something? I've been thinking about how awful teasing can be," I said, remembering how we all made fun of Scotty Wells in the past. "It's just bullying with a different name."

"Okay. I agree with you, but what brought this on?" David asked me.

"Scotty Wells. I ran into him at Magic Beans. I'm afraid that he's been the victim of a malicious prank. Someone stole his trophy the other night—at least, that's what Scotty said. We were talking to each other, and Scotty knows we call him Scooter. He said that people in town think he's just a big joke. It hurt hearing him say those things. I won't be calling him Scooter anymore."

"To be fair, Scooter is kind of a joke," Joe replied. "The guy walks around mooning over other men's wives. He still wears his Spruce Grove Spartans Band jacket from over a decade ago. The guy is like thirty years old, Char."

"I know, but maybe it's time to, I don't know, settle down with the teasing. Yes, Scotty is a bit tone-deaf when dealing with other people. He called me self-absorbed, but I decided to be the bigger person and let it go."

David and Joe exchanged a look, and I could see they were struggling not to laugh.

"Whatever!" I exclaimed. "The trouble is, Scotty might have bigger problems than teasing now."

The two men didn't reply to my obvious prompt. They just stared at the monitor. Whatever they watched, it held their attention.

"What were you two looking at? I sure hope it isn't porn."

TROUBLE BREWING

"Oh, Char! Come here and look!" David beckoned me closer. "Joe and I are reviewing a recording of the football game. The Spartans have some talented players."

I walked over, and watched as David hit the play button on the computer screen. The monitor came alive with the sounds of cheering football fans and the occasional toot of a band instrument. I watched a tall, slim, young Spartans player dash down the field with a football clutched to his side. He crossed the football field in a few seconds.

"Wow! He is fast!" I exclaimed. "Who is that?"

"Aaron Banks. He's a running back and only a junior," Joe informed me, "He wants to graduate early and go to college next year. Arron's got the talent and the grades. He needs a scholarship or two so that he can afford the tuition. There will be scouts in the stands this season—I'm willing to bet Aaron will get a scholarship, maybe even a full ride. There are a couple of other guys—seniors—who are interested in scholarships too. They can't go to college without some financial assistance."

"That's where David comes in, I presume?" I asked. David is loaded.

"Hey, I am happy to help," David replied. "Joe thinks this kid, Aaron, could make it into the NFL one day."

"That's very exciting," I replied. There aren't too many famous people who originate from Spruce Grove. "I never knew you were so into high school football." I squeezed David's shoulder.

"I am now," David replied. He closed the window on the computer monitor and faced me. "Now, what bigger problem does Scotty Wells face?" David had been listening to me.

"Oh. Right," I sighed, grateful for the momentary distraction provided by the football video. "Maybe we could talk over a drink?"

It was after four in the afternoon—not too early for a glass of wine.

"This must be something big," Joe commented, "which is surprising considering we're talking about Scooter Wells." Joe raised and lowered his hand, indicating Scotty's diminutive size.

"See? That's exactly the kind of thing I was talking about," I snarled, "Joe, we need to grow up and stop bullying people. What I have to tell you is potentially serious. It is not the time for distasteful jokes."

"Let's go into the kitchen and get you that drink," David offered to diffuse the tension between Joe and me.

"Good," I said.

"Okay, Char, you have your pint of wine," Joe joked about the generous pour of Pinot Noir in my glass. He leaned against the kitchen counter while I sat at the table.

David busied himself inspecting the contents of the fridge—trying to find a beer for his guest. I already knew he wouldn't find any.

"Sorry, no beer," David said. "I can offer you wine or coffee. Tea?"

"No worries," Joe replied, "I need to get going after I hear Char's story."

I took a fortifying sip of my drink and set the glass on the tabletop.

"As I was saying," I said, "Scotty came into Magic Beans. He was upset because someone stole his trophy last night from the backseat of his car. Scotty wasn't sure when that happened. He thinks he left his car unlocked."

"Did Scotty happen to mention where he went last night?" David interjected. "He was supposed to meet up with us."

"That's what I was about to tell you. After Scotty placed the trophy in the back of his car, he ran into someone he knows—a woman."

"How awful for her," Joe said under his breath. I chose to ignore his comment.

"Scotty didn't say who she was, but the woman invited him for a drink at that sports bar you sometimes go to—the one with the funny name in Crystal Creek."

Joe pretended to cough and said, "false," in that annoying way that guys do when they are kidding around.

TROUBLE BREWING

"No, really. Scotty said they closed the place down and went their separate ways afterward."

"Of course, they did," Joe added sarcastically, "Scooter Wells is every woman's dream man." He rolled his eyes.

"Anyway," I darted eye daggers at my former boss. He didn't like Scotty Wells, that was for sure, "Scotty didn't think about his trophy again until this morning. He planned to take the trophy to his office—only it wasn't in his car."

"Someone stole it," David said.

"Yes. Scotty didn't know if it happened while he was at the bar or after he got home this morning, but the trophy was gone. And weirdly, the trophy was the only thing missing from his car."

"Someone could have taken the trophy from his car at the farm show," Joe offered. He was right. Scotty said he hadn't checked the trophy after leaving it in the backseat of his car. I imagined he was too distracted by the woman who invited him for drinks.

"Okay, I get that he's upset, but Scotty is lucky that the trophy is all the thief took. These days thieves steal catalytic converters and whole cars. I'd say he got off easy," David replied. Joe nodded in agreement.

"But!" I exclaimed.

I lifted my glass and gulped more wine. I drank too quickly and began coughing. I raised a finger to indicate that I had more to say—once I caught my breath. David got a glass of water for me. Joe and David waited for me to speak again. Finally, I took a deep breath.

"Yes?" Joe asked, his voice dripping with sarcasm.

"But," I began again. I cleared my throat and spoke, "after I left Magic Beans, I walked to the police station to give my statement about finding Wilma in the pigpen. I promised Brian I would go in today since I was covered in muck last night. At the station, I saw the potential murder weapon! The thing that killed Wilma Platt!"

"Whoa!" David exclaimed. "What was it, and how did you know it was the murder weapon?"

"How I know doesn't matter," I replied. I thought of Brian with the Ziplock bag that dangled from his grip earlier, "but what the murder weapon was is significant."

"So, tell us, Char and try to stop being so dramatic," Joe implored.

"Scotty called me dramatic too. That's not a character flaw, you know?" I replied.

David shook his head. "Char, what was the alleged weapon?"

"I saw it in an evidence bag," I said, "it was covered in mud—like the mud from the pigpen. I am certain that's where the police found it—in the pigpen."

"If the smell of that stuff was any indication, it wasn't just mud," David said.

Joe chuckled.

I shivered at the memory of the sticky ooze that clung to my shoes, clothing, and hair the previous night. It was not just mud.

"What was the weapon, Char?" David asked again.

"A trophy! It was a trophy, and I think once Mark and Brian check, they'll discover that trophy is Scotty's missing award from the beer brewing contest."

Joe shook his head dismissively. "Don't tell me that you honestly think that Scotty Wells killed Wilma Platt with his trophy."

I shrugged my response. "I honestly don't know what to think. Scotty's trophy is missing. Scotty went missing last night—right around the time Wilma died. Scotty said he was with a woman, but he was weird about it."

Joe chuckled. "I have serious doubts about that."

"Exactly. Scotty said he was with a woman but didn't say her name. Also, when I asked Scotty if he and the woman planned to see each other again, he was rather flippant. He acted like their evening together didn't even matter to him," I said, "Something doesn't smell right about his story. And, it's not just the pig poop that smells."

TROUBLE BREWING

"I agree that the story sounds a bit suspicious, Char, but I am with Joe here," David replied, "I don't think Scotty Wells could kill anyone. Why would he?"

"You were there, guys. You heard the awful things that Wilma said," I reminded them.

"I still don't think Wilma's insults would lead to murder. Do you?" David asked, "And if Scotty killed her, why did he leave the murder weapon—his trophy—behind?"

"We'll see, I guess," I replied before I drained my wineglass, "I put Brian Gold on the case. We should know if Scotty is guilty soon enough."

Joe's eyebrows lifted in amusement. I could tell he thought I was joking.

"What do you mean?" David asked.

"I told him Scotty's story. I imagine Brian is checking the trophy for evidence right now. The plate—that said which prize it was—gold, silver, or bronze—is missing from the trophy. If the plate were intact, Brian would already know the killer's identity."

"I thought you said we shouldn't pick on Scotty anymore," Joe accused as he pointed a finger in my direction, "Suppose the trophy belongs to Scotty. That doesn't mean he killed Wilma."

"I am not picking on Scotty, Joe. I shared relevant case information with the police—that is all. I am sure you agree that if Scotty Wells had anything to do with Wilma's death, he should be found out and punished for the crime."

"Well, yes," Joe agreed, "but I don't think you should get involved. Remember those other times you got involved in police investigations when you shouldn't have?"

I shook my head.

"Again, I agree with Joe," David said.

"Well, it's out of our hands now," I replied, as I considered refilling my glass with wine and crashing on David's sofa for a decade. "Unless..."

"Unless what?" David asked.

"Unless what Scotty told me about meeting a woman for drinks is true. It would be easy enough to find out, I suppose. The killer could have stolen Scotty's trophy and then used it to kill Wilma."

I threw caution to the wind and reached for the wine bottle to refill my glass.

"Do you mind if I crash on your sofa tonight, David?"

"You know you can sleep in the bed," David replied.

"I know, but I doubt I'll be able to walk after I finish this bottle," I replied, "stairs."

Joe shot David a concerned look.

"What?" I asked defensively.

"Char," David grabbed the wine bottle from my hand. A bit of wine spilled on the table. I pushed away the impulse to lick up the spill.

"I think you've had enough. What you saw last night was awful. Don't you think you should talk about it instead of drinking?" He shoved the cork back into the top of the bottle and walked it to the fridge.

"Yeah, why don't you call Cassie?" Joe offered. "I bet she's dying to hear what you think about Wilma's death."

"Maybe later," I replied. I stood from the table. I couldn't have more wine; I would take a nap. "I'm going to go lie down."

"Good idea," David said.

I left the room, kicked off my shoes, and plopped onto David's comfy sofa in his family room. I could hear the garbled sounds of David and Joe speaking in the kitchen. I reached for David's television remote to drown out their voices. I knew they were talking about me.

I heard them talking as David walked Joe to the front door and said goodbye to him. Then David walked into the family room, lifted my feet from the couch, and sat. He rearranged my legs on his lap.

"Want to talk?" He asked.

"I'm sleeping," I grumbled.

TROUBLE BREWING

"No, you aren't. Char, I'm just concerned, that's all. What you saw last night was awful, and unfortunately, Wilma wasn't the first dead body you found since I've known you. Maybe. I don't know. Maybe you should talk to someone?"

"You want me to see a shrink?" I asked. I dropped my arm over my eyes. I didn't want to think about it.

"I don't think it could hurt. I went to counseling as a teenager. I've seen a psychiatrist as an adult. There is no shame in getting help."

"Your mother died when you were little," I said, "and your wife died. Those are both valid reasons to speak to a professional therapist."

"Yes, those things are true, but you don't have to lose a close loved one to be affected by death," David replied. "I think you might actually like seeing a therapist."

I nearly choked on my laughter. Right.

"You would get to talk—a lot—talking is encouraged in therapy. You like talking. Look, I can't force you to go," David said, "but I would like you to consider it. You know that I'm supposed to fly to Europe for work soon. I'd feel a heck of a lot better if I knew you were okay before I leave."

"How long will you be gone?" I asked.

David flies out of the country for weeks at a time. I miss him when he's gone.

"Three or maybe four weeks," he replied, "I won't go if you need me here."

I sat up. "I'll be okay. Really. As you said, I've seen dead people before." I hopped off the sofa to find my shoes.

"What are you doing?" David asked.

"Getting my shoes," I found one sneaker and began looking for the other, "I should go home."

"You've been drinking, Char," David reminded me.

"Pfft. I had one glass of wine," I replied as I located my other shoe. I sat on the second to last step of the staircase to put my shoes on.

"One O'Hara-sized glass," David corrected me.

An *O'Hara-sized glass* is about 12 ounces—give or take an ounce. We don't bother to measure. Someone once told me that a glass of wine is supposed to be 5 or 6 ounces—which is utter nonsense. If that were true, why do glass makers make fishbowl-sized wine glasses?

"Stay. Please?" David begged as he sat on the step next to me and took the shoe I hadn't managed to slip on, "I'll make you dinner, and later, if you feel like it, we can do that thing."

He waggled his eyebrows at me.

I stopped tying my shoe, rested my head on David's sturdy shoulder, and laughed. He won me over. My man knows what I like. "Okay."

"By the way, I did some investigating earlier," David told me.

"I knew it! Why didn't you say anything before? What did you find out?"

"I didn't want to bring it up in front of Joe. He doesn't know that I help you with your investigations, and I'd like to keep it that way," David replied. "I did a deep dive on the internet. I found some old newspaper stories."

"Oh?" I asked, slipping the other shoe off my foot. I set it aside.

"Yes. Did you know that Wilma Platt was partly responsible for Zach Grimes' arrest?"

"What? You're kidding!" I was shocked. If what David said was true, then Zach Grimes had a motive for killing Wilma.

"No. It's true. Did you know Wilma owned rental properties all over Spruce County?" David asked.

"What? Shut the front door! I had no idea. But, how did Wilma figure out what Zach had done?"

"Wilma entered Zach's apartment without his knowledge—an apartment she owned and leased to Zach. Later, Wilma claimed that she entered the place to check for mice, but it was obvious that she was

TROUBLE BREWING

snooping. I guess Wilma found all kinds of evidence linking Zach to his crimes. She contacted the authorities."

"Wait. You said that Wilma had properties all over the county. Was she the landlord for any of the other suspects?" I asked.

"Ding-ding. Give the lady a prize!" David smiled. "Wilma was the landlord for both Poppy and Jack at different times."

"Whoa! Did Poppy or Jack have issues with Wilma? Did she spy on them too?" I could barely contain my interest or excitement.

"I found a letter to the editor of the Spruce Grove Times. It was written by P. F. about six months ago."

"Poppy Flint!" I exclaimed.

"Yep, it appears to be the one and only. In the letter, Poppy alleged that her landlord—actually, she referred to Wilma as a *slum lord*—shut off her heat and hot water. Poppy lost clients because she couldn't keep the studio heated or provide hot water for showers. In the letters, Poppy urged other disappointed renters to come forward. She suggested a filing a class-action lawsuit against the slum lord."

"So, Wilma rented studio space to Poppy?" I asked.

"It appears that way. Poppy never called out Wilma by name, but I did some research on the county property records website. I linked Poppy's former studio address to Wilma's property records. Poppy moved locations a while ago. Her current studio is on Main Street."

"That's interesting. Did anything come out of Poppy's accusations? Or did she move without incident? I can't imagine Wilma liked being called a slum lord."

"No. There were a few letters to the editor over about two months. Then, the letters stopped. I guess the women must have come to an understanding."

"What about Jack Indigo, the tattoo artist? Wilma insulted his intelligence in public," I said.

"Ah, yes, Jack," David chuckled. "It seems Wilma was offended by what Jack had done to the space he rented from her—or rather—what was on display there."

"What? You mean like tattoo illustrations?" I asked, perplexed.

"Not exactly. Jack sublets studio space to other artists. One of the subletters specializes in body piercings." David grinned at me as if he'd just revealed something important.

"Okay. So?" I didn't follow David. Frankly, I didn't understand what would make Wilma upset about piercings. Even I had three piercings in each ear.

"Have you ever been in a place like Jack's?" David asked me.

"No, I don't have tattoos, and I had my ears pierced at the mall. Why? I know you've been in a tattoo parlor—you have that silly hello world tattoo on your chest."

David's face pinkened a bit at the mention of his tattoo. He said he regretted getting the ink, but he never bothered to have it removed.

"Yes. Well, the piercing practitioners often have displays in their studios—like models to show how the piercings will look. Ears, noses, lips, and eyebrows are not the only body parts people get pierced."

"I know David, I am not naïve," I rebuked him, "People get their tongues pierced too."

"What else? Think about it," David replied.

I thought about body piercings for about a second.

"Wait. The piercing studios have models of...those other body parts out in the open?" I asked. I tried not to giggle as I pointed downward with my index finger.

"Indeed, they do," David confirmed. "If you can pierce it, trust me, there's a model for it. I guess Wilma went into the studio and was appalled by something she saw there. She petitioned the county to try to shut Jack down. Wilma said that his shop violated ancient decency laws that still appear in Spruce County lawbooks. The county denied Wilma's petition—the decency laws were ruled outdated and discriminatory. The laws covered many things that should have been removed from the books years ago. However, like Poppy, Jack ended up moving to a new location. That happened before you moved home."

No wonder I had no recollection of the odd things that happened with Wilma and her renters. I was in New York and focused on my troubles when Wilma messed with Jack and Zach. Poppy's encounter with Wilma was more recent, but it sounded like the two women had settled their differences quietly.

"So, what you are telling me, is that pretty much everyone who rented a space from Wilma Platt could be a suspect in her death?" I asked David.

"Well, at least among the beer contestants, that's true," David said. "I have no idea if other renters had problems with Wilma. Odds are, they did."

"What about Scotty? Did he rent a place from Wilma too?"

"That my dear is something that I was unable to confirm. If Scotty rented from the decedent or knocked horns with Wilma in the past, I didn't find any proof of it."

"So, maybe Scotty didn't kill her. Or maybe we're just going around in circles," I said, sighing.

"There is the trophy," David reminded me. "And Scotty could have had another motive to kill Wilma. We just haven't discovered it. Yet."

"That's true," I agreed, "I know what I said earlier, but I don't understand why Scotty would leave evidence behind if he killed Wilma. Not just evidence—the murder weapon. He wouldn't do that, would he? Scotty is odd, but he's not stupid. And anyway, Scotty seemed upset about the theft of his trophy."

"I don't know," David replied. "I suppose if Scotty slipped during the crime and dropped the weapon, he might have lost it. Perhaps he couldn't find the trophy in the mud, and he thought no one else would find it either. Or maybe Scotty intended to go back and retrieve the trophy later."

"And the police found the trophy before Scotty got there to retrieve it. Brilliant!" I exclaimed.

"I do my best," David said with a wink. "Let's try not to convict Scotty without proof."

"Agreed. Have I told you lately how much I love and admire your brain?" I asked with a smile.

"I don't recall. Maybe you should remind me," David waggled his eyebrows at me.

"Did you mean it when you said if I stayed here, you'd cook for me and then do that thing?"

"Every word. You'll have the time of your life, I promise. I need a few minutes to limber up. That lift at the end is a bit hard on my back."

"Okay, you convinced me. I'll stay. You get ready—do whatever you need to. It will take me a minute to find the Dirty Dancing soundtrack."

FIVE

On Sunday, I woke up sore and alone in David's bed. I'd stayed the night at David's place because he'd kept his promise to me. We had dinner followed by dirty dancing in preparation for our wedding. We still hadn't set a date.

Trying to execute the run and lift from the goodbye party scene of the movie was a bad idea. David and I performed the move once before with mixed results. On our first attempt, we went to the deepest part of Crystal Creek so that the buoyancy of the water would help me feel weightless. David caught me that time, but I'd misjudged my launch and dove straight into his face, giving him a fat lip and a black eye. Why David offered to try the move again—without the benefit of deep water—perplexed me. He was undeterred. Saturday night, our second attempt at the dance move went much worse than the first. I ended up with an ache in my side, and poor David threw out his back. Rather than climbing the steep stairs to the bedroom, David slept on the sofa while I slept in his bed.

I rolled out of the comfort of the California King-sized bed at around 9 AM, took a quick shower, and dressed. It was my day off and the perfect time to do some snooping.

David was sound asleep when I descended the stairs. The painkillers that the doctor prescribed for David's back the last time he hurt it helped him to sleep. I knew that if I were quiet, I could slip out of his house unnoticed.

I grabbed my bag and keys, left the house, jumped into my SUV, and drove to my parents' house to mooch breakfast and check on Clouseau. He was staying with them.

"Hi, doll," my dad greeted me as I limped into my mother's fancy kitchen. I could smell something delicious—coffee and my mother's French toast. My dog wagged his tail at me and smiled the way only a dog can.

"Hey, Dad," I replied as I heaved myself onto a stool at the kitchen island and groaned. Clouseau sat at my feet, waiting to get scraps.

"Something the matter?" My dad asked as he reached for a coffee mug and filled it with aromatic coffee.

"Regrets. So many regrets," I replied, shaking my head. My dad's eyebrows raised. When had they gotten so fuzzy? Dad's eyebrows were like twin pepper and salt caterpillars crawling on his forehead. I'd better mention the eyebrow situation to my mother. She would arrange for him to get them shaped before my wedding.

"Regrets? Do you want to elaborate?" Dad set the steaming coffee mug down in front of me. Then he placed a plate and silverware next to me.

"Not really. Where's Mom? I thought I smelled French toast."

"Ah. Your mother is at church. She's trying to have a presence there. Your mother doesn't want to shock Father George when she asks him to preside over your wedding. And you do smell French toast. I have it warming in the oven."

"You made breakfast?" I asked, surprised. I couldn't recall the last time my father cooked anything.

"Your mother didn't have time. I expect your uncle to arrive for brunch soon. I cooked."

"I didn't know that you could cook," I admitted.

"Of course, I can cook, Charlotte. I wasn't always a married old man. I was once a lonely, young bachelor who cooked. I also weighed one-hundred and fifty pounds. I would cook more often, but your mother likes her kitchen..." Dad shrugged and didn't finish his thought.

"Spotless," I finished his sentence for him. "Well, the French toast sure smells good, and the coffee is perfect. Why doesn't Mark's fiancé cook for him? Sarah has a B&B, and I know she cooks for the guests."

"That's something you can ask your uncle—or Sarah," Dad replied. He placed an oven glove over his massive hand, opened the oven door, and withdrew an enormous platter of French toast. My mouth watered.

TROUBLE BREWING

"Why is Uncle Mark coming?" I asked as my dad set the platter on a trivet. I grabbed my fork, greedily stabbed a piece of fluffy French toast, and dropped it on my plate. Then I grabbed another. My dad set a warm carafe of real maple syrup by my plate.

"We didn't have brunch yesterday," Dad shrugged, "it felt like a shame to skip it altogether. Having brunch gives us a chance to catch up. Your uncle is one of my best friends, but aside from our weekly brunch and big holidays, it's surprising how little I see him."

"Especially since he started seeing Sarah," I added.

"Yes," my dad agreed.

"Is Uncle Mark bringing anyone with him?" I hazarded to ask. I wondered if Sarah—Mark's fiancé and my high school nemesis—would be coming with him. If she was coming, I needed to prepare for her snark. I was also curious if Brian Gold would make an appearance, but I didn't mention that.

"I don't know if Sarah is coming," my dad replied. "I made plenty of food."

"Good morning!" My uncle's voice bounced from the back door as he stepped inside the house. I hoped he hadn't heard us talking about him and Sarah. My Uncle Mark is my favorite relative.

Mark walked into the kitchen dressed in civilian clothing. I have to admit, the sight of him surprised me. It seems like my uncle is always in uniform—always working. I noticed that he was carrying something, and it smelled divine.

"Sarah sent over some hot-out-of-the-oven scones and lemon curd."

My mouth watered again. I might not like Sarah very much, but my soon-to-be aunt is an excellent baker.

"But Sarah isn't coming?" I asked.

"I'm afraid not," Uncle Mark didn't elaborate, and I didn't ask for more details. I'd noticed that Sarah rarely accepted invitations to the

O'Hara family get-togethers. I was thankful my nemesis didn't keep Mark from attending all O'Hara family gatherings.

"Good morning!" Another voice sounded from the laundry room—a voice that I knew well.

"Hey Brian, it's good to see you," my dad greeted my former beau. Unlike my uncle, Brian wore his police blues that set off his sea-blue eyes perfectly. Brian and I are no longer involved—I'm with David—but my former boyfriend is still attractive.

"It's good to see you too, Gary. Thanks for the invitation," Brian replied. He turned to acknowledge me. "Char."

"Brian," I felt my face warm despite myself. I looked down at my plate.

"Any news on the case?" My dad asked as he carried two more coffee mugs to the island. Then he grabbed plates, silver, and the coffee carafe. Mark and Brian sat on either side of me.

"We're still investigating. Everything is out for testing. No need to worry. We believe Wilma's murder was an isolated incident."

"But you have a prime suspect," I said without looking up from my plate.

"No, Charlotte. We don't have a prime suspect—yet—but we have," Mark stopped himself and shook his head. "What am I doing? Charlotte, you know by now that you don't need to investigate. No, I'll rephrase that. You know you need to stay out of my investigation."

"Yes, Uncle Mark," I shifted in my seat and felt a twinge in my side. I groaned loudly, making all three men turn their eyes on me.

"Are you okay?" Brian asked.

"Fine," I lied. "Something happened when I was at David's last night. I'm fine."

"Doll, are you sure? You were walking a bit funny when you came in," my dad said.

Brian's eyebrows nearly leaped from his red-hot face. He did his best to look away from me.

TROUBLE BREWING

"Fine," I repeated, "David and I just...crashed into each other a bit hard."

Brian sucked in a deep breath and tried not to laugh.

"David hurt you?" Uncle Mark's voice bellowed.

"No. I mean, yes, but," I shook my head, "it was an accident. He hurt himself too."

"Char, do I need to go up there?" Uncle Mark asked. His voice grew lower. Protective. "Do you want me to talk to him?"

I couldn't help but laugh. "No. It's not like that. David didn't hurt me-hurt me. He would never harm me," I shook my head and groaned again from the pain created by the tiny movement.

"I was too embarrassed to say this, but David and I had a little dancing accident last night."

"Please tell me that's not a euphemism," my uncle replied. "If it is, I don't require further explanation."

"Me either," both my father and Brian chimed in.

"No! See, I got this dumb idea in my head." I laughed again and rubbed my hurting side, "I thought it would be fun to surprise our wedding guests by performing that dance from Dirty Dancing—you know—where Johnny lifts Baby?"

Brian's eyes grew wide, and he burst out laughing. "Char, no offense, but you are probably the last person on earth who should try that move. You're the clumsiest person I know, and David's a bit old to try that lift. I bet he hurt himself."

"Brian! David isn't *that* old! Anyway, I think we are finished with that," I replied. "I can't seem to get the timing right, and poor David is getting battered. Last time, I gave him a fat lip and a blackeye."

"It sounds like you took a few lumps," my dad added. "Maybe you should try a waltz."

"Does that mean the two of you set a date for the wedding?" Uncle Mark asked.

"No. Not yet," I replied. "I'm not in a hurry. There's time. Anyway, you and Sarah got engaged first. When is your wedding?"

My usually cool-as-a-cucumber uncle flushed.

"Uh-huh. Well, you let us know, okay?" I said with a grin.

"We've had a few hiccups, but soon," my uncle replied, "we'll announce a date soon."

"I'll be waiting with bells on," I replied, then I added, "that's not a euphemism."

My uncle shook his head. "You are such a smart aleck."

"Where is David anyway?" Brian asked.

"Um. David threw his back out," I admitted. "I went in too hot, and we fell. He took pills from the last time he tweaked it. David passed out on the sofa. He was asleep when I left."

"Too old," Brian mumbled softly, but I heard him. I poked him in the ribcage.

"Ouch!" Brian yipped. I muffled my laughter—mostly because laughing hurt too much.

"Charlotte, I am glad your mother isn't at home to hear this," my dad informed me.

"Yeah, me too. So anyway, no more lifts—I promise," I said, as the heat from embarrassment rose in my face.

My dad excused me from dishwashing duty because of my injury. I left the house when Brian left—something I had engineered. Clouseau pranced outside with us.

"Hey. Could we talk?" I asked Brian once we'd exited my parents' home.

"Sure," Brian replied.

"Who is the lead investigator in Wilma Platt's death?"

Brian set his hands on his hips, "Me. Why?"

"Okay, promise you won't get mad," I said.

TROUBLE BREWING

"Char, whenever someone says 'don't get mad,' it usually means they know I will be mad when I hear what they want to say. I can't make you that promise."

"Fine. I know something that may be relevant to the case, but I promise you that I haven't done any investigating," I replied, hoping that Brian wouldn't get angry.

Brian shifted. "I'll bite. What did David find on the internet?"

"I didn't say anything about David."

"Char? You know that I know all about David's internet searches. For the record, I'm a damn good investigator too. So, spill it. What is it that you think you know that I don't?"

"Fine. Consider all the beer contestants as suspects in Wilma's death. They each had motives to harm Wilma—well, all of them except Scotty Wells."

"We are looking at everyone, Char, but I spoke to the other beer contest winners yesterday. They all have their trophies. We know who the trophy belongs to," Brian said.

"Scotty, right? He's your person of interest."

"I have to go, Char, but rest assured, I know what I am doing. That's why I have this uniform and a badge," Brian said before he drove off in his police cruiser.

Something troubled me. Why would Scotty tell me that he'd met a woman for drinks at the sports bar if it wasn't true? Was he trying to convince me of his alibi? If Scotty were lying about being at the bar, it would be easy enough to prove—surely someone would remember seeing Scotty there. Furthermore, I was sure that if Brian knew about Scotty's alibi, he would have checked it out himself. My uncle knew Scotty failed to meet up with my friends and me on Friday night. I wondered if Uncle Mark shared that piece of information with Brian.

I looked at the time on my cell phone. It was early—only a little after ten in the morning—too early to go to the sports bar to check out Scotty's alibi myself. The drive to Crystal Creek would only take fifteen minutes—maybe even less due to sparse Sunday traffic. The bar wasn't likely to open until 11 or even noon. I had an idea and time to burn, so I got into my car and drove into Spruce Grove.

"Char, were we supposed to meet up?" Cassie asked me as she stood in her doorway wearing a fuzzy pink robe and slippers.

"No, but I need a favor," I replied.

"Come inside," Cassie opened the door and invited me in.

"Where are Joe and Max?" I asked. I didn't see Cassie's husband or their daughter at first glance.

"Joe is at Magic Beans, and Max had better be brushing her teeth," Cassie said with a raised voice.

"Is something the matter?" I asked.

Cassie shook her head. "Max had three cavities at her last dentist appointment. Three! I found out that she hasn't brushed or flossed her teeth as often as she should. She also joined a candy club at school. Max has been protesting her braces—I told her she is only hurting herself."

"Oh." I arrived at an inconvenient time.

The bathroom door flew open, and Max Binder, all four-foot-three of her, emerged. "I brushed them," she said defiantly. She walked straight up to her mother.

"Open?" Cassie said to Max.

Max opened her mouth wide, and I saw the silvery gleam of new braces on her teeth. Cassie leaned forward and sniffed her daughter's breath. "Okay. Good job."

"I've come at a bad time," I said. I was rethinking my plan of asking Cassie to accompany me to the sports bar. She had her hands full with Max.

"Auntie Char, are we going to go shopping?" Max asked me.

TROUBLE BREWING

I'd promised my goddaughter weeks ago that I'd take her shopping, and I'd forgotten all about it.

"That sounds like a great idea," Cassie broke in, "if you're up for it. I have a bunch of store inventory that I need to log. I would breeze through the job if you took Max out."

"Um." I was speechless. I wanted to check out the sports bar before noon when it filled with patrons. Max stood before me, her big, warm eyes looking straight at me.

"Auntie Char, you promised!" Max whined when I didn't reply. "Char, you said you would take me shopping last month too, and you didn't. You lied."

I felt my heart squeeze. I was a bad godmother.

"You want to go to the store with all the ten-dollar-or-less items, don't you?" I asked, remembering my promise. The new store in Crystal Creek was all the rage with pre-teens. The lure of trendy, cheap goods tantalized poor Max.

"Yes. And you promised," Max replied.

I exhaled. "Well, I am supposed to go to Crystal Creek this morning, but..." I couldn't think of an excuse to shirk my godparent duties.

"Done!" Cassie nearly shouted. "Max, you go and find your sneakers. We don't want to keep Auntie Char waiting."

Max dashed off to her bedroom.

"Thank you so much, Char! You don't know how much this means to me. Max was a real handful at her grandparents' house the other day. Don't even ask me about the football game. You are doing me a huge favor—taking her off my hands for an hour or two."

"I..." I didn't know what to say.

"I know. I know! I sound like such an awful parent, but Max was looking forward to hanging out with you. She misses you. And I need to finish the inventory." My best friend piled the guilt on thick.

"Okay," I replied.

I felt guilty for breaking my promise to Max, and I tried to hide my reluctance to spend time with her. It was Sunday, and on Monday, I would be too busy with work on the tree farm to check out the sports bar. Maybe I could drop by quick—perhaps Max could stay in the car while I went inside. I could check Scotty's alibi and spend time with my goddaughter.

"Thank you, thank you, thank you!" Cassie gratefully replied. She was certainly happy to see Max go. I wondered if I should worry.

"Is there anything special that I need to know?" I asked. If Max made a habit of acting out—being a little tyrant—I wanted to be prepared.

"No, just remember her allergies—Max knows them—and everything is on the list I gave you the last time you had her."

"I have the list of Max's allergies in my purse and children's Benadryl," I said, "but what about her...mood?"

"She'll be fine," Cassie replied, "she saves her rebelliousness for me these days. Joe is a saint in Max's eyes. I swear, I thought I had a few more years before the teen behavior started. She's not even nine yet!"

"They grow up quickly," I replied. "Just wait until puberty."

"Oh Gawd, don't remind me," Cassie gasped. "That's only a few years away."

"I'm ready!" Max announced as she dashed back into the room. While in her bedroom, she'd changed out of the jean shorts and t-shirt she wore. Max stood in front of me dressed in a hot pink dress with large white polka dots and a pair of sequined silver tennis shoes. On her head, Max wore a matching sequined headband. She looked cute and playful. Max didn't look rebellious at all.

"Max Renee Binder, please be on your best behavior for Auntie Char. She might not take you out again if you misbehave today," Cassie warned her daughter.

"I promise," Max kissed Cassie's cheek and reached for my hand. My heart melted.

TROUBLE BREWING

"Let's go, Char."

"Oh, wait," Cassie said as Max and I walked to the door, "what was the favor you wanted to ask?"

I could hardly ask my best friend to go to the bar with me, "It was nothing," I replied.

"See you in a couple of hours?" Cassie asked.

"Yep, I'll text you before we leave Crystal Creek," I replied.

Cassie mouthed thank you one more time before I exited her home.

"Yes!" Max said after I buckled her into the car seat in the back of my SUV. She wasn't big enough yet to ride without one. "I've been dying to go to that store! Jenna got earbuds for eight bucks."

"Earbuds?" I asked as I opened the driver's side door. I didn't bother to ask who Jenna was. "Do you even have a Smartphone?"

"Not yet," Max replied. She began to hum a tune I didn't recognize. I pulled away from the curb.

We arrived at the sports bar about 15 minutes later, and the Open sign in the front window glowed. The bar must have just opened.

"Max, I need to go inside that place and talk to someone," I told my young friend. "You can wait here for a few minutes, right?"

Max crossed her arms over her chest, "Auntie Char, don't you know you aren't supposed to leave young children unattended in the car?"

"Well...yes, but I thought you were big enough," I replied. How old was old enough?

"No, I'm not old enough, and I have nothing to do. Maybe you could leave your cell phone with me."

"Nice try. The last time I did that, you locked all of my apps and changed my ringtone to that shark song," I replied. It took my technology-guru fiancé, David, over an hour to restore my phone to its normal state after Max got her tiny hands on it.

63

Max laughed, "I forgot about that. That was funny!"

"Are you sure you can't wait in the car? I need my phone. I have to show some pictures to the man inside."

Max shrugged noncommittally. "Maybe. Children are unpredictable, Char."

Ugh!

Max was too smart for her own good, the little Dickens!

"Fine, you can come with me," I relented. "This should only take a minute." I stepped out of my SUV and opened the rear passenger door to help Max out of her seat. My little companion had extricated herself from the complicated car seat and was ready to climb out before I had the door open.

"Listen, when we're inside, don't touch anything, and don't talk to anyone, okay?"

"Why not?" Max asked.

"Because these places can be dirty. And, more importantly, people your age aren't supposed to go inside," I told her.

"Really?" Max asked, her eyes brightening.

"Yes, also, and this is very important, Max, don't tell your parents that I brought you here," I said, "if you tell them, your mommy might never let me take you shopping again. You wouldn't like that, would you?"

We walked up to the front doors of Calamity Jane's, and I waited for my young charge to reply.

"Okay, I'll do what you say, but you'll owe me candy. The store we're going to has a self-service candy counter."

"Max, your teeth," I said with a cringe. I imagined Cassie might be angrier with me for buying her daughter candy than for taking her to a bar.

"I won't tell if you don't," Max replied with a grin. The child genius was blackmailing me, and I was falling for it.

"Fine. Shake on it?" I asked as I offered Max my hand. Max put her tiny hand in mine and pumped it.

We walked into the somewhat new bar called Calamity Jane's. The lights were up, and the place didn't look so dirty. Only a handful of patrons sat at the tables, and a burly man with tattoos and a handlebar mustache stood behind the taps. He was filling a glass with foam.

"Hi," I greeted the man. He glanced at me with bored dark eyes.

"Hi!" Max said as she hopped onto a barstool.

"Kids aren't permitted at the bar. She can sit in the dining area," the bartender informed me. He dumped the foam into the sink.

Max slid off the barstool and walked to the nearest table.

"What can I get you?" The barman asked without facing me.

"Information?" I asked. "I wanted to know if you worked here Friday night."

"Maybe, that depends on who is asking."

"Me. I'm asking," I replied, softening my voice. "Listen, this is a bit humiliating. I think that my husband is cheating on me. We have a kid together," I nodded in Max's direction.

"Cute," the barman's voice was flat and noncommittal.

"Yes. Thanks. I think my husband might have been here with another woman Friday night. I need to know the truth," I lied.

The barman exhaled. I could tell he was weighing his options.

"I don't want to make a mistake," I continued, "if he's stepping out now, I need to know."

"Yeah, I worked Friday. Friday is our second busiest night. There were a lot of people here. I'm not sure I'd recognize your man if he were here."

"I understand," I replied, "I have a photo, and my husband is kind of distinctive looking. He's about five-foot-six, and his hair is short. His voice reminds me of a foghorn."

I pulled my phone from my handbag and opened it to a photo I found earlier. The picture of Scotty Wells came from the annual Christmas Pageant. He'd played Joseph.

"This is him," I handed the phone to the bartender.

The man's eyebrows raised in recognition, "Yeah, he was here."

"Was he with someone?" I asked.

The barmen nodded and took a few steps back as if he thought I would assault him—the disgruntled, cheated-upon woman. "He was with a woman."

Scotty had an alibi! I tried not to shout, 'Hurray!'

"Do you know who the woman was?" I asked, hoping for a name or a description of Scotty's companion.

The bartender shook his head at me, "I don't know her name—it's not like I asked. Honestly, the two didn't look like a couple—they were different types—do you know what I mean?"

"How so?" I asked, curious.

"Your husband looked like the buttoned-up type—an accountant or teacher—you know? She looked like more of a free spirit. Not a like white collar woman—a hippy type. She had long, crazy, red hair, floaty clothes. You know the type. The two got along okay, though."

"Oh?" I did know what he meant, and I thought I might know who the woman was.

"Look, I don't make a habit of spying on my customers, and it was busy here on Friday night, but I noticed them. The woman seemed upset about something."

"Really?" I wanted more intel.

"Yeah, but as I said, I wasn't paying much attention," the bartender shrugged. "I can tell you, he got here first, but when they left, they left together."

"They went home together?" I asked, surprised. Scotty left that part out.

TROUBLE BREWING

"That's not what I said, is it?" The bartender leaned against the bar. His blackish eyes narrowed. "I said that they left together. I have an idea what they did once they walked out the door. Your guy paid the bill—used a bank card—and then they walked outside together. I haven't seen them since."

"Right. Okay. Would you do me a favor?" I grabbed a cocktail napkin and a pen from the bar top. I wrote my phone number down along with my first name, "Please call me if you see my husband again—or if you think of anything unusual that happened on Friday."

The bartender raised an eyebrow, "Unusual?"

"I won't rat you out. I want to know what my husband was doing. If he's serious about that woman," I let my voice trail off.

"I'm not making any promises," the barman finally said.

"Also, if the police were to ask for a copy of his bar tab, you could look it up, right?" I asked, hopeful.

"Why would the police ask for his bar tab?" The bartender looked annoyed.

"I don't know. Sorry, I have to go. Max!" I trotted across the floor and took Max's hand. I shouted thanks over my shoulder as we hustled out the door.

SIX

"Wow! Char, look at this one!" Max held up an oversized, inflatable pineapple to show it to me. "Do you want it too?'

I looked down at the shopping cart that I was pushing. I don't know what came over me. I figured Max would be the overzealous shopper, not me! But the items in my shopping cart proved that I was the one with the impulse-control problem. We'd arrived at the store during their summer clearance sale, and I was clearing out the place. Nothing shiny was safe from my grasp! The shopping cart was stacked high with various colorful doo-dads and yard decorations. There was a 4-pack of citronella candles shaped like pineapples, strings of festive outdoor lights, and a set of garish garden Gnomes. My favorite item: beverage glasses shaped like hulled-out coconuts. What harm could an inflatable pineapple bring this late in the game? I nodded to Max, "Yes, I want it. In fact, get two of them."

Max obliged with a smile and set two comical, yellow, plastic, inflatable pineapples in my cart.

"What are you going to do with all this stuff?" She asked me. The pitch of her voice was high, and a bit uncertain. Even Max Binder knew that I was being ridiculous.

"A party?" I answered in the form of a question. The truth was, I hadn't thought things through before I started piling items into the shopping cart. I was like a crow that grabbed anything that caught its eye.

"Is this for your wedding?" She asked. Her eyes brightened. Max loves weddings.

Hmm. Maybe? David and I could have a tropical-themed wedding. It was nearly autumn, and a tropical-themed party should take place outdoors. An outdoor party in Pennsylvania needs to happen when it's warm. If I wanted a tropical-themed wedding in Pennsylvania, David and I would have to wait to until at least the end of June.

"We'll see," I replied with a noncommittal shrug. I lifted a sun tea pitcher, inspected it for damage, and set it into my cart. "Everything is so inexpensive, it can't hurt to prepare, right?"

Max shrugged her shoulders, "I'm eight years old. I don't know."

I won't tell you how much I spent on clearance party items. I had to make two trips from the store to my car. There was a set of four Adirondack chairs marked down 40% I spied next to the exit—I couldn't leave them behind. The clerk had to summon someone from the warehouse to help me carry my items to the SUV. Even with half of the rear seat folded down, the merchandise barely fit in the cargo section. There was still room for Max, of course.

I pulled away from the curb and felt the heat of embarrassment rise to my face. What was David going to say when I pulled into his driveway with my SUV loaded down with plastic junk? I couldn't take my purchases to my cottage—there wasn't enough room for everything. Also, my mom would freak out if she saw what I bought.

I shook my head and resolved to give myself a break. A tropical wedding sounded like a lot of fun. I glanced into the rearview mirror and discovered that Max had fallen asleep. I'd worn out the little terror—at least Cassie would be happy. I hoped that my little charge kept her end of our bargain, and she didn't tell her mom about our trip to the sports bar. That wasn't one of my proudest moments.

I'd bought Max about ten bucks worth of mix-and-match candy, so she'd keep quiet about our visit to the bar. We hid most of the goodies in her new pink, sparkly, backpack. I told Max that there was no way that her mom would believe that we left the store without a little bit of candy. Max kept a modest-sized bag of treats clutched in her hands.

With Max fast asleep, I had about 15 minutes of me-time during the drive home.

I thought about the bartender and what he'd said about Scotty and the mystery woman he'd shared drinks with on Friday night. Based on the bartender's description, I was pretty sure I knew who the woman was, and I wondered why Scotty had lied to me.

I fumbled in my pocket for my phone without taking my eyes off the road. I had Scotty's number saved. I developed the habit of saving phone numbers when people called me—that way, I'd recognize callers and I could avoid their calls whenever I wanted.

I told the smart person inside my phone to dial Scooter Wells, and I waited for our call to connect.

"Charlotte?" Scotty picked up immediately—almost as if he was waiting for a phone call.

"Hi, Scoot...Scotty. Do you have a second?" I asked.

"Um. Sure. What's up?"

"I need to ask you something," I began, "I know who you were with at the bar on Friday night."

"Oh?" I imagined Scotty's face contorting as he thought of a cover-up lie to tell me.

"Poppy Flint? Were you with Poppy?" I asked.

"No," he answered too quick and too sharp. I knew Scotty was lying. As a creative fibber myself, I knew the signs of an amateur liar—the lady doth protest too much and all that. Shakespeare definitely had things right.

"I *know*, Scotty. There were witnesses at the bar," I explained. "They saw the two of you together."

"I...are you spying on me, Charlotte?" Scotty sounded flustered and accusatory—more signs of someone caught in a lie.

"No. I am not spying. Look. I understand if you think you can't admit it. Poppy is a married woman," I replied. "I know that getting caught must sound awful, but Scotty a woman died. You can't cover this up."

Scotty exhaled. "It wasn't like that, Charlotte."

"Do you admit that you were with Poppy Flint on Friday night?" I asked as I played a detective.

"What is this? An interrogation?" He protested.

"No, but if you were with Poppy, and I am pretty certain that you were, that might give you an alibi for the time of Ms. Platt's death."

"Who said I needed an alibi, Charlotte?" Scotty objected.

"Come on, Scotty, why won't you tell me?" I asked. "I'm on your side here."

"That's a first," Scotty said. "Since when have you cared?"

"I mean it. After we spoke the other day, I developed a new perspective. Scotty, I am convinced that you didn't kill Wilma. Don't ask me how I know this, but you are the police's number one person of interest. That is why you need a strong alibi."

Scotty exhaled again. "This is all getting out of hand." He took a beat before he spoke again. "Fine, but if I tell you the truth, you can't say anything to anyone."

"Scotty, admitting that you were with Poppy on Friday night could save you. Don't you think you should say something to the police?" I asked. "Poppy will confirm your story, won't she?"

"Charlotte, I am innocent. Friday night I shared a couple of drinks with a friend. I am confident that the police will figure out that I didn't do anything wrong."

"Do you watch the news, Scotty?" I asked with cynicism. "These things don't always turn out the way we think they will."

"I know! I know!" Scotty's voice rose. He was worried.

"Then tell me what happened Friday night. Maybe I can help you," I offered.

"First, Poppy and I are NOT having an affair, okay? She's not my type. There's always been someone else someone who is unattainable..." Scotty's voice trailed off.

Despite my new compassion for Scotty, I cringed when I realized he was talking about my bestie—Cassie. She was the unattainable woman for whom Scotty Wells pined over. Scotty couldn't see me through the cell phone—if Scotty could see me, he'd see the world's biggest grimace on my face.

"Scotty?" I asked when he remained silent for too long. "Are you still there?"

"Charlotte, I can't say anything about Poppy because she's in trouble and I promised I would help her. When I told you that I met someone at the farm show, it was Poppy. It was you who assumed that it was a date, and I didn't bother to deny it. It felt good to hear that someone thought that a woman asked me out," Scotty said. "Poppy asked me to meet her because she wanted to talk away from eavesdroppers—you know that Spruce Grove is full of them."

Scotty was right. The Spruce Grove grapevine is like a noxious weed.

"What kind of trouble is Poppy in?" I asked as I took a sharp bend in the road and looked into the rearview again to make sure Max was asleep. She was.

"Poppy wouldn't say. She only told me that she needs to get out of town for a while. She needed to sort some things out. I got the feeling that something bad happened to her."

"Oh. That's too bad. But what does that have to do with you? Why did Poppy seek you out?" I asked. Perhaps Scotty was still lying about how well he knew Poppy Flint. Like the barman had said, Scotty and Poppy are about as opposite as two people can get, but we all know that sometimes opposites attract. Look at me and David.

"I took a couple of yoga classes with Poppy earlier in the year," Scotty explained. "I had bad sciatica from sitting at work all day, and Poppy tried to help me. Anyway, we used to talk after class over glasses of cucumber water. I guess told Poppy about my cabin. I have a sweet cabin upstate," Scotty said.

"Yes, I remember," I said with an eye roll. Scotty likes to talk about his cabin. It would surprise me if anyone in Spruce Grove didn't know about Scotty's weekend place.

"Poppy remembered the cabin too. She asked if it was in use and if I would be willing to let her stay there while she worked a few things out. I told Poppy that I was about to close up the cabin for the season. She offered to pay rent if I let her stay there."

"What kind of trouble Poppy is in? Did she offer any details?" I asked, curious.

The Flints were newer residents in Spruce Grove, and I didn't know too much about them. Poppy ran the yoga studio. Mick did custodial work—taking care of small maintenance projects in various shops and offices in Spruce Grove. Mick struck me as a quiet, cerebral type with a lot on his mind and not a lot to say. Poppy is a free spirit—the kind of person who organizes fireside chants and dances under the moon during the winter solstice.

"I didn't ask Poppy too much. I didn't think her problems were my business," Scotty said.

"I guess not," I admitted. I noticed that I'd reached the stretch of highway where cell signals were spotty. I needed to finish up our conversation or risk losing Scotty. "Did you agree to let Poppy stay?"

The next thing I heard was a click. Our call dropped.

I had no recourse but to keep driving. Max was still asleep. Her little mouth moved a bit like she was chattering as she slept. She was cute when she wasn't being a terror. Maybe I would have one someday.

Once I drove out of the cell phone dead zone, I redialed Scotty. This time, Scotty didn't pick up. My call went straight to his voicemail. *'This is Scott Wells, Assistant Principal of Spruce Grove High School and craft beer brewer. I am sorry I missed your call...'*

Ugh! I disconnected the call without leaving a message. Scotty was avoiding me.

After I dropped Max off at her house, I drove back to the farm. I was hungry because all Max wanted to eat for lunch was candy, and I couldn't stomach more than three pieces. I sauntered into my mother's kitchen hoping that she was home and cooking. The kitchen smelled sweet and spicy. I recognized the smell of my mother's Arrabbiata sauce. Mom had a bumper crop of tomatoes, and she busied herself canning sauce for the future.

Clouseau shimmied up to me as I entered the room. I crouched to greet my dog.

"Hey little buddy," I said to Clouseau as I stroked his curly head.

Clouseau's little curly tail wagged, and he sniffed my hands. Then he sneezed and hit his nose on the hardwood floor and that caused him to sneeze again. Each time he sneezed, Clouseau hit his nose and sneezed again. I lifted the poor dog to prevent him from knocking himself silly.

"There, there," I comforted my pup, and he stopped sneezing.

"That dog," my mother said without further comment. She stood at the stove stirring the sauce. "Where were you all day?"

"I had plans with Max Binder," I replied, "after I had brunch with dad and the boys."

My mom tutted her tongue. "Can you believe this mess? I know he meant well, but your father does not know how to clean a kitchen."

I let my eyes rove the pristine kitchen. The countertops shined and the stainless-steel appliances sparkled. "I don't see anything wrong."

"Of course, you don't," my mother said with a shake of her head.

"Anyway, I have to admit, Dad makes some pretty tasty French toast."

My mother shot a warning glance in my direction. Mom was very comfortable in her position of Chief Cook and Wine Glass Washer, and she wasn't about to be replaced by my father or anyone else.

"Dad's is not as good as your French toast, but it was definitely edible," I corrected—after all, I was on the hunt for a free meal. I didn't want to insult the cook.

"Dinner is at six," my mother, the mind reader, said.

I looked at the clock. It was only a few minutes after 3. My tummy grumbled.

I carried Clouseau to one of his many doggy beds—the one on the cusp of the threshold between the laundry room and the kitchen, and I set him down. I walked to the kitchen pantry and retrieved a box of graham crackers, pulled one from the box, and shoved it in my mouth.

"Charlotte, did you wash your hands? You touched the dog," my mother scolded.

"*Mmm mune*," I replied, my mouth full of crackers.

"I can't understand you with your mouth full!"

She shook her head again, so I walked to the sink, washed my hands, and swallowed the cracker.

"I said, 'I'm immune'—at least to Clouseau's cooties. He is my second brother. We live under the same roof, sleep on the same furniture, and share food. Clouseau and I practically share DNA at this point," I said as I dried my hands.

Ignoring my impromptu genetics lesson, my mother asked, "What did you and Max do today?"

We'd moved beyond my ill manners. Thankfully, my mother's tirades are generally short-lived. Patty O'Hara knows that battling me and my father on our lack of manners is pointless.

"We went to that store with all the stuff," I said as I popped another cracker.

My mouth grew dry. I needed a glass of milk. I reached for a tumbler from the cupboard and walked to the fridge. When I opened the refrigerator, I was horrified to see only nonfat milk. "Mom, where's the good stuff?" I asked holding up the offending carton of milk.

"Your father is on a diet," she replied. She left out the *again*. My mother puts my father on diets so often that she's going to need to start calling the diets something else.

I sighed and poured myself a glass of the opaque liquid. Beggars can't be choosers.

TROUBLE BREWING

"You have to be more specific than 'the store with the stuff,' Charlotte if you want me to know where you were today. You are a writer—sort of—you should be more precise in your descriptions."

"Ugh. I haven't written an article for Around the Town in months, Mom," I leaned against the kitchen counter and sulked. "No one wants to be featured in my blog anymore."

"That's because you write things that are unflattering," my mother offered as she stirred the pot.

"I said one uncharitable thing about a meal I had at Le Petit Croissant. I had no idea how much feedback I'd get."

The French-inspired diner closed a month after I wrote an article that said that the pastry that I'd gotten there was stale. I wasn't their only unsatisfied customer.

"Well, you'll think of something to write."

"Maybe. Or maybe it's time to hang up my blogger's hat. I will have to if I don't come up with a by-line soon. The natives get restless for my unique perspective on things," I sighed. "I would write about Wilma Platt, but so far, no one is saying anything interesting about her death."

"Charlotte!" My mother scolded. "You don't want to write about that poor woman, do you?"

I shrugged. Was it my fault that Wilma Platt's death in the pigpen was the most interesting thing that happened in Spruce County in months?

"You could write an article about wedding planning. Those are always nice," my mother offered. I knew she had ulterior motives. My momzilla wanted to plan my wedding, and so far, I hadn't invited her to help me.

"I could," I sighed again. I didn't want to risk turning my blog—which is an entertainment blog—into a diary of my wedding planning escapades. There weren't any escapades at the moment—wedding-related or otherwise. I hadn't even picked out a wedding gown. That was when I remembered all the plastic junk in my SUV, and I sighed yet again.

"Where did you say that you went with Max?" My mother asked me.

"I took her to that trendy 'tween store in Crystal Creek. It's the place with all the budget-friendly plastic stuff," I replied.

"Oh, good grief! I don't like those places," my mother lamented. "Plastic waste is so bad for the planet. You must have had nothing to do. I hope you didn't buy too many things for Max—not that she doesn't deserve a treat. I don't think Cassie wants to clutter her cute home with those kinds of things."

"No, rest assured, I didn't buy much of anything for Max. I got her a cute backpack for school and a tiny bag of candy."

I didn't dare mention the tiki party in the back of my SUV. I needed to figure out what I was going to do with all the tropical décor that was weighing down my car and fast! I didn't want Patty O'Hara to see my stash.

"Oh. That's nice," my mother replied.

"Yes, and our excursion gave Cassie some time to get work done. She'll be happy," I replied.

I shut the box of graham crackers and carried it back to the pantry. After I drank the last of the nonfat milk, I rinsed my glass and placed it in the dishwasher. "I should get going. I have a lot to do."

"Oh?" My mother raised a skeptical penciled-in eyebrow.

"Wedding planning," I fibbed. I needed to get to David's place and find somewhere to stow my purchases.

"What about dinner?" My mother asked.

"I have a few hours. I'll be back."

"What is all this stuff?" David asked me as he lifted a set of jingling, gaudy, bird-shaped windchimes from my car and stared at it.

"Don't ask," I replied, "I was thinking tiki-themed wedding earlier. Max Binder was my accomplice. I don't suppose I can blame an eight-and-three-quarters-year-old for having bad taste. Looking at these things now, I don't think a tropical wedding in Spruce Grove is going to work."

"Okay," David replied. He was so patient with me.

"Anyway, I had an interesting day," I continued.

"Oh?" David helped me unload one of the chairs and immediately grasped his lower back.

"Sorry," I replied with a cringe. "I'll finish unloading. Why don't you rest?"

David didn't argue with me. He plopped down in one of the Adirondack chairs and sighed. "This is surprisingly comfortable," he said of the chair.

"Right? I got a huge discount for buying the set. I thought we'd put them outside on the patio. Near the firepit you are building." At least the chairs were something I could keep.

"Sure. Now, what made your day interesting? Did you buy an entire flea market or something?"

I chuckled. "No. I went to that newish sports bar in Crystal Creek—you know the one—Calamity Jane's."

David nodded, "yes."

"I interviewed the bartender, and he remembered seeing Scotty on Friday night. He remembered Scotty's date too." I lifted one of the inflatable pineapples and shook my head. What was I thinking when I bought them?

"Wait. I thought you had Max Binder with you?" David asked. "Where was Max when you were in the bar?"

"Um. Well, Max wouldn't let me leave her in the car..."

"Of course not," David said as if it was obvious that leaving an eight-year-old in a parked SUV outside of a bar was a bad idea.

"So, I took Max into the bar with me," I said.

David's eyebrows lifted.

"There was hardly anyone inside the bar," I continued, "and we weren't in there long. I couldn't leave Max in the car."

"Still. I can't imagine your best friend would like hearing that you took her daughter to a bar. You know they have a wet t-shirt contest on Friday night and foxy boxing on Wednesday."

"Okay," I said, "I wasn't aware of those details, and I didn't know that you knew them either."

"We weren't always a couple, Char," David reminded me.

He was right. David was a free agent when he moved to town. I was pursuing Brian when David relocated to Spruce Grove.

"Anyway, those details were a surprise to me as well. What if Max tells Cassie where you took her?" David asked me.

"Max and I already sorted that out. I bribed her," I said.

"Right...How?"

"Candy. Lots and lots of candy.

David chuckled.

"As I was saying, the barman remembered Scotty, and from the description of Scotty's date. Scotty was at the bar with Poppy Flint."

"Yoga studio Poppy?" David looked skeptical. "I can't picture them together."

"Yes, I know it sounds strange, and Scotty insisted that they weren't there on a date. Poppy wanted a favor from Scotty and someone to talk to. She said that she was in some kind of trouble, and she asked Scotty if she could rent his cabin."

"The place you refer to as the murder cabin?" David asked me.

I'd made a habit of calling Scotty's cabin the murder cabin as a kind of joke. How could I know that Scotty would be implicated in an actual murder?

"Yes. That's the one."

"Okay, so maybe Scotty has an alibi for Wilma's death," David replied.

TROUBLE BREWING

"Exactly! What a relief. The problem is Scotty refuses to tell the police about his alibi. Poppy swore him to secrecy—which is odd, right? Why doesn't Poppy want anyone to know where she will be? Why won't Scotty use Poppy as an alibi?"

I finished unloading my purchases and wiped the sweat from my brow. I still had to lug the items into the garage.

"You have a point. Then again, we have no way of knowing when Wilma died. If he got the timing right, Scotty could have killed her and still gone out with Poppy," David offered. He tilted his head like he was thinking. "Or he could be covering up for Poppy. Could Poppy Flint be a killer?"

"Poppy?" I couldn't imagine the friendly yogi as a killer. "I don't see it. If Poppy killed Wilma, why would Scotty help her?"

"I can think of at least one reason a guy like Scotty might keep Poppy's secret," David said.

"Scotty insisted that he and Poppy aren't having an affair. If that's what you are thinking. I am sure that Scotty is aware of Poppy's big, strong, handsome, husband. I believed Scotty. I don't think Scotty and Poppy are having an affair, and I no longer believe that Scotty killed Wilma."

"Did Scotty agree to rent the cabin to Poppy?" David asked. He stood from the chair intent on helping me move the junk I'd purchased. He grimaced with the effort. I waved him off even though my dance injury hurt too.

"I don't know. I was in that cell phone dead zone, and our call dropped. When I phoned Scotty back, my call went straight to voice mail."

"Oh well," David replied. "The case is in the police's hands. I am sure Brian Gold will figure everything out. Wilma's murderer will be in prison in no time."

"Really?" I began carrying some items into the garage, and David followed me.

"Sure. They might be a bit unconventional, but in my experience, the Spruce Grove Police Department always gets their man—or their woman." David rubbed his back, "So, not to change the subject or anything, but what do you want to do about our wedding? We don't need to go tropical, but what other themes would you consider?"

"I'm not sure. There's no rush though, right?" I asked.

"No, I suppose not," David replied as he stared at a string of margarita lights. "What would you like for dinner?"

"Whatever Mom is cooking. She's expecting us at six," I replied.

"Great." David rubbed his lower back.

Dinner with my parents is always chaotic, but I was thankful that David wouldn't feel obligated to cook for me. His back was bothering him. I don't offer to cook often because I'm a horrible cook.

"You should take another painkiller before we go over to chez O'Hara. Also, based on our injuries that we should definitely skip my dirty dancing idea. Between your back and my achy side, we're only half of a person. I guess that my dream of being 'Baby' to your 'Johnny' was a bit of a stretch. We should do something else for our first dance as newlyweds."

"Agreed," David said. I could see the relief on his face. "Perhaps we can do a normal slow dance. Or a waltz. I can handle that."

"Agreed," I replied as I feigned a waltz around David's garage.

One, two, three. One, two, three.

"I would like us to be able to enjoy our honeymoon uninjured." I winked at David and winced at the pain in my side.

SEVEN

Monday

Despite my painful side, I rose early Monday morning and walked to work. I promised my mother that I'd help with the billing in our office first and then work on the farm in the afternoon. I left David snoring in his bed, and I changed into a semi-cute outfit of dark skinny jeans, a plain white t-shirt, and black low-court sneakers. I put my long, wavy brown hair up into a high ponytail, and slashed some red lipstick on my lips for color.

It didn't take long for me to post the billing, print the invoices, and slip them into envelopes. O'Hara's tree farm has a handful of clients who buy trees for landscaping throughout the year. The rest of our income is from the sale of Christmas trees, and we accept direct payment for those.

I stood from my office chair and stretched to get the kinks out of my neck and back. "Ouch!" I exclaimed as I felt the ache in my side once more.

My mother looked up from her computer. The glasses she wore made her eyes look owlish and twice their normal size. "What is wrong?" She asked.

"I pulled a muscle in my abdomen in an unfortunate dancing accident," I replied as I rubbed the side of my tummy. "It hurts."

"I don't think I want any further details," my mother said. "Are you finished with the billing?"

"I am, and it's getting close to noon. I thought I'd zip into town for some lunch. Would you like me to bring anything back for you from Magic Beans or Abby's Bistro?"

"No, thank you. Your dad and I are going to meet at the house for leftovers in a bit. You're welcome to join us," my mother said as she removed her glasses and set them aside.

"Thanks, but I have an errand to run while I'm in town."

"Okay. You are helping dad with the farm this afternoon, right?" My mother asked me. I'd been shirking my duties a lot lately.

"That's the plan," I reached for my shoulder bag and slipped it over my left shoulder.

"Will you be over for dinner again tonight?" My mother asked.

"I'm not sure of our plans yet—if that was an invitation."

"It is an invitation for you and David," my mother replied. "I wanted to talk with the two of you about the wedding. Father George has availability next June. If you want a June wedding, you need to schedule now. I was going to bring it up last night, but David seemed a bit off."

A narrow miss! Thanks to the painkillers that David took, we dodged a momzilla wedding inquiry.

"Yes, David hurt himself dancing too, so I asked him to take a painkiller before dinner last night. He was groggy," I grabbed my car keys from the desk. I hoped Mom wouldn't keep me much longer.

"Tell David to be careful with those pills," my mother cautioned.

"I will. I'll let you know if you'll see us at dinner tonight."

Obviously, David and I would not be accepting the dinner invitation. I wasn't ready to talk to my mother about my lack of wedding plans.

I reached the business district of Spruce Grove in ten minutes. Rather than going straight to Magic Beans, I parked my SUV on Main Street and walked downtown. It was hot outside—88 degrees and damp. The humidity caused the little wisps of hair that broke free of my ponytail to curl into coils and stick to my face. I'd long since given up trying to control my crazy hair.

Poppy's yoga studio was only a few blocks from where I'd parked. If what Scotty had told me over the phone was true, Poppy could be his alibi for Wilma Platt's death. Surely, Poppy wouldn't want Scotty to risk arrest. I decided I should speak to the free-spirited yoga instructor and see if she was willing to talk to the police.

When I reached Poppy's studio, Namast-Stay, I noticed the sign on the door said Closed. I peered through the darkened windows. It seemed odd to me that the studio was dark at noon. I expected to see a classroom full of middle-aged men and women contorting themselves into pretzel shapes. All I saw in the dark window was my reflection.

I thought Poppy might be in the locker room at the back of the studio. I know the layout and the clientele of the studio because Cassie dragged me to a beginner's yoga class about a month before. I hadn't returned. My friend and I were the youngest yoga participants by about ten years—which was good for me because most of the students were about as flexible as I am. I'm as flexible as a fence post.

The part of the yoga experience that turned me off the most was the mention of the sacrum and pelvic floors. *How does one breathe from the sacrum?* I shivered at the thought. Also, I learned that yoga sometimes causes people to fart! A sophisticated-looking woman dressed in expensive spandex released excessive wind while performing downward-facing dog. I couldn't contain my laughter. Oddly, everyone in the class glared at me instead of the farter. As I said, I haven't returned to the class.

I reached for the doorknob and was surprised when it turned in my hand. I opened the door and stepped inside. The giant ceiling fan above my head whooshed and stirred the air. "Hello?" I called out.

No one replied.

I closed the door, not wishing to let the cool air out of the studio. I stepped further inside. It was so quiet that I could hear my sneakers on the wooden floor. Usually, Poppy required her students to remove their shoes, but I wasn't there to take a class.

"Hello?" I called out again—and once again, no one replied.

I stepped up to the women's locker room and pushed the door open. Like the main studio, the locker room was dark, cool, and quiet. I found the men's locker room in the same state. There was another room at the end of the hall—a business office—flanked by a rear exit that led to an alleyway. Most of the buildings in downtown Spruce Grove were set up in this fashion. The alleyway was wide enough for a garbage truck to drive through on collection day.

Once again, I called out a greeting, "Hello?" and again, there was no response. I approached the closed office door and hesitated. I could see a thin band of light beneath the door. If someone was in the office, why didn't they answer me?

I tapped the office door tentatively with my balled fist, "Poppy?"

No one answered. I reached for the doorknob and opened the door. The room was larger than I guessed, and it was lit by a table lamp on an old, heavy-looking wooden desk that faced the door. If I hadn't been looking closely, I might have missed the pale feet that poked out from behind the massive desk.

"Poppy?" I asked in a lower voice.

It occurred to me that the yogi might be doing Shivasina—AKA the dead man's pose—the usual final pose in a yoga routine. But it would be odd for Poppy to perform yoga in the office rather than the studio.

"Poppy?" I repeated. I rounded the desk.

It took me a moment to realize what lay before me on the floor. It was Poppy stretched out behind the desk. She wore a white flowing tunic and matching white pants—both spattered with russet stains. Blood. Poppy's fiery red hair flared out around her. Her arms bowed in odd angles, but it was her face that made my stomach flip and sweat form under my arms. I plastered my hand to my mouth to try to prevent myself from vomiting as a small, black housefly landed on Poppy's pulverized face. I ran from the room and down the hall to the studio. I threw open the front door and collapsed on the sidewalk as I tried to catch my breath. I grew dizzy. I knew I was close to fainting.

TROUBLE BREWING

I don't know how long I sat on the cool concrete of the sidewalk. I waited for a surge of nausea and dizziness to pass but knew that I needed to dial nine-one-one as soon as possible. Whoever had beaten Poppy to death might be lurking nearby.

The sound of tires humming on the hot asphalt of Main Street caused me to look up. Had I called the police and forgotten? No, the large, orange truck that pulled up along the curb wasn't a Spruce Grove Police Department cruiser. It was a civilian's vehicle.

I heard the engine click off and a car door shut. Then I saw a person round the front of the SUV. His jet-black hair shone in the late August sun. Instead of his usual work coveralls, he wore a pair of dark jeans and a nice dark blue button-up shirt. His mouth formed a smile as his dark eyes sparkled down at me.

"Charlotte? You look like you've seen a ghost?" Mick Flint said as a greeting. "Are you okay?"

"Mick?" was all I could manage.

I fished my cell phone from my pocket and held it in front of me. I needed to report Poppy's death. I didn't want to do that in front of her husband.

"Are you here to see Pops? She was supposed to meet me for lunch at Abby's about thirty minutes ago. She never showed. I guess she's running late." Mick stepped closer. "She probably forgot to set a reminder on her phone. You know Poppy, she likes to eschew all technology while she's practicing her craft. She avoids cell phones, computers, televisions, and even the radio." He grinned again as he reached for the door.

"Don't go in there!" I shouted as I scrambled to my feet. I couldn't let Mick see what happened to his beautiful wife.

"Why not?" Mick's smile receded.

"Please don't," I begged as I grasped his muscular forearm with my hand. "I need to call the police."

Mick's eyes shot from me to the door. His voice grew loud with concern.

"What's happened? Where's Poppy?" He grasped the door knob.

"You can't go in there, Mick," I protested. He shouldn't enter a crime scene. He shouldn't see his bruised and bloodied deceased wife.

Mick flung my hand off his arm and tore the door open. I heard the sound of his boots as they pounded across the hardwood floor. I dialed the emergency number and reentered the studio. As my call connected to the 911 dispatcher, I heard Mick shout, "No! Poppy! No!"

"Mick is rattled," Brian's voice rang in my ears. "The poor guy."

It wasn't me that Brian was speaking to. I was lying in the back of an ambulance with an oxygen mask dangling from my face. I vaguely remembered someone grabbing me while I was in the yoga studio.

"Yes, that is probably shock," Anthony, one of Spruce Grove's local EMTs replied. "Mick refused a ride to the hospital. I can't make him go if he doesn't want to."

The two men stood outside of the ambulance. Both had blue nitrile gloves on their hands, and both wore disturbed expressions on their faces. I closed my eyes and listened to them speaking.

"I understand," Brian replied. "We'll meet up with Mick after we clear the scene."

"I've been an EMT for a while now, but I will never get used to scenes like this. It looked like someone beat the stuffing out of that poor woman," Anthony said.

"It does," Brian confirmed.

"Do you think Poppy's and Wilma Platt's deaths are related?" Anthony asked.

"Hard to say," Brian replied, his voice hushed enough that I had to strain to hear his words. "Someone beat Wilma with a blunt object, and it appears that Poppy was punched or kicked to death."

TROUBLE BREWING

My throat tightened upon hearing Brian's words. I remembered the fly on Poppy's pulverized face. I coughed. Brian and Anthony turned in surprise—like they had forgotten that I was there.

"Hey," Anthony's gaze fell on me as he climbed into the back of the ambulance. He removed a glove and he pressed his fingers to the pulse point on my wrist, "How are you feeling? You gave us a bit of a shock when you fainted. It's a good thing that Officer Gold was there to catch you when you fell."

I slid the mask from my face and nodded. "I'm feeling a bit shaky."

"I bet. You've had a couple of big shocks in the past few days," Anthony replied. "Have you ever fainted before?"

"Yes," I said. I felt my face warm a bit at my admission. Fainting always left me feeling embarrassed. "Once when I was about thirteen and Brian Gold fell and cut his head. There was a lot of blood. He had to have a butterfly bandage on the back of his head. I fainted once while I was waitressing in New York. I was exhausted and dehydrated, and the diner was super busy and hot. All the customers kept asking me if I was pregnant—which was embarrassing—I wasn't pregnant then. I'm not now either."

"Well, your pulse is a little fast, but your blood pressure is okay. I won't insist you go to the hospital if you promise you'll visit your GP in the next couple of days. I'm not a doctor, but I suspect you might have had something called a vasovagal response. You should speak to your doctor to make sure everything is okay."

"I will," I promised—and I would definitely look up *vasovagal response* on the internet.

"Good," Anthony said. "Do you feel well enough to try to sit up?"

I nodded and set the oxygen mask aside. Anthony helped me sit up and then, he helped me stand. We took it slow.

"I can drive Char home," Brian offered. He stepped into the ambulance.

"I have my car," I protested.

"It's locked and safe. I checked," Brian replied in a gentle voice. "You could use some rest. I'll drive you to the cottage. You can retrieve your car later or have someone pick it up for you." He was right. I knew I shouldn't drive.

I considered asking Brian to drop me off at David's place instead of my cottage, but then I reconsidered. If I showed up weak and faint with Brian as my escort, David would certainly ask a bunch of questions. I would have to admit that I was investigating Wilma Platt's murder. It was better to let Brian drive me to my cottage. I could see David later.

"Are you ready?" Brian asked.

"Yes." I let Brian take my arm and lead me out of the ambulance. We thanked Anthony and Brian walked with me to his cruiser. Brian helped me into the front seat, and then he rounded the vehicle and took the driver's seat.

"Are you okay?" He asked.

"I think so. I can't believe I fainted."

"It happens. As Anthony said, you are likely a bit overwhelmed. You've had a rough couple of days. I'll get you home, make you some tea, tuck you into your sofa, and I'll even bring that nutty dog over for you too. Does that sound good?" Brian asked, his voice as soft and gentle as a kitten's mew.

"Yes."

Brian's plan sounded perfect.

"Good. Let's get you home," Brian squeezed my knee with his right hand before he started the cruiser.

I was snug on my sofa with Clouseau clutched to my side and a cup of steaming tea on the coffee table in front of me. Brian plopped down onto my loveseat—something that I hadn't expected. He sighed as he sunk into the comfort of the squishy cushions.

"What are you doing?" I asked.

TROUBLE BREWING

I tried not to sound like an ingrate. Brian had gone above and beyond in his effort to look after me. It surprised me that he looked like he was planning to stay with me.

"I'm taking a load off. Do you mind?" He asked.

I noticed that he was holding a steaming cup of tea.

"I know if I head back to the station right now, I'll pull another five or six hours. I need a little break. I've been on-call for the past two days."

"They won't miss you at the police station?" I asked.

"Nah, your uncle knows I am looking after you. If he needs me, he'll call."

"Okay." I didn't know what else to say.

I couldn't remember the last time that Brain and I were alone together for more than a couple of minutes. It felt odd to be alone with my old friend. "Are things really that busy at the station?"

Brian nodded. "You have no idea. Five years ago, we were overwhelmed with new recruits. Now, we're trying to convince people to begin a career in law enforcement. We started a recruitment campaign at the community college. We lost a few officers recently. I guess they don't want to be cops anymore. It's a sign of the times, as they say."

"I had no idea," I replied sitting up.

"Yeah, it's not great," he exhaled. "We'll get through it, but two suspicious deaths in less than ninety-six hours is rough on a small force."

"I believe it," I shook my head. I couldn't believe I stumbled on two dead bodies in such a small timeframe. "You don't think there will be more, do you?"

"I don't know, Char. It's hard to shake the feeling that Ms. Platt's death is related to Poppy Flint's."

Brian was right. Poppy and Wilma were two women who on the outside, seemed to have nothing in common. But they were both at the beer competition, and they were both beaten or bludgeoned to death.

"Is Scotty a suspect?" I asked.

"Char..."

"I know, I know. You aren't supposed to talk about open cases."

"Let's talk about something other than the case," Brian's voice was practically a plea.

"Sure. What do you want to talk about?" I asked.

Brian took a sip of his tea and crossed one leg over the other so the top knee jutted out to one side. "How are the wedding plans going?"

I shook my head, "Maybe we should talk about something else."

Brian chuckled.

I flushed.

"I saw Weaver last weekend," Brian smiled when he mentioned the little girl that he'd once thought of as his daughter. She was about a year old—a fun age.

"Oh! How is she?" My mood lightened.

"Great. Weaver is doing well."

Brian pulled a cell phone from the pocket of his slacks and tapped at the screen. He handed me the phone. He had opened a photo of arguably one of the cutest babies I've ever seen.

"Oh," I squealed with delight, "she gets more and more adorable. Look at that smile! Oh, I want one!"

Brian's eyebrows shot up, "Oh?"

"You know what I mean. Babies and toddlers are so cute. Then they turn to kids, and it gets complicated. They develop attitudes."

Brian chuckled. "Maybe you should wait a bit before you reproduce?"

"Yes," I replied with a laugh. "Do you ever think about it—having kids, I mean?"

"I think seeing Weaver periodically is enough for me right now. I'm not even in a relationship, and I'm not looking to get involved. I don't know if biological kids are going to be part of my future," Brian admitted.

"I understand."

I realized that Brian and I were talking—having a friendly, casual conversation without any of the discomforts of our breakup stopping us. It was nice.

"Are you feeling any better?" Brian asked as I returned his phone to him.

"I am," I confirmed. "Thanks for looking out for me."

"I'm glad you feel better," he drained his tea and stood. "I should probably get to the station. I've got to write up some reports." Brian closed the distance between us. "Try to get some rest." He leaned in and kissed the top of my head.

"I will," I promised. "When will you have more information on Wilma's death?" I hazarded to ask. Brian surprised me with his response.

"It takes a while to get the DNA results back. We put a rush on them. Hopefully, we'll get a clue about who killed Wilma soon. I know that you're worried about Scotty. I don't understand it, but I know that you're worried."

"I believe he's innocent."

Brian shrugged. "I'd feel better if Scotty answered my calls."

"Brian, I know you aren't going to like this, but I went to Crystal Creek yesterday to check on Scotty's alibi, and he does have one. Sort of. The bartender I spoke with said he remembers seeing Scotty at the bar Friday night. He was with a woman. I know that doesn't necessarily prove Scotty's innocence, but it must count for something."

Brian nodded and placed his policeman's hat on his head. "I spoke to the bartender too. And you're right, from the look of things, there was very little time between Wilma's death and Scotty's appearance at the bar—but we can't rule him out yet."

"Brian, I am sure you're planning to ask me this when I am feeling better, but I'm going to tell you this now. I was in Poppy's studio today because Scotty was at the bar with her. I thought if I spoke to Poppy, she'd give Scotty an alibi for Friday night."

"I see."

"What if the person who murdered Wilma killed Poppy too? If it is the same killer—Scotty has links to both women. What if Scotty isn't the killer? What if the killer is after Scotty too?"

"I considered that. Look, Char, I'm a good cop—I'm honest and I try not to let my personal feelings affect a case. I promise that I will do my best to find the killer—whoever he or she is," Brian said. "It's what I do."

"I know."

I remembered that my phone call with Scotty dropped, and I wondered if a bad signal was responsible or if something else was at play.

Brian walked to the door.

"Brian," I said, stopping him, "thanks for everything. I've missed our friendship. Talking with you today felt...good."

"Char, I never stopped being your friend. As far as I'm concerned, you and I are good. Okay?" He replied before he turned the doorknob.

"Okay."

With Brian gone, I reached for my phone and dialed Scotty's number again. My call went straight to voicemail. I decided to leave him a message.

"*Scotty, it's Charlotte O'Hara. I don't know where you are, but we need to talk. Please call me.*"

I considered telling Scotty that Poppy was dead, but then I decided not to. First of all, that tactic felt rude. Leaving a message over the phone to say Poppy was dead was insensitive. Furthermore, I didn't want to frighten Scotty. If Scotty was avoiding me—and the police—telling him that Poppy was dead could push him deeper into hiding. I would wait and see if Scotty called me back, and if I didn't hear from him soon, I'd make a new plan.

I got up from the sofa and locked the front door—the push lock, the chain, and the deadbolt. I was very tired. I walked back to the sofa and lay down next to Clouseau. I allowed myself to drift off to sleep.

EIGHT

I woke at seven Tuesday morning to the sound of my landline ringing. The incessant jangling of the old phone was harsh on my sleepy ears. I wasn't used to getting calls on the old line—everyone uses my cell phone number these days. I hopped from the sofa, waking Clouseau who'd snuggled with me all night. I darted to the kitchen to answer the call.

"Hello?" I said into the receiver. Clouseau circled my ankles and huffed. He needed a potty break. I stretched the 20-foot phone cord and walked to the door, releasing the three locks—the deadbolt, the push lock, and the chain. I propped the door open for my dog. He raced outside and lifted his leg against the corner of my cottage. I swear the look on Clouseau's face was sheer delight.

"Char? Are you there?" It was David's voice on the phone.

"David!"

"Are you okay? When you didn't return to my house last night, I called around. Brian Gold said you were resting at the cottage. I tried calling your cell phone but you never answered. I figured you must be napping so I waited a while and dropped by. I tapped on your door. No one answered."

"You could have let yourself in," I replied as Clouseau finished in my yard and raced back to my kitchen. He wanted his breakfast.

"I would have but you must have locked all the locks. I peered through the living room window and saw you asleep and decided that I should let you rest."

"Sorry about that. I fell asleep on my sofa and didn't awaken until you called. Why didn't you call my cell?"

"This morning I tried your cell and my call went straight to voicemail. Are you okay? Brian told me you fainted yesterday. You didn't hit your head, did you?"

I pulled my cell phone off the kitchen counter. I hadn't plugged the phone into its charger. The battery was dead.

"I'm so sorry. I didn't mean to worry you. I forgot to charge my phone, and yesterday was a bit frantic."

"What happened yesterday?" David asked. "Brian didn't offer any details. Are you sick? Should I come by?"

"I'm not sick. I guess you could say that I was overcome by stress. I fainted. I didn't hit my head or anything. Brian caught me when I fell—he was there, obviously. David, I found Poppy Flint dead in her yoga studio yesterday, and now Scotty Wells is missing."

"Oh wow! Char, I am so sorry. I didn't know what happened. I can jump in my car right now. I'll be there in five minutes."

I exhaled and looked at my reflection in the stainless steel of my refrigerator's door. My hair was in knots. My skin looked pale. "I need a shower and an OJ first."

"Are you sure? I can come and get you. You can shower here—I'll be around in case you feel faint again. I'll make you breakfast," David offered.

"No, I can shower here," I protested. David didn't need to see how I looked that morning. "Aren't you curious about how Poppy died?" I asked my fiancé. I know I would want to know what happened if I were in his position.

"Oh, of course. I want to make sure you are okay first."

"I am. Or I will be after a long shower. David, Poppy was beaten to death. Wilma was bludgeoned and now Scotty is missing. I have to admit, I'm worried about him."

"Yeah, it doesn't look good for Scotty. You were with Brian yesterday. What did he say?" David asked.

"The usual. Brian doesn't want me interfering with his investigations. Also, he told me that it takes a while to get DNA evidence back—I already knew that. Brian interviewed the bartender that I spoke with at Calamity Jane's, so at least he's aware that Scotty and Poppy were at the bar together on Friday night."

"But, that links Scotty to Poppy in a new way. She's dead… and so is Wilma Flint. And now he's missing," David recanted.

"I know." Things felt grim.

"That's not good news for Scotty," David said. "Scotty could be a suspect, or he could be a victim. All three of them—Wilma, Poppy, and Scotty—were at the beer contest. I'd be shocked if that connection isn't more than a coincidence."

I let David's words resonate for a moment. Scotty could be dead? I hadn't even thought of that.

"Wait. Do you think something happened to Scotty too? Oh my gosh! David, that could mean that all the contestants are in danger."

"Or it could mean that one of the other contestants is the killer," David offered.

"Oh my gosh! You're right, and there are only two remaining—unless all the entrants are suspects. There were about ten, altogether." I twisted the phone cord around my hand. The two remaining contestants from the final round of judging—aside from Scotty if he was alive—were Jack Indigo and Zach Grimes. One of them could be the killer.

"I imagine Jack and Zach will be getting visits from Spruce Grove's finest today," David said.

"Yes, and Mick Flint too. He was so bereft when he saw Poppy's body yesterday, that he left the scene with one of the officers. Brian said that he'd interview Mick at a later time. Anthony, the EMT? He wanted to take Mick to the hospital for observation, but Mick refused treatment. Anthony said that Mick was in shock." I didn't bother to tell David that Anthony suggested that I get checked out too.

"I didn't realize that Mick Flint was with you," David replied.

"He wasn't. I ran into Mick after I found Poppy. Mick and Poppy had a lunch date, and Mick was there to pick her up. I tried to stop him from going into the studio. I didn't want him to see Poppy. Her face was... it was awful, David."

I felt myself swallow as I recalled the crime scene. If it hadn't been for Poppy's distinctive clothing and her beautiful red hair, I don't think I would have recognized her.

"That's it. That's enough talk about awful things for now. Char, get showered and dressed. I'm stopping by to pick you up in twenty minutes. Then, I am going to pamper you the rest of the day."

"David, that isn't necessary," I protested. I didn't put my heart into my objection. I was being polite. I wanted David to rescue me.

"Nevertheless, get into a comfy outfit, and prepare to be waited on," David said.

"But your back," I reminded him. "I don't want to hurt it again."

"I'm fine, Char. We won't be dancing. I will be there in twenty minutes, okay?"

I glanced at my reflection in my refrigerator door. "You'd better make it thirty minutes," I replied as I swiped a snarl of hair from my forehead.

"Okay, a half hour. I will see you then."

"There. How does that feel?" David asked as he rubbed my feet. I reclined on his sofa with my feet in his hands. I had a book by my new favorite mystery writer in my grip and Clouseau was sleeping in his doggy bed chasing bunnies in his sleep.

"Wonderful," I replied, "but I imagine you have better things to do than wait on me."

"Better things than taking care of you?" David asked as he kneaded my foot. "Never."

"But what about that feasibility report you need to write?" I reminded him. "Isn't that due by Friday?"

TROUBLE BREWING

"It will wait," David replied as he increased the pressure of my foot massage. "This won't be the first time I have to pull a couple of all-nighters to finish a report, and I am certain it won't be the last."

I retracted my feet from his grasp. The massage began to hurt. "No. I am fine. I'm resting, I have something great to read. Clouseau is napping. You should get some work done. If I need anything, I'll tell you."

"Well, the truth is, I do need to go to the overnight shipment place in Crystal Creek. They're holding a package that I need to sign for." He shifted his eyes to the Swiss watch on his wrist. "I didn't want to leave you alone."

"No. I'm fine. That shipping place closes at five. You should go and get that," I said.

"Are you sure?" David snuck another glance at his watch. It was already mid-afternoon.

"Go," I insisted.

David jumped to his feet, "Well, I could drive to Crystal Creek in fifteen minutes and be back in forty-five minutes—top."

"Actually," I said sitting up, "if it wouldn't be too much trouble...No never mind."

"What is it?" David asked—eager to do something to please me.

"I don't want to be a pain," I replied, smiling.

"Wait. I bet I know what you want. Ice cream from that new place—*Drips*—am I right?" David asked.

To be honest, I hadn't thought of what I was going to ask David to get for me. I needed a way to bide my time. You see, after hours of sitting on David's sofa, I was a bit bored. I wanted to investigate, and I knew David would never sign off on that so soon after my stupid fainting spell.

"That's it!" I lied. "I've been thinking of their Fox Prints ice cream since noon," I replied.

"Fox Prints?" He asked.

"Yes. It is malt-flavored ice cream with bits of peanut butter crisp, chocolate, and butterscotch chips. It's all swirled together."

"Hmm," David scratched his chin and then laid his hand on his midsection. "I hate to admit it, but some good old Rocky Road sounds good to me."

"You are not going to mention your diet again, are you?" I asked. "You look perfect, David."

My fiancé smiled and shook his head. "So, I'll pop over to pick up my package, then I'll run into the city of Crystal Creek and get a pint of each. Does that sound good?"

Before I could say, yes, David spoke again.

"Although, if I am in Crystal Creek, and I am picking up dessert, I should get us something for dinner too." He scratched his chin again, considering.

"Yes. You might pick up that three-course meal deal from Trois Filles," I suggested. I knew that the fancy restaurant didn't open its doors until 5 PM. I was buying myself enough time to interview my suspects if I could find them.

"Well, now I am hungry!" David proclaimed as he slipped his wallet into his back pocket. "Damn the diet! But will you be okay if I leave for a few hours?"

He grabbed his car keys from the table and let them jingle in his hand. He'd already made his decision.

"Of course," I replied. "I fainted from stress—nothing else. Look at me. I had an hour-long foot massage, I'm reading a great book, and I am curled up on the sofa. No more stress."

"Okay. I'll go, but I want you to lock the door and set the alarm after I leave. The killer is still out there. It doesn't pay to take any chances," David said. He walked over and kissed my forehead.

"I'll lock this place up as tight as a drum," I replied.

"Good. If I time things right, I should be back by six. Call if you need anything." He kissed me again and said goodbye.

TROUBLE BREWING

You might be wondering if I felt guilty lying to my fiancé like that. The truth is, I did feel a twinge of guilt, but I thought that if I told David what I wanted to do—investigate on my own—he would get upset. I was protecting him.

I waited a full five minutes after I heard the rumble of David's Italian sports car pull away. I hopped off the sofa, ran my fingers through my hair, and reached for my handbag. Then I remembered: I didn't have my car. I masterminded an entire excuse to get David out of the house. Now I was carless. I knew from experience that I was unlikely to have another couple of hours to investigate any time soon. Cassie was too busy to drive me and there was no way my parents would sanction my investigation. I did the only thing I could think of. I took David's favorite vehicle—his vintage pickup truck—ole Blue.

Thanks to David's internet search, I knew where Zach Grimes lived, and Jack Indigo's tattoo parlor was right in the heart of downtown Spruce Grove. I would stop in and offer my condolences to Mick Flint between the visits to Zach and Jack—if I could find him. I decided to visit Zach first.

"Yes?" Zach answered the garage door of his sketchy apartment—which was a one-car garage that the owner converted into a studio apartment.

Speaking of sketchy, Zach didn't look his best. Zach's salt and pepper hair was standing on end, and his chin and cheeks were rough with stubble. His graying white t-shirt and torn blue jeans were not bespoke—they were a product of dirty work and frequent wear. A musky, warm odor hung in the air of his darkened dwelling.

"I'm Charlotte O'Hara," I told Zach as I peered past his shoulder. There was a large, silver vat behind him that I recognized as a tank used for brewing beer. The receptacle took up a lot of space leaving enough room for a small camping cot, and an old folding table and chair at the corner of the room. The tank looked expensive and large for a small home-brewing operation. Zach was serious about his craft.

"Is that for making beer?" I nodded in the direction of the tank.

"Yep, that's my fermentation tank," Zach confirmed in a gruff voice. "How can I help you?"

"Oh. Right. I have a blog. Around the Town?" I wondered if he'd heard of my blog site. "I wanted to interview the participants in the farm show's home brewing contest. I'd love to hear your take on whether Spruce Grove might become a hub for the craft brewing industry."

"Are you recording this conversation?" Zach's eyes narrowed landing on my chest as if he expected me to be wearing a wire. There wasn't much else for him to look at in that region of my body. I could have been imagining Zach's glare. Why would he think I wore a wire?

"No," I replied.

I hadn't thought about what I would say to Zach and Jack to gain their trust. Writing a blog episode about brewing was a fly-by-the-seat-of-my-pants idea.

"I'm old school. I listen closely during my interviews and write everything down later."

Zach nodded like my answer eased his mind.

"I find that people are less natural when they know their words are being recorded. It's all a matter of trust," I explained.

"Yeah," Zach ran a beefy hand through his messy hair. When he extracted his hand from his ruffled mane, I noticed that two of his knuckles were scabbed over. I also noted a tattoo of a red heart on the back of his hand. "The thing is, Charlotte, I wish you would have phoned me first. I have an appointment I need to get to. I don't have time for an interview."

I didn't believe him. I mean, who goes out to an appointment looking as scruffy as Zach did? Also, those scabs on his knuckles? Was it possible that they were from beating someone?

"Oh, right!" I replied as I took a cautious step back from the man. Those beefy hands looked big enough to do some serious damage. "I

TROUBLE BREWING

was on my way to interview Jack Indigo, and I remembered that you lived along the way. I don't have your phone number."

Zach nodded as if he was considering the veracity of my words. Could he detect that I was lying?

After what seemed like an eternity, he reached around his back and pulled a worn leather wallet from his back pocket. From the wallet, he extracted a business card and handed it to me.

"The number on the card is my cell phone," he said as he stepped out of the garage apartment and shut the door. He managed to push me out the doorway in the process.

"Oh, thanks." I let my eyes skim the high-quality, cream-colored business card. Killer Brewing Company, LLC. I felt a shiver run up my spine.

"Call me if you want an interview. I guess a story about my brewery could be good for business. I have to get going. I have an appointment, and I don't want to be late." Zach said as he jingled a set of keys. His eyes darted to the blue pickup parked at the edge of the driveway. "Is that your ride?"

"Uh-huh," I said.

"Nice." Zach took several steps forward to get a better look at ole Blue. "These are pretty rare these days. 1972. Original paint. No putty. I bet it has the big V-8."

"*Yes?*" I replied, unsure.

I'd always thought of David's pickup truck as an old, reliable vehicle—a tool to get a person from A to B. David was sure fond of the truck. I guess ole Blue was more valuable than I'd realized.

"Well, I guess when I see that truck around town, I'll know who is driving her," Zach and ran an admiring hand down her hood. "Very nice." He let out a low whistle that sounded vaguely inappropriate.

"Thanks," I replied with a shudder. It felt a bit like ole Blue had suffered an assault, and I found it difficult to breathe. I remembered that Zach was accused of many crimes but had only served time for one of them. I wondered if assault was on the man's rap sheet.

"I'll see you around, Miss O'Hara." Zach walked away from the pickup and got into an old, gray beater car. He fired up the engine and drove away.

"Not if I see you first," I replied, under my breath.

I didn't know where Mick and Poppy made their home, aside from *somewhere downtown*. I couldn't ask David if he knew the address. The last thing I needed was for David to figure out that I was investigating Wilma and Poppy's deaths when I was supposed to be at home resting.

I drove down Main Street with my eyes wide looking for Mick's hard-to-miss truck. The pickup was big and orange with a backseat and dually wheels. A distinctive blue logo for Flint Services adorned the sides of the truck. I doubted that Mick would be at work since Poppy had recently died. Furthermore, the enormous vehicle wouldn't fit inside one of the tiny, ancient one-car, garages that were common among the Victorian-era homes in Spruce Grove's downtown area.

It didn't take me long to find Mick's truck, but *where* I found the vehicle took my breath away. The truck was parked in front of Poppy's studio, Namast-Stay. The yellow police scene tape still hung from the doorway.

I parked my SUV and walked a short distance to the yoga studio. The door was propped open with old red brick, and I wondered if Mick was inside.

Without touching anything, I peeked into the studio and called inside. "Hello?"

Within a second or two, I heard the unmistakable sound of heavy work boots crossing the hardwood floors. Soon, Mick Flint's dark, bloodshot eyes peered down at me through the crack in the door. He didn't bother to open it.

TROUBLE BREWING

The redness in Mick's eyes caused me to question my motives. When I started out that morning, I told myself I was going to offer Mick Flint my most sincere condolences. With the grieving husband before me, I realized I arrived unprepared and empty-handed. What was I going to say to a man who had so obviously been crying over the loss of his wife?

"Mick?" I asked unsure of what I should say.

"Charlotte, what are you doing here?" Mick asked from behind the door.

"I saw your truck, and I thought I should check on you. Are you okay?" I asked. The stupidity of my question hit me at the same time that it hit Mick.

"How can I be okay, Charlotte? Poppy is gone—that guy—Scotty Wells killed her. Did you know that he is missing?"

"I heard something like that," I confirmed. "Are you supposed to be here? I thought this was a crime scene."

"The police have what they need. Did you know that the police don't clean up crime scenes? I have to figure out what I am going to do. Poppy rented this space. She signed a six-month rental agreement. There are three months left on it. I can't afford the rent and I sure as hell don't teach yoga."

"I can't imagine that the owners will hold you to the contract—not after what happened here," I advised Mick.

I imagined that whoever owned the studio would be worried about a wrongful death lawsuit. After all, there didn't appear to be any type of security system in the studio. Perhaps an armed burglar alarm or better locks would have saved Poppy's life.

"Hmm. Maybe you're right. I hope so." Mick straightened. "You know Scotty, don't you?" He asked me. The new widower leaned against the door jam, and I noticed an odd-looking tattoo on his wrist. Was that an Ace of Spades? The tattoo reminded me of the Zach Grimes's heart ink.

"Yes, I mean, Scotty and I aren't close or anything, but we went to school together. He was behind me by a couple of grades."

I was ashamed of myself for denying what was probably a new friendship with Scotty Wells, but if you were in my position, you would do the same thing.

"Did you ever hear anything about him and Poppy?" Mick asked me.

"Um." I didn't know how to answer Mick. There was no way that I was going to betray Scotty.

"I don't mean it like that. I doubt Poppy would have an affair with a wimp like Scotty. What I mean is, why would he kill my wife? I can imagine that he killed Wilma Platt because she was an awful old woman. I'm trying to figure out Scotty's motive for killing Poppy. She wouldn't harm a fly," Mick replied. "Maybe you know how that little guy thinks—why he'd kill someone."

"I really don't know," I said. "Let's not forget, Scotty Wells is innocent until he's proven guilty," I reminded Mick.

Mick's dark eyebrows lifted, "We can't prove his guilt until someone finds him and drags him back to town and gets him to talk."

"Scotty isn't a suspect in the case. He's only a person of interest."

Mick's eyebrows lowered. "Maybe you should get a move on, Charlotte. I need to close up here."

Suddenly, I realized how my comment about Scotty's presumed innocence must have sounded to Mick. Of course, he was angry. He was distraught. My words were insensitive.

"Oh, gosh. I didn't mean that," I said. "What I meant was, we shouldn't rule out other suspects. If we focus on Scotty Wells and it turns out that he didn't kill Poppy, well, the real killer could get away."

Mick leaned in. "Is there another suspect? Have you heard anything? Because the police haven't told me a thing."

I threw my arms out in exasperation. "No, I don't actually know anything. I'm spit-balling here."

TROUBLE BREWING

"Of course, you don't know," Mick replied, but he sounded unconvinced.

Like most of the citizenry of Spruce Grove, Mick would know that Officer Brian Gold is a friend of mine, and that Chief Mark Wright is my maternal uncle. It was fair of Mick to think I knew more about the case than I was admitting.

"I am sorry for your loss, Mick. If you need anything at all, please don't hesitate to ask."

"Thanks," Mick said, glibly.

His eyes hardened, "I need to get going so..." he pointed his chin towards the street—a subtle invitation for me to leave.

"Right," I replied. I turned to walk away, but then I spun around and faced Mick again. "Anything at all. The townsfolk of Spruce Grove loved Poppy, and we're here for you. Don't hesitate to ask for help if you need it."

Mick nodded and then he kicked the brick away from the door and let it shut him inside the studio. The poor man. I wondered what he would do without Poppy. I decided that after a reasonable amount of time, my friend group and I would try to include Mick in our activities. He could use the support.

I arrived at Jack Indigo's tattoo parlor a few minutes after I left Mick.

Jack's receptionist, Chloe, informed me that Jack was with a client, but that he would be free in a few minutes if I wanted to hang out and wait for him. I told her that I would stay and have a look around.

I walked around the studio and looked at the art on the walls. Creative designs in all kinds of colors and shapes covered nearly every inch of the pale green walls. I stepped around and admired the various ethnic-looking tattoos, animals, and text art that adorned the walls. I never considered getting a tattoo before, but looking at the images, I could understand the appeal.

Then, my eyes fell on a large glass cabinet with a very prominent piercing display. The models were shockingly realistic with various skin tones and a variety of studs and rings clinging to them. I cringed in imaginary pain when I realized which body parts were punctured.

"Are you here for ink or a piercing?" A pleasant tenor voice asked from behind me.

I spun around and saw Jack Indigo grinning at me. His bare arms were decorated with green vine tattoos and a serpent's tongue peeked out from the neck of his black tank top. "I know you," he continued, "you used to work at Magic Beans. I've never seen you in here, though."

"I don't work at the coffee shop anymore. I wasn't fired or anything," I felt myself blush. "And I have a couple of piercings—in my ears—no tattoos."

"Christmas tree farm!" Jack added with energy. "That's where you work these days."

"Right."

"So—ink or piercing?" He asked me again.

"Interview?" I replied with a question. "I have a blog—Around the Town."

"I've read it. It's not bad. That piece on public vaping was interesting—but I didn't agree with your argument. Is this about the murder?" Jack asked.

"Um, about brewing? But if you wanted to talk about Wilma..."

"That woman was a nut—that's all there is to it. What harm did it cause to Wilma if adults want to get their bodies pierced?" Jack said. "It's a shame that she's dead, but I am not surprised. She didn't treat people very well."

"Right. Anyway..."

"You'd look great with a nose stud," Jack stepped forward and stared at my nose. "What's your birthstone?"

"Um. A sapphire?" I replied.

TROUBLE BREWING

"Wow. That's exactly the stone I'd recommend for you. Isn't that funny?" Jack crooked a finger at me, inviting me to follow him. Intrigued, I shadowed him through a door and into a sterile-looking room with a pair of massage tables in the center of it. One of the tables was occupied by a young man who was getting a tattoo of a lion on the back of his shoulder. A young, pretty woman with bright pink hair was wielding the tattoo needle. She was nearly finished as she dabbed at the man's back with a roll of cotton.

"Have a seat." Jack gestured to the empty table drawing my attention away from the woman and her client.

"Uh, okay." I sat on the table and Jack pulled an industrial-looking chair on wheels from the corner and sat across from me.

"So, Wilma Platt died at the farm show after she insulted all the craft beer contestants. The police think they've found the murder weapon," I began.

Suddenly, it felt like I had a topic for my blog. I felt my spirit lift. I could name the blog entry *Trouble Brewing in Spruce County*.

"Yeah, I heard," Jack stood and walked to a sink in the corner of the room. He washed his hands and dried them on a paper towel. Then he slipped a pair of examination gloves over his hands. "Are you allergic to anything? Latex, minerals, plant extracts?"

"No. I am only allergic to penicillin," I replied. "Anyway, I am operating on the angle that Wilma died due to her protest at the beer crafting contest. Now Poppy Flint is dead and Scotty Wells is missing. All three of them were at the contest," I said as Jack stood before me. "Congratulations on winning the gold, by the way. I hope I can try your beer soon."

Jack nodded his appreciation. He didn't seem overly enthusiastic about his win—not like Scotty. "I'm a hobby brewer. I don't think I'll be trying to catch a break in the beer industry."

"Oh, I think that Zach Grimes is trying to make a go at it. He only won the honorable mention certificate."

111

"Mmhmm. May I?" He lifted his gloved hands toward my face.

"Um?"

He touched the side of my nose lightly. "I was thinking that a 4-millimeter stud could go here. Something small and classy."

"I really don't think..." I sputtered before Jack interrupted me.

"Would you like to hear about Wilma and Poppy? I'm pretty sure you aren't here to talk about beer."

Jack leveled his eyes at me, and in the corner of my eye, I saw the pink-hair woman help the man with the lion tattoo off the table and usher him out of the room. I had no witnesses if Jack decided to hurt me.

"I would like your thoughts, yes," I replied.

"So, your nose or somewhere else?" He kept his eyes on my face, but I felt my entire body grow cold.

I could tell by Jack's expression, that he was serious. He was convinced that I was getting something pierced that day, and all I could think about was those damned piercing models in the front of the studio.

"You see, Charlotte, it's all about trust." Jack grabbed a cotton swab and doused it with an antiseptic liquid that he poured from a brown bottle. "I want to trust that what I tell you won't come back to haunt me. As you pointed out, people from the beer contest are dying left and right. In return for my cooperation, you," he dabbed my nose with the swab, "will trust that I won't hurt you. Right?"

"Um..." I felt a bit muddled by Jack's logic.

Jack backed off and raised his hands in the air. "Or you can leave."

"Do you know something—about Wilma or Poppy?" I asked.

"I might," he replied.

"How much will it hurt?" I asked—referring to the piercing that Jack seemed determined to give me.

"It will feel like a pinch," he winked at me.

TROUBLE BREWING

"What do you know?" I asked wondering if he was telling me the truth.

"After." He grinned and reached for the needle, and I hoped I wouldn't faint again. Jack leveled the needle and told me his thoughts on the murders.

"So, do you see? Wilma Platt had a lot of enemies, but if I were to bet on her killer, my money is on Zach Grimes. He had motive and opportunity. Now Poppy is a bit of a mystery. She tended to keep to herself—which makes me think that she had something going on. You know the old saying: still waters run deep," Jack said as he handed me a mirror. "Poppy and her husband were newlyweds—sort of. I think they got married shortly after he moved to town. That was around a year ago—maybe a little more."

I took in Jack's words as I stared at my reflection. The piercing on the left side of my nose was flawless. I'd never considered a nasal piercing before, but I liked it. It hurt more than a pinch when he pushed the needle through.

"But what about you?" I asked. "Some might argue that you had as much motive to kill Wilma as Zach. You had to move your entire business and faced possible closure because of Wilma's rant about the piercing models."

"Have you ever heard the saying that there's no bad publicity?" Jack asked as he wheeled his chair back from me, and stood. He walked to the trashcan and threw his gloves into it along with a wad of cotton.

"Yes. I've heard that saying before. I'm not sure I believe it."

"Well, in my case, it was true. It turns out that a lot of people in the county welcomed a tattoo and piercing parlor. The publicity that Wilma gave me helped my business. I owe the woman a word of thanks. Zach on the other hand ended up in prison because of what Wilma said about him. So, what do you think?"

"I like the piercing," I admitted. "I'm not sure about your theory on Zach Grimes, though."

Jack shrugged. "I put a temporary stud in. Keep it clean. You'll notice some swelling but that will go down in a week or so. When you're healed, I can find you a nice sapphire stud," Jack replied.

"Okay," I agreed as I jumped off the table. My mother was going to hate my new look. I wasn't sure what David would think.

Jack walked me to the front desk. I hoped he wasn't expecting payment. After all, I hadn't asked for the piercing, and I imagined that there was some kind of credentialing organization that wouldn't be happy to hear that Jack Indigo bullied me into getting my nose pierced.

Jack grabbed a business card from the desk, "You know where you can find me. If your friends are interested in skin art, have them come see me," he handed me the card.

I placed the card into my bag. "I can't imagine my friends coming for more than ear piercings."

"But you'll be back," Jack said with utter confidence.

"I will?" I asked, dubious.

Jack nodded, knowingly. "Piercings and tattoos are a bit addictive. You'll see what I mean."

I shook my head. I didn't think I'd get a tattoo or another piercing.

"Thanks," I said as I walked to the door.

"I can't wait to see the blog post," Jack said before I exited the studio.

Suddenly, I thought of something. "Jack, I noticed that Zach Grimes and Mick Flint have interesting tattoos. Zach's is a big red heart on the back of his hand. Mick has an Ace of Spades on his wrist. Did you give them their tattoos?"

"No," Jack told me. "I've seen Zach's ink—it's definitely not my work—prison ink if you ask me. I didn't give Mick his tattoo either."

I left the tattoo parlor with a lot on my mind. My nose ached a bit, and frankly, that was a problem. When I'd left David's house hours

TROUBLE BREWING

earlier, I didn't have a nasal piercing. How was I supposed to explain the new hole in my body to David? I was meant to be at home resting.

NINE

David arrived home bearing delicious-smelling hot food and a couple of pints of ice cream. I was ready for him. I dimmed all the lights in the house, closed the curtains, and lit a few candles for ambiance and shadows to hide my new nose stud. I considered removing the gold stud from the hole in my nose, but I feared that pulling it out would hurt. Besides, I was more worried about an infection setting in than getting caught. An infection would be more painful down the line. The stud remained. I hoped that romantic lighting and avoidance behavior would help me hide the nose stud from my fiancé.

David found me curled up on the sofa—pierced-nose-side down against the cushions. I pulled a fluffy throw up to my chin.

"You look cozy," David said as he left the bags of food on the coffee table and approached me. "The whole house looks cozy. What's up?"

"Nothing," I lied. "I thought it would be nice to have a candlelight dinner."

"Sure. I'm game. How are you feeling?" David leaned forward and brushed the long bangs from my eyes. I did my best to hide my nose from him.

"I'm fine. I got some rest. It helped. I don't feel woozy at all."

"That's good," David stepped back and reached for the bags. "I hope you're hungry. I brought a lot of food. I'll go set the table, and let you know when everything is ready."

"Thank you," I said.

Once David was out of the family room, I sat up and considered how I could hide my nose from him while we ate. Despite the candlelight, he was bound to see the stud if I sat across from him at the small kitchen table as I usually did. Fortunately, I had an idea.

"Do you want to eat in here? We could watch a little TV," I offered, "or listened to music."

I knew that David would agree to hang out with me on the sofa. All I had to do was make sure that David sat on my right side. How hard could that be? On further reflection, I realized that my fiancé had to stay on my right until the following day. Then, I could pretend that I got the piercing while I was in town for my usual coffee and meet-up with Cassie.

"Okay. I'll plate the food and bring it in. I got vegetarian cassoulet and the field greens salad. There's a loaf of French bread with whipped butter, and haricots vert. They included dessert too—something chocolate and gooey. That's besides the ice cream that I picked up," David happily chattered.

"It smells delicious," I said.

"We could start with a drink. I bet this bottle of Chardonnay would pair well with the cassoulet. What do you think?"

David stepped into the family room and held up a bottle of wine for my inspection. I don't know much about wine other than I like it. I nodded.

"Okay. I don't think one glass would hurt," I agreed.

"Only one glass? Are you sure you don't have a concussion from earlier?" David asked with a playful chuckle. David knows that I don't usually stop at one glass of wine if I am staying in for the evening. On a good night, I'll have two glasses of wine—three if I am PMS-ing.

"I don't want to drink and drive," I replied. "I was going to ask my dad to drive me to town so I can pick up my SUV. It's been on Main Street for over twenty-four hours. I don't want to get a parking ticket."

David shook his head. "Char, it can wait. Your uncle isn't going to let anyone write a parking ticket for you after what you've been through. And anyway, if you insist on getting your car tonight, I can drive you. There's no reason to bother Gary or Patty."

"No, that's okay," I deflected. I couldn't ride to town with David—he would be on my left side—my wrong side—he'd see the piercing and start asking questions. "You're right. I can wait until tomorrow to get my car. I'm sure that Uncle Mark wouldn't let me get a ticket."

David shrugged and went back to the kitchen. A few minutes later, he returned with two generous glasses of wine and placed them on the table. He sat close to me on the sofa and draped his left arm over my shoulder, pulling me closer. He kissed the shell of my right ear, and I jumped.

"Is everything okay?" David pulled back.

"Yes, of course," I replied. "You just took me by surprise, that's all."

"I guess I got the wrong idea. I saw the candles, and you invited me to snuggle up on the sofa...I guess I thought..." David winced and lowered his voice, "it's been a while..."

"Oh! Sorry!" I said, flustered and jumpy. David thought the candlelight meant that I wanted a night of romance. All I wanted was to keep my secret from him for another 12 hours.

"Char. What's going on?" David's voice was suspicious. He caught me! I should have known that I couldn't pull one over on David—he's a genius.

I exhaled. It was time to come clean with him.

"David, I can't lie to you," I said as I turned to face him.

"Char? You have me worried. Did something happen? Is it Brian?" David asked.

I exhaled again, more from my shame than from anger at David. He should know that Brian had nothing to do with my mood. Brian and I were friends—we hadn't been more than friends in over a year.

"No. It's not Brian. I lied to you today. Remember when I asked you to get the food for me? It was all a ploy to get you out of here. I promised you that I would stay put here in your house, but I ran into town as soon as you were gone."

"Oh. Well, you seem to be okay," David's words were slow and measured, "no harm done. Although, I wish you didn't think you had to lie to me about wanting to go out. I could have gone with you."

"No, you don't understand. I went into town and spoke to Zach Grimes, Mick Flint, and Jack Indigo," I admitted, "and Jack gave me this." I pointed my forefinger at my nose—or rather the stud in my nose. "I was trying to hide it from you."

"What did he give you?" David asked as he narrowed his eyes. I guess that it was so dark in the family room that my fiancé couldn't see the tiny stud.

I reached around and switched on the table lamp by the sofa. "Jack kind of quid-pro-quo-ed me, and now I have this," I said as I pointed to my nose again.

"Huh," David leaned in to get a closer look. "Did it hurt?"

"You have no idea! And now it's swollen," I shook my head, "Jack said piercing my nose would feel like a pinch. I'd like to know who taught that man what constitutes a pinch. This is cartilage! Needles don't go through it without a fight."

David swallowed a chuckle. I fought the urge to remind my fiancé of the ridiculous tattoo on his chest. The tattoo should say 'Hello World' in binary code, but the tattoo was only a series of ones and zeros. David chickened out before the tattoo artist finished.

"But why did you do it?" David asked.

"As I said, Jack acted like I had to let him pierce my nose in exchange for the info I was seeking," I shrugged. "Jack said that it was a matter of trust—it felt a bit like a warning, if I am being honest—which I am, now. I am so sorry that I lied to you earlier."

"Well, that is weird—making you suffer to hear his story," David replied. "Did Jack tell you anything worth knowing?"

"Yes. Maybe. I don't know," I stammered.

Thinking back, I felt like I hadn't learned much at all from Zach or Jack. One man made my skin crawl, and the other made me feel threatened. "I don't know how useful any of it was. I probably should have stayed in as you asked me.

"Do you hate it?" I gently touched the stud. "I can let it grow in if you don't like it."

"I don't hate it," David admitted, finally smiling from his chocolate eyes to his slightly crooked mouth. "It gives you a bit of an edge. Honestly? It's kind of sexy."

"That's what I think too, but I wasn't sure you'd want a wife with a nose stud. You're an international philanthropist. I doubt many of your business partners or their spouses wear nose studs," I replied. "Also, I wasn't sure if I could carry it off, but I like it."

"If you like it, I'm fine with it. Trust me, no one from Moore Reach will mind the stud. We're a pretty open-minded group. So, what did Jack tell you?"

I took a few minutes to tell David everything Jack and Zach said to me. I decided that I hadn't learned anything new—except that I was a bit afraid of Zach Grimes and that Jack seemed to enjoy piercing my flesh a bit too much. I could envision either one of them as a killer.

"Are you mad at me—for breaking my promise?" I asked.

"No. But I do have a question for you. How did you get to town?" David asked as he reached for the wine and gave me a glass. "Your SUV is on Main Street. I'm assuming you didn't walk to town."

"Oh, that. I borrowed ole Blue. I hope you don't mind."

"No. That's fine. What's mine is yours—you know that," David said.

I nodded gratefully and took a fortifying gulp of wine. It tasted good.

"By the way, I had no idea that Blue was such a collector's item. Zach Grimes literally couldn't keep his hands off of her."

"Yep, Blue is a special truck, but usually only true gearheads recognize her for what she is," David replied. "Most people think she's a hunk of metal and tires."

"Then Zach must be a gearhead. He told me that when he sees the truck in town, he'll know I'm around. I didn't tell him that the truck belongs to you."

David shifted in his seat. "I'm not sure that I like the sound of that. Why would Zach Grimes need to keep an eye out for you? Do me a favor? Stay away from that guy. We don't know what he allegedly did before he got arrested—aside from money laundering—which is bad enough. We still don't know who killed Wilma Platt or Poppy Flint. I don't like the idea of you being alone with Zach."

"You don't even have to ask me to keep my distance from that man," I replied. "I have no desire to be alone with Zach—or Jack, for that matter."

"Good. I'll go grab the salads," David said as he set his wine glass on the coffee table. He reached for the TV remote and handed it to me. "Your job is to find something for us to watch while we dine. Maybe there's a classic with your favorite leading lady, Audrey, in it."

"I dropped the remote onto the table and set my hand on David's forearm. "Or we could eat later." I fluttered my eyelashes at my fiancé.

"Aren't you hungry?" David asked. He completely missed my clue.

I shook my head and waggled my eyebrows at him. I loved that David didn't hate my nose piercing. He said it was sexy. I leaned forward and gazed up into his brown eyes.

"Ah. Yes, dinner can wait," David said. He sat down, wrapped an arm around my shoulder, leaned in, and at that exact moment my cell phone rang and simultaneously vibrated in my pocket.

"Sorry!" I said, reaching for my phone.

Politeness dictated that I needed to turn off the ringer and focus on my fiancé. This was 'David and me' time. As I extracted my phone, I glanced at the caller ID. The number that appeared surprised me. "But first, I should take this," I said, apologetically, and I stood from the sofa to answer the call. David exhaled loudly.

"This is Charlotte," I said into the phone. I walked to the edge of the room to distance myself from David. He didn't need to know who I was speaking with.

TROUBLE BREWING

"Hi, this is Roger from Calamity Jane's Sports Bar in Crystal Creek."

It was the bartender calling. I couldn't believe my luck!

"Hi. Have you seen my husband? Is that why you phoned?" I asked as I lowered my voice and cupped the phone a bit too late. David heard me and jumped from his seat.

"Husband?" David whispered as he approached me. His face crumpled in confusion. I guess I failed to tell David that I pretended that Scotty was my husband when I visited the sports bar.

"Not exactly. I haven't seen your husband in person since Friday night," Roger replied. "The thing is, I was reviewing my surveillance video. A tagger has been painting the walls outside with lewd images, so I installed the cameras a while back. I didn't catch the little bastard who painted the graffiti, but I saw your man and that hippy-dippy chick on Friday night's recording. They weren't alone."

"What do you mean?" I asked.

"Someone was outside. It looked like they were waiting for them to leave," Roger explained.

"Did my husband or the lady he was with speak to the person?" I asked.

"No, he or she hid in the shadows. I got the feeling that the couple was being watched. The watcher had his or her hood up and everything—like they didn't want to be seen. I didn't get a good look at them, but whoever it was had a lot of interest in your husband or the lady. They watched them from the shadows while your husband and his friend hugged goodnight and got into their vehicles. Then he or she disappeared."

"Did you see the watcher get into a car or where they went?" I asked. Maybe Roger could describe the vehicle to me.

"Nah. As I said, the third person sort of disappeared. They probably went around the other side of the building. I don't have cameras there."

"Oh." Disappointment flooded me.

"Anyway, you asked me to call if I saw anything, so I did," Roger said.

"I appreciate that," I replied. "You're certain that the third individual was waiting outside—he or she didn't leave the bar?"

"Nope, whoever it was, they weren't in my bar."

"Okay. Thank you for calling," I said as I drew the phone away from my ear. I wondered if Brian knew about the bar's surveillance system. Did he also see the person lurking in the shadows? Did he know who was spying on Scotty and Poppy?

"So, what are you going to do about your fellow?" Roger asked, startling me. I thought he'd hung up.

"Honestly, I'm not sure. I guess I need to find him before I'll know what I'm going to do," I replied.

"Good luck with that," Roger said, and we said goodbye.

I turned around and found David leaning against the foyer wall. He was staring at me. His eyes were dark. "Char, please tell me that Kyle Stalls isn't in town making trouble."

"Kyle? David, why would you think my ex-husband is in Spruce Grove?"

"I heard you say husband at least twice. Who phoned you?" David asked.

I waved a hand dismissively.

"Oh! That was Roger the bartender from Calamity Jane's. He called to tell me some news about the case. Roger said that someone was watching Scotty and Poppy when they left the bar Friday night. He caught them all on his surveillance camera. I told Roger that Scotty was my philandering husband. I thought that would make me a sympathetic character and that he would share information with me. I guess I was right."

"Who was watching them? Did Roger say?" David asked.

"Roger had no idea. The point is someone seemed to be stalking the two of them. Which means, the stalker might be the killer, and Scotty Wells is innocent."

David crossed his arms over his chest.

"You have to admit, that's a bit of a stretch—and an unidentified person lurking in the shadows is not a heck of a lot of go on. I mean, if you were actually a detective investigating the case, you would need more proof than shadowy figures to accuse someone. Luckily, you aren't a detective."

"No, I'm not a detective," I agreed. "Except…" Before I finished my sentence, David spoke.

"Char. You know how I feel about this," David's voice implored. He uncrossed his arms and gently placed his hand on my shoulder.

"You feel left out when I don't include you?" I asked. David and I shared interesting adventures in the past. I hadn't invited him to assist me in my current investigation.

"No. Char…come on. Is it so awful that I want you to be safe?" David asked. "Do you think that I'm wrong for wanting you to let the police do their job without your involvement? Without *our* involvement?"

"No."

I was involved in the case, whether David liked it or not. I found both of the dead women. It was me that Scotty was talking to—or had talked to—before he disappeared like a thief in the night.

"Do you agree that the Spruce Grove Police Department is competent enough to catch Wilma and Poppy's killers? You must know that they will eventually find Scotty Wells—whether he was involved in the murders or not."

"I suppose so…" I agreed with reluctance.

"Good. Case closed," David said. "Why don't we have some dinner?"

"Sure," I replied feeling a little defeated. All it took was one phone call to cause a rift and ruin my romantic aspirations for the evening. I thought by now that David knew me better. How could I stop investigating when I knew I was close to proving that Scotty was innocent?

We ate our dinner in silence as an old black-and-white movie flickered on David's TV. After dinner, I helped David clear and rinse the dishes before he set them into the dishwasher. He dried his hands on a dishtowel and turned to face me.

"I have an early day tomorrow," David said. "I need to join a meeting online at four in the morning."

"Right," I said.

David's nonprofit—Moore Reach—was taking off. That meant that David was taking off too. He hopped planes left and right. When he was in Spruce Grove, David spent a lot of time answering phone calls in the middle of the night and attending early morning internet meetings. That was my fault because I wanted to my fiancé close to me. I was the reason he took early meetings and late-night calls. If David were in Europe with his team, he wouldn't need to keep odd hours.

I drew a deep breath. "Maybe I should go home so you can get some sleep before your meeting. Could you drive me to the cottage?"

"Of course," David said. "And in the morning, after my meeting, I can pick you up and drive you into town to retrieve your car."

I shrugged. "I can have Dad drive me. It's not a big deal."

"Okay," David readily agreed. He reached for me and hugged me to him. I felt his lips touch the top of my head, and he whispered, "are we okay?"

"Sure," I whispered and hugged him back.

I pushed down the nagging thought that David and I were anything other than okay. David and I argued about two things: my habit of getting myself involved in the police's business and my ex-boyfriend, Brian Gold who happened to be a police officer.

TEN

The following day, I retrieved my car and ran some errands. While driving home from Crystal Creek in my SUV, I thought about David. We needed to set a wedding date and start planning the event. There was no reason for the two of us to have a long engagement. We weren't kids. The sooner we married, the sooner I could travel with David when he left the country. We wouldn't need to be apart anymore. Getting married would help reduce the strain I noticed in our relationship.

The warble of my phone ringing pulled me from my thoughts. My phone was safely tucked into my vehicle's cupholder, and I hazarded a glance to check the caller ID. I didn't recognize the incoming phone number. I put my eyes back on the road and let the call ring out. A few seconds later, a beep let me know that the caller left a voicemail message for me. I decided to wait until I was home before I checked my messages.

Earlier that morning, my dad and I conducted supply checks in the barn. We discovered that we were running low on some minerals that we use when planting trees. I offered to drive into Crystal Creek to stock up on supplies. Before I headed to Crystal Creek, my dad drove me into town so that I could pick up my SUV. I used the opportunity to talk to Dad about my latest predicament—wedding planning.

Unlike my mother, who is a confirmed Type A personality, my dad is much more easygoing. The differences in my parents' personality types are why I gravitate to my dad so much. When I need to talk about something that I think is important, I talk to my dad. Dad hears my tales of woe, and he is able to point out the silver lining in the black clouds hovering over my head. My mother, on the other hand, hears my stories and gets nervous and critical of me.

"Are you having doubts, doll?" My dad asked when I told him that I worried about how often David and I argue about the same things again and again.

"There's no rush to get married if you aren't ready," my dad reminded me.

"I know that Dad, and I love David," I replied. "I know that you and Mom are smitten with him. It's just that I don't always think David trusts me, and that hurts. When something happens, I anticipate his disappointment in me, and I lie to him. I lie about stupid things too—like my nose piercing."

My dad nodded but refrained from commenting about the stud that protruded from my swollen nose. I don't think Dad liked my new piece of jewelry.

"I am the same person I was when David met me, and now that we're engaged, it feels like he wants me to change." I shook my head.

My dad glanced at me and cleared his throat. I anticipated words of wisdom from my father.

"Charlotte, your mother and I love you more than anything. And yes, David is a great partner for you. What we wish is for you to be happy and safe. We will support whatever you decide to do, but don't expect us—or David—to ever stop worrying about you. That, my dear, is love. If you can't accept David's love and he can't accept you for who you are, then the two of you should slow things down."

I shook my head.

"Dad, I don't want to slow things down with David. Things are slow enough already. I want him to understand me. David treats my opinions dismissively when he imagines that I put myself in danger. He makes me feel like a child. It's like he doesn't think I can take care of myself. I never scrutinize David in that way."

My dad nodded his head.

"After an uncertain childhood, it makes sense that David is afraid of losing you. He lost his mother at a young age, and his first wife passed away. That may be why he's so adamant about protecting you."

My eyes darted at my dad.

TROUBLE BREWING

"I'm not excusing David's behavior," Dad added, "I'm giving him the benefit of doubt."

"Has he said something to you?" I asked with suspicion. My dad and David are close. "Did David say that he's worried about me or something else?"

"No, but I know David worries about what could happen to you if you keep investigating crimes. I worry too."

"I'm not 'investigating'," I replied with defiance.

Okay, I was snooping a little, but it wasn't like I was putting myself in harm's way intentionally.

"Whatever you call it—snooping, investigating, keeping an eye out—David worries about your well-being. You're engaged, you're planning your lives together. Both of you have talked about having children one day. I can understand why David worries about you. What will happen when you have kids? Are you going to drag them along during your investigations? Charlotte, how will you keep your children safe if you're nosing around looking for criminals?"

"Okay, first of all, that's a kind of sexist statement, Dad. I forgive you for assuming that as a woman I am merely capable of caring for my hypothetical kids and nothing else. You are from a different generation and you might not know any better. Plenty of female cops have families. I hope they aren't scrutinized like this. It's a well-known fact that women are better at multitasking than men."

"That's not what I..." my dad sputtered and gripped the steering wheel tighter.

I interrupted him before he could finish his sentence.

"And B, when David and I have kids, I will expect him to be home more often than he is now. I can't have my husband jet-setting and leaving me alone with squalling babies. For the record, we've already talked about that. When David and I have children, he's going to be an involved father. He'll bathe, feed, and change the babies, and he'll love it."

"Okay, then I will remove myself from the conversation, and finish by saying, 'I love you, dear daughter.'"

"I love you too, Dad."

Was that it? Was everyone afraid that I was irresponsible and incapable of caring for myself and my future children? Was marrying me off my parents' strategy to protect me? I huffed as I pulled into my family's driveway and switched off the SUV's engine. I had things to do. I would worry about wedding planning later.

I locked up my car and took the walking path from my home to the barn. I needed to get the ATV and load its trailer with my purchases from the farm goods store. I was sliding the big barn doors open when I remembered that I had a phone message.

I pulled the phone from the pocket of my work slacks and checked my messages. The number of the caller was unfamiliar to me. I pressed the phone to my ear and listened to the brief message that the caller left. It wasn't a message, but rather it was a series of sounds—bangs, clicks, and a human voice? When the message ended, I replayed it so that I could listen again. Did I hear my name in the message? Was there a faint *Charlotte* before the call disconnected?

I glared at my phone as if staring at it would give me the answers I was searching for. On a normal day, I would go into my cottage, fire up my laptop computer and do a reverse phone number search, but I didn't have time. I had work to do. Like my wedding plans, I shirked my farm work too often.

Since I couldn't do the research myself. I did the next best thing. I dialed Cassie Binder. What good is having a best friend who was once a high school librarian if you can't phone and ask her to do research on occasion?

"Hey, Char, how are you feeling? David stopped by for his latte this morning, and he said you were under the weather," Cassie answered.

"I'm fine. Thank you for asking. Actually, I am super busy on the farm. Dad and I have to fertilize the trees. The mineral tests we did last week showed a drop in the nitrogen levels in our soil. That's not important right now. May I ask you a favor? I got the weirdest phone call. Could you do a reverse phone number lookup for me? You know that if I do the search, I'm likely to get sidetracked and fall down an internet rabbit hole for hours."

"Sure. I'm in my office now. What's the number?" My friend asked.

I rattled off the phone number and cradled my phone between my ear and my shoulder as I boarded the ATV.

"It's a call coming from a landline," Cassie said. "The five-seven-zero area code is a wide area, I'm afraid."

"Yes, I saw that. Any hits?" I asked.

"No, not yet. But wait. A friend showed me how do use Canadian directories for reverse lookups. Sometimes those are better. Hang on."

I waited as I fired up the engine of my ATV and drove it through the garage doors and down the lane toward my SUV.

"Bingo!" Cassie called out. "Char, what did the message say, exactly?"

"That's the weird part. Whoever called, didn't say anything except my name—or maybe he said my name. The message was only a few seconds long, and it sounded like utter chaos at the end of the line. It was probably a butt dial," I replied.

"I doubt it. I don't think it's possible to butt dial from a landline, is it? If it is possible, I don't want to know about it. Anyway, that call came from a landline registered to Walter Wells."

"Walter Wells?" I asked, feeling surprised. "Wasn't that Scotty's father's name?"

"Yes. Walter passed away about three years ago—shortly after Scotty lost his mom. Char, do you know what?"

"No, tell me," I replied. Mind reading is not my strong suit.

"Char, I bet that the call came from Scotty's cabin. If I remember correctly, the cabin is upstate—and within the five-seven-zero area code. Give me another second. I bet I can find the address," Cassie went quiet for a minute. I pulled the ATV up to my SUV and began unloading the bags of fertilizer from my SUV and placed them on the trailer.

"Direct hit!" Cassie called into the phone. "I thought that the Wells' cabin address would be a PO box because it is so rural, but I found a physical address. I Google searched it online. The place is pretty remote."

"Could you send the information to me? Give me a pin drop of the address or whatever?" I asked.

"Sure," Cassie replied. "The address is on its way."

"Thanks, Cass."

My phone beeped when I received the information.

"Char, what do you plan to do with the address?" Cassie asked me.

"Scotty is missing. He must be hiding out in his cabin waiting for everything to blow over. I am going to go see him," I replied. "I will try to persuade Scotty to tell me more about what happened between him and Poppy Flint on Friday night."

"Don't you think that you should call him first? Find out what why he called you," Cassie suggested. "I mean, has it occurred to you that Scotty may be hiding out because he's guilty?"

I gave Cassie's words consideration.

"No, Cassie. My gut tells me that Scotty is innocent. He might even be afraid. I've given this a lot of thought. There's a distinct possibility that Scotty is the murderer's next target. They killed Wilma and Poppy. Scotty might be next."

"If that's the case, shouldn't you call the police?" Cassie suggested. "If Scotty is in danger, then you will need backup."

"There's no need for that. For better or worse, I'm the person Scotty is reaching out to. I know that if I phone Uncle Mark or Brian Gold, they will dismiss me as being crazy. Or worse, they'll go in with sirens shrieking. They could lead the murderer to Scotty's hideout. We can't risk it."

TROUBLE BREWING

"Char, I don't feel good about this," Cassie admitted.

"I'll be fine. I'll call Scotty and tell him I'm on my way. And when I find Scotty, I will do my best to convince him to come back to Spruce Grove with me."

"If you say so," Cassie replied with reluctance.

"I'll call you when I get to his cabin," I said. "Thanks for finding the address for me."

As soon as I hung up with Cassie, I tried calling the phone number for Scotty's cabin. He didn't answer, in fact, the phone rang and rang. It didn't matter, my mind was set. I was going to drive north and find Scotty and make sure that he was safe—after I begged off work.

I drove over three hours to reach the remote border town between Pennsylvania and New York where Scotty's family cabin was. It took another thirty minutes to find the narrow, gravel road from the address that Cassie forwarded to me. There weren't any other cabins or homes around. I thought the tree farm was remote and rustic, but Scotty's cabin hid deep in the middle of nowhere.

My SUV thumped and bumped over the potholes and loose gravel as I made my way down the quiet, country road. Ancient oak and maple trees grew on either side creating a hidden passageway. I thought that Scotty's tiny car must struggle over the rough terrain. There was no way he drove the little roadster there. Perhaps he had a second vehicle that he used to reach the cabin. At any rate, there was no vehicle parked outside of the rustic, log cabin when I pulled up to it. In fact, the cabin was quiet, and it appeared that there were no lights on inside. I glanced at my phone. I knew I should call Cassie and David to let them know where I was. My phone had no signal. The call would have to wait.

I hoped that I wouldn't need to make a phone call. I mean, what would I do if I found another body? I would have to drive to the nearest town to report the death. I wasn't exactly sure where the closest town was. Then I remembered that Scotty had a landline inside the cabin. I let out a sigh of relief. Everything would be okay.

I climbed the concrete block steps and approached the door. It was a heavy-looking, solid oak. I knocked. "Scotty? It's Charlotte O'Hara."

There was no answer. I knocked again. An icy shiver ran up my spine as I remembered that the last time I went knocking on a quiet door, I'd found Poppy Flint's body. I reached for the doorknob and found the door unlocked. I pushed it open.

The cabin was sticky, dark, and warm inside. A musty smell enveloped me.

"Scotty?" I called out as I stumbled over something unseen on the floor. I illuminated my phone and discovered that I'd tripped over an old black telephone. The receiver was off the hook as if someone threw it aside. That was weird.

"Scotty?" I called out. I stopped and listened.

Was that something rustling in the dark? My pulse quickened as I imagined creepy crawlers—mice, spiders, or snakes—crawling around in the dark. I yipped and hopped into the air. Calm down, Char! I told myself as I walked toward a door across the room. I heard the rustling sound again coming from a room that I imagined was the bedroom.

"Scotty?" I called again as I reached for the doorknob.

I drew a deep breath, and I pushed the door open. "Scotty?" I whispered into the darkness.

A *"Harrumph!"* answered me.

"Scotty?" I whispered as I ran my hand along the wall hoping to locate a light switch. I found a switch and flicked it on. In front of me was a twin-sized bed, the duvet was smooth, and the pillows plumped.

"Harrumph!" Scotty's voice answered from the other side of the bed. He was alive!

I ran around the bed and found an overturned chair with a gagged Scotty Wells tied to it with a black telephone cord!

TROUBLE BREWING

"Scotty!" I shouted as I knelt by his side. I pulled the gag from his mouth. Scotty's skin looked gray, and droplets of sweat and blood clung to his forehead. His left eye was swollen and blackened.

"Charlotte," he whispered, "you came."

I grabbed the cord that secured his hands to the back of his chair. I tried to untie the cord, but it seemed to get tighter with my effort. The old black phone cord wrapped around the chair's spindles and then coiled around Scotty's wrists. His ankles were bound to the chair's legs.

"You need to cut it," Scotty implored, "he'll be back soon."

"Who? Who did this to you, Scotty?" I asked as I jumped to my feet intending to search for something sharp enough to slide through the thick cord. Aside from the small bed and the chair that Scotty was bound to, there was nothing useful in sight.

"There are steak knives in the kitchen," Scotty said with a gasp, "quickly, Charlotte!"

I darted from the room and ran to the small galley kitchen. I tore drawers open until I found a steak knife, and I ran back to Scotty. I began sawing at the cord that bound him to the chair.

"Scotty, what happened?" I asked, "the last time we spoke, you hung up on me. How did you wind up like this?"

"I didn't hang up," Scotty replied. He grimaced as he peered over his shoulder and watched me sawing the cord with the dullest knife I've ever held.

"I was walking in the alley behind the yoga studio. He tried to grab me, but I had pepper spray on my keyring. I sprayed him. The spray didn't stop him! He hit me over the head. When I came to, I was in his car, and he demanded that I tell him where the cabin is. I guess I passed out after that. I woke up chained to a beam in the living room. The chain was only long enough for me to reach the bathroom. I was alone. Our old phone is still connected, and I was able to reach it. I called you, but I guess he was lurking outside. He stormed inside, grabbed me, and pulled the phone's cord right out of the wall. He whipped me with the

135

cord until I fell to the floor and begged him to stop. I thought I would be okay, but then he started kicking me. I guess I blacked out again. When I woke up, I discovered that he tied me with the phone cord to this chair."

Oh my gosh! Whoever the man was, he was a monster. I needed to get Scotty out of there!

"Why didn't you call the police? Why did you call me?" I asked. Scotty had one chance at freedom, and he'd called me.

"The police think that I killed Wilma and Poppy. You are the only one who believed that I am innocent. He set me up, Charlotte."

"Who? Scotty, who did this to you?" I dragged the knife over the cord again. The handle popped off the knife, leaving me with an old, serrated blade with nothing to hold it.

"I did," a low voice growled from behind me.

I turned slowly. I still hadn't freed Scotty from his binds. If I had to face a killer, I knew that I was on my own, and all that I had to defend myself was a useless, broken, steak knife.

He pointed a gnarled, wooden cane directly at my face. I knew that cane. It had belonged to Wilma Flint. Perhaps he'd taken it from her as a trophy. I know that murderers sometimes keep things that belonged to their victims.

His normally handsome face scowled, and his eyes darkened as he tapped the end of the cane on the floor. Thunk. Thunk. Thunk.

"I brought Scotty here. Everyone thinks he killed Wilma and Poppy—that he beat them to death. Scotty's silence allowed me to get away with murder. He could have gone to the police and told them about Poppy, but he didn't—out of loyalty to her." He stopped speaking long enough to release a long, cold, guffaw that sent shivers down my spine. Then, he spoke again.

"Scotty is here, in his beloved cabin to kill himself out of remorse for what he did. He was going to set this place on fire, wrap a cord around his neck, throw it over the rafters, and go down in a blaze of glory. But then you came along," he smiled eyeing me wickedly. "So, there's been a change of plan. Scotty is going to kill you before he takes his own life. The investigators won't find enough evidence to prove that Scotty didn't kill himself or you. They won't find much at all aside from your charred bones. This old hunk of wood will burn hot—with a little help."

"You don't have to do this," I implored as my eyes skimmed the room for a better weapon. The broken knife I had was dull and lacked a handle. The blade wouldn't likely penetrate the thick denim coveralls that he wore. There was nothing in the room that I could hoist as a weapon—no Ming Dynasty vase, no scissors, no weighted bookends. There are always weapons available to the heroine in the old murder mysteries I read. I saw nothing that I could use to fend off our would-be killer.

The killer stepped forward. His boots sounded heavy on the hardwood floor. I could sense that he would have no qualms about beating me over the head with that cane—like he'd hit Wilma. Or he would kick me with those boots as he had with Poppy. I could imagine the scenario. He would beat me on the floor of the old cabin. It would take a while to knock my lights out, and he would take pleasure in it. Then, he would kill Scotty before he set the cabin on fire to destroy any trace of himself.

He shook his head dismissively at me. "I do have to do it. I have to kill you both. You left me no choice. I am aware of your reputation, Charlotte. You pretend you're a sweet, dim little actress," he stopped to let his words sink in.

I felt the heat of anger rush through my veins. I don't pretend—I mean, *I am not dim*! How dare he?

He continued. "Charlotte, everyone knows that you are a snoop, and you have the ear of the Chief of Police. He's your cousin or uncle or something. Don't worry, I will make sure you're unconscious when it happens. You will die from smoke inhalation before the flames get you."

He backed out of the room quickly, and I heard the click of a lock on the door. Scotty and I were trapped in the bedroom, but at least our would-be killer was gone for the moment.

I returned my attention to Scotty and grasped the knife's blade. The old knife dug into my skin as I sawed furiously at the old-fashioned telephone cord. "Help me, Scotty. You need to try to pull the cords tighter. They are too tough and thick for this knife."

Then, I smelled fuel. Scotty's frightened eyes met mine. "He must have found the kerosene tank."

"Hurry!" I cried.

I heard a woosh as the fuel ignited. A few seconds later, I heard the sound of tires kicking up gravel in the driveway. Mick Flint was getting away!

"Scotty, you have to move!" I cried.

Scotty's eyes were like globes. "Charlotte, I can't. Mick smashed my knees and kicked me in the back. I'm having trouble feeling my legs."

Thick grayish smoke billowed through the crack beneath the closed bedroom door. I abandoned my post next to Scotty and yanked the duvet from the bed. I dammed the crack under the door with the cover to buy myself more time to free Scotty.

There was a small window across the room. The curtains were drawn against the sunlight, and I hadn't noticed the window before.

"Scotty, we need to get out that window," I told him. I grabbed a pillow from the bed and removed the pillowcase. I wrapped the case around my right hand like I'd seen actors do in movies. I walked to the window, turned my head sideways, closed my eyes, and I threw a punch.

Crash! The window shattered. I looked at the opening. The center of the window broke but long shards of glass—jagged like a dragon's teeth—remained in the window frame. With my covered hand, I pulled a glassy tooth from the frame.

TROUBLE BREWING

I jogged back to Scotty and used the glass as a knife. Finally, the cord began to fall away from Scotty's wrists and ankles. I ignored the wet redness that seeped through the cloth on my hand.

"You're free!" I shouted.

I noticed that smoke from the fire exited the front of the cabin and wrapped around the back of the house. The smoke was coming through the window.

"This is it, Scotty," I shouted as I reached to pull him from the floor. He yelped and collapsed as soon as he tried to put weight on his legs.

"I can't!" He cried.

"Scotty, you'll forgive me later for saying this, but you need to stop being a wimp for once in your life. You can be the biggest dork in Spruce Grove after we get out of here, but right now, you need to move!"

Scotty isn't a tall man. Lord knows he was teased about his height in school. Scotty's lack of stature helped save his life that day. I stepped behind Scotty, and I reached under his arms, forcing him to stand. The screech he failed to muffle made me realize how much agony he was in. I couldn't let Scotty's pain stop us—not when we were so close to freedom.

Scotty leaned against me as I backed up to the wall. The window was low, and with a little help from me, Scotty went through the opening first. I barely heard Scotty over the roaring fire when he called my name, "Hurry, Charlotte!"

I dragged my torso through the narrow window and felt the remaining broken glass scrape my flesh as I slid through to the outside.

We scrabbled as far as we could from the building, exhausted, bleeding, and panting. Lying beneath an old oak tree, I felt a *woosh*. It was like the cabin sucked the oxygen from around us. Then, flames engulfed the entire building.

I looked at Scotty. Sweat and blood covered his face, and the pupils of his eyes were large and dark. His mouth opened, then closed. If

Scotty spoke to me, I didn't hear him. All I could hear was the blood pounding inside my head as we watched the Wells family cabin disintegrate in front of us. Then everything went silent.

ELEVEN

"Charlotte? Can you hear me?"

"Let me sleep five more minutes, Mom," I mumbled to whoever was touching my face, and lifting my eyelids. I fought to close my eyes, but someone opened them again.

"Charlotte?" His face was blurry.

"Is she awake?" A second man's voice sounded relieved.

"I think she's coming around," the first man replied in a gruff voice. "Charlotte? Time to wake up, kiddo, the Calvary is here."

I turned my head toward the voice. Everything from my head to the tips of my toes hurt. "Uncle Mark? You're blurry." My voice was soft and scratchy.

My uncle emitted a relieved chuckle. "You scared us, kiddo. Your eyes are blurry from the smoke, that's all."

I felt pressure on my right hand—the one I'd cut when I tried to rescue Scotty Wells. I dared a sideways glance at it. Brian Gold smiled as he held something—a cloth—against my hand. "You've got a couple of bad cuts."

"Glass," I whispered. "And a broken knife."

"You'll be okay," my uncle said, "we both had first aid training, and Brian took the volunteer EMT course."

Brian smiled again from his place by my side. There was something different about how he was looking at me.

"How did you know I was here?" I croaked as I attempted to sit up. Uncle Mark placed a hand behind my back to steady me. I realized that I was still under the oak tree, but Scotty wasn't with me.

"Where's Scotty?" I asked against the sandpapery sensation in my throat. I coughed.

"He's with Officer Collins," my uncle replied. He reached for a water bottle and handed it to me. "Small sips," my uncle instructed. I took the bottle with my uninjured hand and slowly drank.

"Office Collins is with the local county fire department and has EMT certification. She knows Scotty from when he used to come here as a kid. She'll look after him while we wait for the ambulance to get here," my uncle explained. "They're on their way."

"He's hurt bad, isn't he?" I asked.

My uncle's eyes darted to the ground, confirming my suspicions.

Brian spoke, "Scotty has some broken bones and possible spinal trauma. He took quite a beating."

"Frankly, we're surprised he's alive," Uncle Mark added. "He is lucky you found him."

"Oh my gosh. I forced him to walk." I felt guilty tears gather in my otherwise dry eyes.

"Char, you had no choice," Brian's voice was low and calm, "did you see the cabin?"

I looked over his shoulder. All that remained of Scotty's beloved retreat was ash and smoke. A few firemen were busy putting out hotspots with hoes and water. Despite the high-vis vests they wore, I hadn't even noticed them before.

Tears flooded my eyes, and I didn't bother to rub them away.

"How did you find us?" I repeated my earlier question.

"Cassie Binder. She called us after she didn't hear from you. She thought something was wrong, and she was right."

I stared at my blurry uncle.

"You came here on a hunch?" It was hard to imagine that my uncle would waste police time on a gut feeling. My uncle always told me that he needed hard evidence not gut feelings to solve a case.

"Cassie said that you were in contact with Scotty. She told me about the phone calls, and I contacted the local authorities. We're working together. It would sure be a lot easier if we knew who we were after," Mark said.

"You don't know?" I drew a deep breath.

TROUBLE BREWING

I realized, only Scotty and I knew the killer's identity. Everyone was looking for Scotty Wells when the real killer walked among them—pretending to be a grieving husband.

"It was Mick Flint—Poppy's husband. I don't know why he killed her, but it was him. He hurt Scotty, and he set the cabin on fire with the two of us inside it. Mick was framing Scotty for Poppy and Wilma's murders."

"Right." Uncle Mark turned to face Brian, "Can I leave you here with Charlotte? I need to put out an APB on Mr. Flint."

"Absolutely, Chief," Brian replied. His sea-blue eyes met mine, and he offered me another shy smile. "The ambulance should be here soon."

"I'm okay," I whispered.

"No, you aren't okay, but you will be," Brian said.

"And Scotty?"

Brian shook his head, "I don't know. He's conscious at least. He even said a few words to Officer Collins. He didn't say anything about Mick Flint, though."

Brian smiled again, "I think Scotty and Officer Collins have a history together. Scotty called her Tink—you know—like Tinkerbell? And she got all red in the face."

"Really? That's kind of sweet." I drank more water.

"Yeah, and, get this. Officer Penny Collins looks a lot like Cassie—you know, cute, blonde and blue-eyed? Only Penny is a lot taller and jacked up."

"Jacked up?" I felt my eyes squint, trying to place the reference.

"Like a bodybuilder," Brian said, smiling. "She's a firefighter—a lot of them work out."

"Gosh, where was Tink when I was trying to get Scooter out of the burning cabin? I could have used her back there," I said using their nicknames. Scooter and Tink seemed to go together.

"I have a feeling we will be seeing more of Penny Collins," Brian admitted. "The way she took over Scotty's care. There's some old chemistry there. Good for Scooter."

"Yes. Good for Scooter," I replied as I heard the sound of a siren in the distance.

"Okay, I need everybody out," the male nurse said to all my visitors, "Miss O'Hara needs some rest. One of you can stay." He walked slowly out of the room and waited for the crowd to disperse.

Most of my favorite people were in my small room—breaking hospital rules. My parents, Cassie, Joe, Uncle Mark and his fiancé, Sarah, and Brian Gold gathered around me. David was notably absent, but everyone was too polite to mention it.

"Who should stay?" Sarah asked as she grasped Uncle Mark's hand. I guessed that she wanted to get back to whatever she was doing before I interrupted her busy day. Sarah and I have a combative past and we still haven't completely worked through it. It didn't surprise me that my future aunt (who is the same age as me) wanted to leave.

"I'll stay, if that's okay with the rest of you," Brian piped up. "I'm off the clock, but we still haven't located Mick Flint. I can keep a watch over Char until a guard shows up."

"That's a good idea," my dad replied. "I'll feel better knowing that Charlotte is under the close eye of a Spruce Grove Police Officer."

"I'll feel better too," my mom added as she brushed my bangs from my eyes. "Why don't the rest of us meet up at our house? I can make us dinner."

"Thank you, Mrs. O'Hara, but we need to pick up Max from her grandparents' house," Cassie replied. "They've had her twice this week, and Max can be a real pistol these days."

TROUBLE BREWING

"Bring Max along," my mom added, "it will be nice to have a child in the house. Lord knows when we'll have another one around. I'll make spaghetti."

"Sounds great," Joe offered. "Char, feel better soon, okay? We'll come and check on you during visiting hours tomorrow."

"If I am still here," I replied. "I can't wait to get home and sleep in my own bed."

"Don't give the nurses a hard time, Char," Cassie leaned in and kissed my cheek. "Do what they tell you."

Since she was so close, I whispered in my best friend's ear, "Where's David?"

Cassie pulled back a bit. She waited for the rest of the crowd to leave the room. Brian stood by the door, waiting.

"I don't know, honey," Cassie whispered. "I tried calling David, and Joe went around to his house. His truck wasn't in the driveway."

Cassie noted my worried look.

"Don't worry. I left about a dozen messages for David. He'll show up. I bet he is someplace where he doesn't have a good phone signal. You know how it is around here—dead zones everywhere," Cassie tried to reassure me.

Or, I thought, David is angry at me for ignoring his request to stay out of the investigation. He was going to dump me, and I couldn't blame him. This was all my fault.

"You're probably right, Cassie," I replied going along with Cassie's optimism. "Or he's doing internet research and he hasn't even looked at his phone."

"Yep, that's it," Cassie agreed. "Once he hears my messages, David will be by your side. Guaranteed." This time, Cassie shot a concerned look toward Brian. Brian's face remained stoic.

"I'll see you later," she brushed the top of my head and walked over to Brian. Cassie whispered in his ear, and he nodded. Then, Cassie left. I could hear the voices of my loved ones as they exited the corridor.

Brian stepped closer and dragged a chair over with him. "You don't mind if I stay, at least, until your fiancé arrives? Or one of our officers?" He sat beside me.

I shook my head. "I don't mind. It will be too quiet and lonely here by myself. You don't know where David is, do you?"

"Not a clue," Brian reached for my left hand and held it in his. His skin was warm against mine.

"Why do they always keep hospitals so cold?" I asked.

"It's one of life's mysteries," Brian replied, smiling again. "I know he would want to be here—David, I mean."

I shook my head. I was doubtful. "How can you know that?"

"Because I would want to be here if I were him," Brian leaned in, "I *want* to be here."

Despite the cold hospital room, I felt my face grow warm. "You *are* here, and that means so much to me."

"I won't leave your side," Brian said, "until you tell me to go."

"Then I guess you'll be here as long as I am," I said, wincing; the ache in my side returned.

"What's wrong? Are you in pain? Is it your hand?" He asked. I read the concern in Brian's face.

"It's nothing. It's my side. It's from my dancing accident a couple of days ago. I don't understand why it hurts so much. The pain is getting worse over time instead of better."

"Your side?" Brian asked sitting up straighter. "Show me?"

I felt my face grow warmer. The place where my side hurt was low on the right side of my abdomen—diagonal from my belly button. I rested my hand where the pain was radiating. A swell of nausea rose in my throat. "Here," I said rubbing the side of my tummy.

Brian's sea-blue eyes widened. "How long has your side been bothering you?"

TROUBLE BREWING

"A few days," I replied. "I first noticed it when David and I were doing a dance move—or trying to. I pulled a muscle or something. I sort of feel like barfing."

"Mind if I try something?" Brian stood and hovered over my hospital bed.

"Okay?" I was feeling a bit unsure.

Brian laid his hands on the spot that hurt. "Can you lift your knees to your chest?"

I laughed at him, but Brian looked insistent.

"Brian, why?" I asked.

"Please?" He asked. "Trust me. Lift them."

"Um, okay," I complied with Brian's wishes and raised my knees to my chest. I hoped that the bedsheets covered my bottom. I was clad in one of those unflattering hospital gowns and nothing else.

As soon as I lifted my knees, Brian pressed down on my gut where I felt the pain. I didn't notice any increase in the pain until he pulled his hands away.

"Ow! What the heck, Brian? What did you do to me?" I demanded as I let my legs drop down to the bed. I squashed the sudden urge to smack my old friend for hurting me.

"Char, I don't think you pulled a muscle. I think you're having appendicitis. You never had your appendix removed, right? I mean, I don't remember seeing a scar back in the day."

"Appendicitis? I am not eight years old, Brian. Kids have appendicitis—not adults!" I protested, ignoring Brian's scar remark. I was already upset. I didn't need to add embarrassment to the list of emotions I felt.

"Uh, yeah, adults definitely have appendicitis too. Stay here," Brian pulled away from me, "I'm going to get a nurse."

"Wait. Brian, if I need to have my appendix out, will they make me stay here longer?" I asked. I really wanted to get home to my cozy cottage. I didn't want the annoyance of a childhood health concern to keep me away from my home longer.

"Try to relax, Char, I'll be right back."

Brian jogged from the room.

"Well, Charlotte, I am happy to say, we removed your appendix without any complications. We used arthroscopic surgery," the surgeon told me a few hours later. "Thanks to Officer Gold, we caught it before the appendix had a chance to rupture. You are a lucky lady."

"Funny, I don't feel so lucky," I groggily replied.

Can you blame me for feeling less than lucky? Over the last several days, I'd found two dead bodies, was confined by a killer, survived a fire, misplaced my fiancé, and had my appendix removed. That's a lot for a woman who lives in a town where nothing ever happens.

The surgeon smiled, "I recommend two nights in the hospital. You can use the rest after your injuries and the operation. I'll write a prescription for an antibiotic for when you're released. I expect you'll be able to return home the day after tomorrow barring any complications, of course."

"Oh, thank goodness," I replied. "How likely are complications?"

"Not very likely at all—if you obey your medical orders. Anyway, your friend is hoping to speak to you, but only for a minute. I'd like you to get some rest," the surgeon said as he walked from the room.

"Hey, how are you feeling?" Brian asked as he entered the room. He scratched the soft amber stubble on his cheeks. He held a bunch of mixed daisies in a pink plastic vase that he bought at the hospital's gift shop. He set the flowers on my table and smiled.

"I'm sleepy," I replied. My voice still sounded scratchy. "I don't think the anesthesia has worn off yet."

"You're probably right," Brian sat in the chair next to me. "And it's been a long day."

TROUBLE BREWING

"Have you been waiting here the entire time?" I asked. It was dark outside, and Brian was still dressed in his police uniform.

"I told you I wasn't leaving you," Brian reminded me.

I nodded as I remembered the conversation we'd had before Brian diagnosed my wonky appendix. "I owe you a big thank you," I finally said, "for diagnosing my appendicitis. So, thank you, Brian. And I forgive you for causing me excruciating pain for a second. Where did you learn to do that?"

"That's something I picked up while riding around in the ambulance during my EMT training," Brian said. "I never diagnosed one before though. You're my first. Again."

"Again?" I asked wondering what he meant.

"First appendicitis. First love," he smiled and flushed. "You have no idea, Char, how worried I was about you today—first at the fire, and then here."

"I'm okay now," I replied. My voice was a whisper. "And you're here." David was conspicuously absent.

"As I said, Char, I won't leave until you tell me to," Brian said.

"Well, I think you've played the knight in shining armor long enough today. You look tired, and if I know my Uncle Mark, he'll have you out looking for Mick Flint first thing tomorrow."

"You're probably right," Brian scratched his face again. "Officer Jim Stevens arrived while you were in surgery. He will be keeping watch right outside the door for the rest of the night. Just in case."

"You mean you could have left already?" I asked.

Brian shrugged. I knew that he meant what he said. Brian wasn't going to leave until I told him to.

"Brian, you should go home now, and get some sleep. I need to sleep too—doctor's orders."

"You still haven't heard from David?" Brian asked as he stood from his chair, finally giving up his post as my bodyguard. He covered a yawn with his hand.

"No," I whispered. "I think he is angry with me."

Then, something happened that would change everything. Brian leaned in and closed his eyes, and his lips headed my way. I twisted in reaction. Somehow our directions got mixed up. What should have been a chaste kiss on my cheek landed on my lips instead.

The kiss only lasted a second, but neither of us pulled away immediately. The kiss reminded me of the first kiss we shared when I was sixteen—my very first kiss. Suddenly, a flood of emotions rained over me. Brian stared down at me, his mouth formed a surprised O, as he straightened to his full height. "Um, I guess I slipped," his voice was an embarrassed squeak.

"Me too," I said against the rocks that formed in my throat. I didn't know what else to say.

"Char!" David's voice bellowed as he jogged into the room. "I came as soon as I heard. Are you alright?"

"I'll text you later," I said to Brian. His face reddened as he beat a hasty retreat toward the door. He stopped when he reached David.

"Glad you made it. She's going to be okay, with time," Brian said to David before he exited the room. David didn't reply to Brian. He stepped toward my bed.

"Char, I am so awfully sorry," David began as he dropped into the chair that Brian abandoned a moment before. Had he seen us kiss? If David had seen Brian and I, he didn't make mention of it.

"I was in a place with no cell service. When I finally got into range, my cell phone came to life with about fifty missed calls and messages—most of them were from Cassie. She said that Mick Flint tried to kill you. The last message was from Brian. He said you had acute appendicitis. My God, are you okay?"

"If you think my appendicitis is cute, boy are you going to love my liver," I replied with a joke.

Twin pangs of guilt and anger hit me as I remembered the kiss.

TROUBLE BREWING

"I'm okay, now. But David, where were you? It's been hours. Mick Flint nearly killed me, and he gravely injured Scotty Wells."

David drew a breath and exhaled. I could tell by his expression that someone—probably Cassie—had filled him in on everything. "Charlotte, I have a confession to make."

My insides grew watery as I anticipated David's next words. I told myself not to flinch when he uttered the phrase that I dreaded hearing. *We shouldn't get married.*

True, I'd had my doubts about marrying David—especially recently—when everything we talked about seemed to spiral into an argument. We hadn't shared a romantic moment in weeks. Everything was wrong. And I kissed Brian just seconds before David entered the hospital room. The kiss was an accident, but I couldn't deny that I felt nostalgic about Brian. I didn't deserve David.

Faced with the possibility of David ending our romance and disappearing forever, I was petrified of losing him. I wanted to cling to him like a life raft in a sea of circling sharks.

"Charlotte, I am sorry. I was conducting my own investigation. While you were out there saving Scotty Wells' life, I was on the dark web looking for clues. I now know that I should have been here—or there—with you. I am so very sorry. Can you forgive me?"

"David," I whispered. "Of course, I forgive you, but I don't understand why you didn't tell me that you were investigating too. You know I would have helped you. Why didn't you tell me? And where were you? What place has the dark web but no cell service?"

David lowered his eyes and shook his head. "I can't, Char."

"You don't want to tell me, or you can't?" I asked.

I will never forget David's next words:

"Charlotte, there are some things that you are better off not knowing about me." He raised his head and it felt like his chocolate brown eyes bored right through me. "There are things and people from my past that I wish I could erase."

My stomach fell to my knees. "I don't understand. What are you trying to tell me, David? What things from your past are you trying to forget?"

David shook his head again. He reached a strong hand out and set it on my forehead. "You must be tired. After the surgery, after everything. I'll go see if I can find a friendly nurse to get me a cot. I'll sleep here next to you tonight. I promise I won't leave you again."

I grabbed his wrist determined not to let him leave before I knew what he was talking about before.

"David, I am certain that I don't understand what you are talking about—your past, I mean. I thought you told me everything. You are an orphan who worked his way through college doing construction. College was where you met your business partner George and your lovely wife Anne. You started your tech company, and then Anne died. You came to Spruce Grove after you sold your company to heal and start over again. What haven't you told me?"

"That isn't important right now, Char." He gently slid my hand from his forearm.

"Honestly, David, I thought you disappeared earlier because you were angry with me. I thought my heart would break when everyone that I love was here to see me at the hospital except for you. I thought you came back to break things off." I felt tears fill my eyes. "I am so relieved to see you and that you want to stay with me. I hope one day, you can tell me what is troubling you."

David nodded to reassure me. "I'll tell you everything when the time is right. But, Char, why would you ever imagine that I'd break up with you? If you think back, I've always been the one pressing for us to get married—even after we argue. I want to make a life with you."

"After our disagreement, and after everything that happened today, I thought I'd messed up everything." I stopped speaking to let a yawn escape my mouth. "I broke yet another promise to you. When you didn't come to the hospital, I thought you were finished with me. If you broke up with me, I would only have myself to blame."

David stood and bent forward. He pressed his lips gently to my forehead. When he straightened, he said, "You won't lose me that easily, Charlotte Virginia O'Hara. I am devastatingly in love with you." He grasped my hand—the one that bore the beautiful sapphire engagement ring that he gave me when he asked me to be his wife.

"Really?" My voice cracked at the realization that David Moore was actually in love with me. He wasn't angry with me. He hadn't come to the hospital to break my heart but to make sure that I was okay.

"Charlotte, I'm all in, as they sometimes say in poker."

"Funny, I really do feel like people see me as a bit of a gamble. If you marry me, David, I will do my best to give you *better-than-house odds*," I replied, using the tidbit of knowledge I have about poker.

David chuckled at my promise.

"You know what?" He asked.

I shook my head. "What?"

"Let's do it. When you get out of here, and you're feeling better, let's jump on the first plane to Las Vegas. We'll have an Elvis impersonator marry us. The hell with big ceremonies, tuxes, and white wedding dresses. We don't need any of those things to be happy. We always said we just need each other. What do you think?"

"David, I've been dreading the wedding ceremony. And in all fairness, my days of white weddings are long gone. My mother clings to the hope that my *virtue* magically returned on the day that I divorced Kyle Stalls. She really didn't like Kyle."

Suddenly, despite everything that had happened, I came down with a case of giggles. I only stopped laughing at my stupid joke when I realized I risked tearing a suture.

"My days of white weddings are over too, Char. Besides, I want a marriage, not a wedding ceremony. And you're the one I want to spend the rest of my life with. So, what do you say to Las Vegas?" David asked. His eyes gleamed.

"I say, *I am all in*, fiancé."

TWELVE

A couple weeks rolled away, and I was beginning to feel like myself again. I healed from my surgery and the cuts I received when I escaped from Scotty's cabin. I was well enough to travel and cleared for my honeymoon in Las Vegas.

"Okay, which swimsuit should I take?" I asked Cassie as I held up a pretty but conservative blue one-piece in one hand and a tiny black bikini in the other. In the past, I never would have considered the bikini, but working on the tree farm has its perks. I was in great shape from the hard labor of cutting and planting trees.

"They're both nice bathing suits. There's no rule against packing both, you know. But are you supposed to swim so soon after surgery?" Cassie cocked a skeptical eyebrow at me as she lifted a slinky blue dress from my discard pile.

"I'm cleared for all activities, but I plan to soak up the sun and get rid of my farmer's tan. I agree with you. Both swimsuits are nice, but I have a surgical scar now," I looked down at my midsection and frowned. I was wearing a t-shirt and jeans that covered the incision site, but I could still see the fresh, pink scar in my mind's eye.

"You'll be fine. I don't worry about my C-section scar. You shouldn't worry about your scar either," Cassie replied. "I can't believe the two of you are going to tie the knot without us. I really wanted to stand up for both of you." Cassie plopped onto the King-sized bed in the guestroom of David's house, and sulked.

I'd moved a bunch of my things into the spare bedroom after I was released from the hospital. Actually, my dad moved them for me. I was too embarrassed to ask my father to put my clothes and things in the main bedroom that I shared with David. We weren't married yet. I doubted that Gary O'Hara believed that I was staying in the spare bedroom until after the wedding. I wanted to save him and my mom the embarrassment of having a harlot for a daughter. (Insert eye roll here.)

I placed both swimsuits into my suitcase and smiled at my friend. "I know you want to be there, but David and I realized that we've been dancing around the whole wedding thing for far too long. Who says we need a big wedding? We want to make things legal and get on with our lives."

"I suppose I understand," Cassie said as she twisted a strand of her golden hair between her fingers. "And I don't mind telling you that I'll be glad to see you get out of town for a little while. With Mick Flint at large, it's not a bad idea to lay low for a while. Who knows where he is?"

"David agrees with you," I said as I plunked onto the bed beside my bestie. "That's why I am already living here. We didn't want to officially move in together until after the wedding. I spent half my nights with David before everything happened with Mick and Scotty. Mostly, David and I were trying to appease my mother. You know she doesn't approve of pre-marital shenanigans—regardless of how old David and I are. But with Mick Flint missing, David didn't want to take any chances with my safety. He has a top-of-the-line security system here."

My dog, Clouseau, jumped up on the bed to join us, and he licked the tip of my nose, making me laugh. "Also, I have my ferocious guard dog with me."

Cassie laughed. "I'm glad you're safe. Have you decided what to wear to the altar?"

"Ha! Altar makes it sound like David's going to kill me as a sacrifice. What's with all the Medieval wedding references? Altars, maiden names, giving away the bride. It's all so old fashioned! I am relieved to elope. And yes, I have picked out the dress. David hasn't even seen it yet. I found it at that fancy consignment shop in town."

TROUBLE BREWING

"So? Are you going to show your dress to me?" Cassie asked with impatience.

"It's the dress in the plastic cover hanging in the closet," I replied, lazily. I hadn't had my mid-day nap and it was nearly five in the evening. In a few hours, David and I would jump into his car and drive to the airport. We would arrive in Las Vegas later that evening, have a nice dinner, and get hitched in the morning before we boarded a flight for a two-week honeymoon. David hadn't told me the destination of our honeymoon—it was a surprise—one of many.

Cassie hopped off the bed and ambled to the walk-in closet. I could hear the zipper on the garment bag as she dragged it down.

"Oh, Char! This is perfect! It's stunning! I can't believe you didn't show it to me before." Cassie returned holding out the dress by the hanger. She stood in front of the full-length mirror that hangs from the bedroom door and placed the dress in front of herself as if she were trying it on. Cassie is several inches shorter than me, so the skirt of the dress fell below her knees instead of above them.

"Do you really like it? And, more importantly, will it be okay for the wedding? I mean, most brides don't wear black to their own nuptials."

"Well," Cassie spun around still clinging to the dress, "first of all, you aren't most brides. You are Charlotte-freaking-O'Hara, and you are a badass."

I felt the sting of tears in my eyes. Cassie always knows what to say to me.

"Secondly, you are going to look like Audrey H. in this dress. All you need is a tiara, long gloves, and one of those old-fashioned cigarette holders."

"I've already packed those things," I said with a smile and a wink. "Except for the cigarette holder—I don't smoke, and I doubt that Audrey would smoke either."

"You're right, obviously," Cassie carried the dress back into the closet and returned a few seconds later. She sat on the bed beside me. "I wish we were going to be there—especially now. I'd love to see you waltz down the aisle in that beautiful dress."

"Well, don't worry. Mom said that she is throwing us a party when we return. You'll be there. Everyone will. I will wear the dress then."

"I will be at the party. All our friends are invited. Speaking of which, do you want to talk about Brian?"

"Brian? Why?" I anticipated my best friend's next words. I busied myself by unpacking the clothes from my suitcase. I started re-folding them.

"Come on Char. I've known Brian almost as long as I've known you. He told me what happened at the hospital. The two of you kissed."

I shook my head and tried to pretend the kiss wasn't a big deal. There was no point in denying what happened. I hadn't spoken to Brian about it. I thought we were both too embarrassed to say anything. I guess I was wrong.

"So, it's true?" Cassie asked. She already knew that Brian would never lie to her.

I nodded, "What did Brian say? Does Joe know? I haven't told David. I thought about telling him, but then I decided there was no point. It was one, innocent kiss."

Cassie shook her head and placed her hand over mine so that I would stop unfolding and refolding my clothes. "Joe doesn't know. Brian and I agreed not to say anything to him or anyone else. But…" Cassie paused.

"What? Say it, Cass."

"Brian thinks he's the reason you decided to rush the wedding and elope with David. I think he's right. One minute you had no immediate plans to marry, the next minute, you announced that you were eloping. That sounds like more than a coincidence to me."

TROUBLE BREWING

"Nonsense," I replied, but I couldn't meet my bestie's eyes because her words held some truth. I loved David but I knew that I would never stop loving Brian—at least a little bit. I decided that the best thing to do was nip it in the bud and get married.

"Joe thinks there is still a spark between the two of you," Cassie offered, "and I think there is too. I've noticed the buzz coming off of both of you on the rare times that we're all together—even though I'm team David."

"Cassie, as you know, Brian and I have a long history together. That must be the energy that you sense between us. You also know that things never seemed to come together for us—no matter how hard we—particularly me—tried. I don't think Brian and I were meant to be. Things happened so organically between me and David. That is why I am marrying him—that, and also because I love him—David, I mean."

"Uh huh. I know you love David, and he adores you, Char, but if you still have feelings for Brian, don't you think you should wait?"

"Cassie," I laughed, "I don't have those kinds of feelings for Brian anymore. Hey, is this a ploy to get me to have a church wedding here in Spruce Grove?"

"No, and you know it isn't, Char. I'm not joking around. You deserve to be happy."

"I am happy, Cass, and I will be even happier after David and I tie the knot. We're talking about splitting our time between here and Italy. Once we're settled, we want to start a family. Trust me, Cass, this is for the best. When David and I are official, Brian and I will be okay—as friends."

Cassie shook her head as if she disagreed with my logic, but to her credit, she didn't argue with me. Instead, she changed the subject. "Have you heard anything from Scotty?"

"No. Have you?" I asked. It surprised me that Scotty hadn't reached out after our ordeal. I thought we shared a new bond.

"I haven't heard from Scotty. But I heard that he is doing okay. He's in a rehab hospital. Scotty isn't walking, but they think he will walk again soon."

"That's amazing news!" I said, feeling happy for the man who we used to make fun of.

"It is, and that firewoman from up north? Her name is Penny Collins. I met her at Magic Beans. She's been back and forth visiting Scotty in the hospital. She came into the shop and struck up a conversation with me like she'd known me for years. She's a real hoot. Penny and Scotty are kind of an item now. I guess they used to be summertime sweethearts when they were little kids. Penny or Tink—that's what Scotty calls her—said that Scotty's family stopped going to the cabin when he was fourteen because his parents got divorced. Anyway, Scotty and Penny plan to rebuild the cabin when he's better." Cassie stopped to take a breath, "I don't think you and David are the only ones with wedding bells in the future." Her voice sounded like a song. "Penny and Scotty are *in loooooove*. I wonder if they'll settle here or up north."

"I am happy for both of them," I replied. I hoped that Scotty would heal and have a wonderful life with his new love.

Cassie's phone beeped and she pulled it from her pocket. "Gah! Look at the time. I have to go. Max had gymnastics today, and I have to go pick her up at the studio." She bounced off the bed again and Clouseau eagerly followed her.

I extracted myself from the comfy bed and followed Cassie out of the room so that I could show her out and re-arm the alarm once she was gone. "How are Max's gymnastic lessons going, anyway?" We trudged down the wide staircase.

"Great! Her coach says that Max has a lot of potential. She has the energy, and Max says she likes flying through the air."

"We might have a future Olympian on our hands," I replied.

TROUBLE BREWING

"Normally, I'd poo-poo that idea and act modest, but Char, Max's coach thinks she might have what it takes to be a competitive gymnast. Can you imagine? I'm willing my daughter to stay short like me and not grow tall like her father. Small stature may give her an edge."

"That's amazing about Max, Cassie. You must be so proud." We hovered by the door. It's always so difficult to say goodbye to the people we love the most, even when it's only for a short while.

"I am proud—and thankful. I never would have enrolled Max in the gymnastics program if it wasn't for your mom suggesting it. Gymnastics became a way for Max to burn off all that energy. It's working out well. She comes home hungry and exhausted and rarely sasses me or argues about her bedtime anymore. The coach is all about self-discipline. I considered introducing Brian to Coach Nelson, but I changed my mind when I saw what a ball-buster she is." Cassie looked down at the delicate watch on her wrist, "Oh shoot, I don't want to be late picking her up. The coach makes them do crunches and push-ups if we parents are late for pickup."

"Well, then, give me a hug, wish me congratulations, and I will see you in about fifteen days," I said as I reached out to hug my dearest friend.

"I'll miss you!" Cassie hugged me, and then she patted Clouseau on the head. "Let me know if there's anything I can do for you while you're away. And congratulations, Char. I hope everything turns out beautifully and you get a nineteen-sixties era Elvis instead of a nineteen-seventies one to marry you."

"Here's hoping," I replied with a giggle. I imagined the wedding photos we would have—snapped by a giftshop employee. It didn't matter what the photos looked like. I had a giant photo album from my first wedding, and I never dragged it out of the box in the top of my bedroom closet to reminisce. Admittedly, that might have something to do with the groom in those photos. I could imagine a time in the future, showing the silly Elvis wedding photos to my children and explaining to them who The King was.

I opened the front door and waved as Cassie left the house. Once she was safely in her car, I shut and locked the door then jabbed the security code into system to arm the alarm. David was out running last minute errands and I'd promised that I would stay safe.

I turned to face my dog. I got down on the floor so that we were eye-to-eye—Cavachons are small. "I'm going to miss you too, little buddy. I'd love nothing more than to have you stand up for me and David when we get married, but I think we're leaving the country afterward. You don't own a doggie passport yet."

Clouseau whimpered. I knew that he wanted to be there to see David and I get married. Afterall, Clouseau liked David from the start.

"I promise we'll find something for you to do at the reception when we get home, okay little buddy? Maybe I can find you a tiny doggie tuxedo."

Clouseau wagged his curly tail. He accepted my offer.

"Shake?" I asked him. Clouseau rolled over and showed me his belly instead. "Good enough."

It was getting late. David would be home soon, and still hadn't finished packing.

"I have to pack. Want to help?" I asked my little friend.

Clouseau yipped and darted up the staircase. I followed him slowly. I wasn't in pain from surgery anymore, but I didn't want to risk an injury before my honeymoon.

Back upstairs, I grabbed my toiletries and shoved them into a giant zip bag. I placed the bag into the internal pocket of my suitcase. I grabbed my favorite sneakers, and my black heels. I stuffed those into the bottom of the bag. Next came my clothes—David promised a warm destination for our honeymoon so I knew I could pack lightly. Swimsuits, shorts, t-shirts, skirts, and of course my Audrey-inspired dress. I struggled to pull the zipper closed, but somehow managed to

TROUBLE BREWING

secure my bag. I set the bag on the armchair in the corner. My suitcase was bulging like an overstuffed sandwich. David packed hours before and his suitcase looked small, crisp, and neat compared with mine. Oh well.

I walked into the closet and slipped into a cute mid-thigh, flared skirt and short sleeved blouse. I pulled a pair of strappy, low-heel sandals onto my feet. I only needed to apply make-up and straighten my hair, and I would be ready to become Mrs. David Moore. Or Mrs. Charlotte Moore. Definitely not Charlotte Moore-O'Hara—heaven forbid! Moore-O'Hara sounded too much like a gathering of my nutty relatives. I didn't know what I would call myself yet.

Suddenly, Clouseau's little ears rose, and he let out a yip. A car was approaching. I knew that it must be David, and I wasn't ready. I jogged into the attached bathroom and ran a hand through my wild waves. I didn't have time to straighten my hair. I checked my teeth to make sure they weren't stained with lipstick, and I patted my outfit to straighten it.

Moments later, I heard the front door open with a bang, and all heck broke loose. A screeching *Weee Weee Weee!* sounded throughout the house—setting my teeth on edge. It was the security alarm going off.

Frightened, Clouseau scrambled under the bed to hide.

I waited a beat for David to disarm the alarm, but he didn't.

"David?" I yelled over the shrieking alarm. I walked from the room and into the upstairs hallway. I peeked down the stairs only to meet the near-black eyes of Mick Flint as he jogged up the staircase taking two steps at a time.

I retreated from Mick's approach and darted into my room. I slammed the door only to have it meet with resistance. The door wouldn't close. Looking down, I saw one of Mick's big, steel-toed work boots blocking the path of the door.

"Get out!" I screamed as I threw my entire bodyweight at the door, willing it to shut.

Mick scowled and threw his more considerable weight on the other side. I staggered as the door caught me in the shoulder and knocked me to the floor.

Mick wasted no time. He entered the room and closed the door behind him. I heard the lock click before he turned to face me.

"Hello, Charlotte," Mick shouted as I fumbled trying to get back to my feet.

"The alarm is going off," I yelled at him. I finally stood and backed to the other side of the bed. The only thing between me and my would-be-killer was a hybrid California King and about a dozen throw pillows. "The police will be here soon."

"The security company will call first," Mick informed me as he took a step closer to me. "And when they do, you'll answer the phone. You will tell them that you are staying at your boyfriend's house, and you accidentally set off the alarm. Then, the nice person at the alarm company will ask if you are okay and they will ask you to give them the secret code. I'm sure you know the code, don't you, Charlotte?" He stepped up to me.

The alarm box was on the wall right next to me—above the bedside table.

I nodded my answer. "May I turn it off? It's hurting my ears." I was thinking about Clouseau who was hiding under the bed. His poor ears!

"Sure, but don't type any of those emergency codes. I know all about alarm systems, and I'll know if you type nine-one-one." Mick was so close to me that I could feel his warm breath on my face. That's when I noticed the knife he clutched in his right hand and the length of rope coiled around his shoulder. The knife was large and shiny.

I typed the alarm code into the system, and the shrill noise stopped, but the phone on the bedside table began to ring.

TROUBLE BREWING

"You know what to do," Mick said. "If you try to let them know I'm here, I'll slit your pretty neck."

I nodded that I understood him and lifted the receiver to my ear.

"Hello?" I answered, trying to calm my voice.

"Hello. This is Irene from Nordic Security. We've had an alarm tripped at 1010 Spruce Lane. Are you okay ma'am? Would you like me to alert the police?"

"I'm okay," I exhaled when I realized I was holding my breath. Mick pressed his body against my back and ran the blade of the knife up my shoulder and across my neck. I knew he would kill me if I didn't follow his demands.

"I'm David Moore's fiancé, Charlotte O'Hara, and I am sorry, I tripped the alarm when I got home," I lied.

"Could you give me the security code please?" Irene asked.

"Yes," I said. "Um. I need to remember it, ha, ha. Setting off the alarm was a shock. I'm a bit frazzled."

Mick reached his free arm around my waist and pressed himself against me harder. Then he ran the knife's cool blade down my cheek and kissed the spot. He smelled of motor oil and sweat. My stomach churned.

"The security code is my birthday," I told Irene. David chose my birthday as the code so that if I tripped the alarm, I'd remember it. But I had an idea. "My birthday is April seventh," I lied. My birthday is in September, but I was banking on Mick not knowing that.

"Did you say April seventh, ma'am?" Irene, the security professional asked me.

"That's correct," I replied. I prayed to the God that I'd abandoned long ago that Irene understood my intention. I was telling her that there was an intruder in the house.

"Okay, ma'am," Irene replied. "That's what I needed to know."

I hung up the phone.

"Good girl," Mick said as I set the receiver down. He believed my lie! Mick spun me around so that we were face to face.

"What do you want?" I demanded.

"What do you think I want?" Mick asked me. He held the knife between us.

"You want to kill me, but you were dumb to come back here. The cops have no idea where you are. You could have disappeared forever," I told him.

"I don't like to leave messes behind, and you, my dear, are a mess. Besides, disappearing takes money, Charlotte; that's something I don't have. That damn studio of Poppy's wiped me out."

"If you want money, my fiancé is David Moore. He's rich. He'll give you whatever you need to start over," I said as I tried to buy more time. I knew that giving the security person the wrong code meant that she would call the police. David was on his way home. I needed to hold on.

"Well, maybe when I am finished with you, I'll make a bargain with your fiancé. Then I'll kill him too. I did my research. I know who David *really* is. I bet he has a safe in this Mc Mansion and it's full of cash."

"There is a safe and money," I confirmed, "but I don't know the combination to the safe, and David won't pay you if you hurt me."

"I'm not going to hurt you, Charlotte. I'm going to kill you," he grinned at me.

I heard my pulse pounding in my ears. I wanted to run, but Mick struck the side of my head, and I lost my balance. I sunk into the plush bed. My ears rang from the hard blow to the side of my head, and I felt discombobulated.

"Before I kill you, I will tell you why Ms. Platt and Poppy had to die." Mick said as he stood over me and pointed the knife in my direction.

"I wish you would," I replied. Dizziness made my brain feel fuzzy, but I did my best to focus. "Why did you want to hurt Scotty? What did he ever do to you?"

Mick laughed at me and shook his head as if I was some naïve little girl. "Oh Charlotte, what you don't know could fill a book!"

I felt myself scowling at his insult. "Even so, why did you kill them?"

"That would have never happened if it weren't for that old snoop—Wilma Platt. She was no better than a Medieval land baron. She owned half the rental spaces in Spruce Grove's business district. Wilma charged high rent, but she didn't keep up with the basic care—heat, water—things that everyone needs."

"I might have heard about that, but those are the kinds of problems you solve with the aid of a lawyer. You don't kill people," I replied.

"Come here," Mick waggled the knife in my direction. "Sit on the edge of the bed."

I knew I should try to run, but my head was still reeling. I doubted I'd make it three feet before Mick caught me. The knife he held looked so shiny and sharp. I did as I was told. I would come up with my escape plan while Mick tried to justify murdering two people and hurting Scotty. I needed to keep him talking.

"Good girl," Mick said as I sat on the edge of the bed. "Don't try anything, or you'll be seeing Wilma and Poppy very soon."

Mick knelt before me and bound my ankles together with a length of the rope that he hacked from the coil he carried. It was an odd move, I thought. If I were tying someone up, I would have started with their hands rather than their feet.

"I didn't know Wilma," Mick said, as he cut another length of the rope—a longer one this time. "Months ago, when Poppy said that her landlord had turned the heat off in her yoga studio, I gave the old woman the benefit of the doubt. I thought there was a mechanical problem with the boiler. I decided to offer Wilma help. I know how to fix things."

"That was nice of you," I said to keep Mick talking. There was nothing nice about the murderer who stood before me. He'd had me and everyone else bamboozled for months.

"What can I say? I am a nice guy," Mick quickly formed a loop with the new length of rope and tied a slip knot in it. "The minute I laid eyes on the woman, I knew I'd seen her before. That silver hair, the cane, and that craggy face? I remembered those."

Mick lifted the rope and slipped it over my head. He pulled the end so that the noose was snug around my neck but not too tight. I could still breathe and talk.

Instinctively, I reached up and grasped the rope. My hands were still untethered, but Mick made it nearly impossible to escape from him. As long as my ankles were bound, I couldn't run. I knew that if I could get the noose off and untie the rope at my ankles, I could try to fight him off and run. Mick smacked my hands away from the noose. He pressed the knife to my cheek. "Behave yourself, Charlotte, or I swear, I'll gut you now and let you bleed out. I couldn't care less. You're the one who wants to know why they had to die."

I swallowed hard. I needed a better plan. I had to get my ankles untied—which seemed impossible with Mick looming over me. I had to distract Mick long enough for the police to arrive.

"The problem was," Mick continued, "Wilma Platt recognized me too."

"From where?" I asked.

"From a federal trial that I'd appeared in about three years ago. You see, Wilma was on the jury."

"And you? Were you a juror too?" I asked.

Mick laughed at me. "You are a bit thick in the head, aren't you?" Mick remarked with a laugh as he gave the rope a tug. "Think Charlotte. Would Wilma Platt care if she recognized another juror?"

"What did you do?" I asked, "To have to sit trial in a federal court?"

TROUBLE BREWING

"Nothing. I am innocent," Mick laughed again, and a chill ran down my spine.

"Isn't that what criminals always say?" I retorted.

"A jury of my *peers* decided that I was innocent. There wasn't enough evidence to convict me. That's what matters. Isn't democracy grand? The problem was, Wilma Platt couldn't let it go. First, she threatened me—making me pay her five hundred dollars a month to keep my little secret. When she taunted Poppy at the brewing contest—Wilma's insults weren't about Poppy—they were about me."

I recalled Poppy's taunt the night of the Farm Show. *"Poppy your third eye is blind."* The older woman was talking about Poppy being blind to Mick's true identity.

"I guess I didn't see you at the brewing contest," I said, thinking back to that Friday evening. With his size, rugged handsomeness, and muscular build, it would be difficult to miss Mick in the small crowd.

"I wasn't at the competition. Poppy was funny about having me see her there—in case she didn't win. I was waiting for the mud bog to start—right down the midway. I know what happened at the contest because Poppy told me everything later. Wilma and Poppy had a little chat before the contest, and Wilma told Poppy who I am. The old bat told Poppy about my past. I suppose Poppy was a bit shocked to hear that I was a kidnapper and an arsonist."

I tried to steady myself.

"Was it you who spied on Poppy and Scotty at Calamity Jane's bar that night?"

"I wasn't spying," Mick spat, "Poppy was my wife!"

"If you weren't spying, then why were you hiding in the shadows like a coward?" I taunted.

Mick pointed the knife at my neck.

"You have got some mouth on you, Charlotte. I guess I didn't notice that before—back when you used to serve me at Magic Beans, I always thought you were kind of cute. I mean, yeah, you have small tits, but you've got a nice ass. I don't particularly like mouthy women."

I snarled at him. What a pig!

"When did you realize that Poppy believed Wilma about your criminal past?"

"That night—Friday. I decided I needed to cover my ass. I had to convince Poppy that Wilma was mistaken. I realized I had to get rid of Wilma so she'd keep her mouth shut. Can you imagine my luck when I found the old bat leaning over the pigpens? I smacked her over the head with her own cane. I lifted her body over the fence and threw her in the mud. That was a fitting end—Wilma Platt could wallow in the mud that she was so fond of slinging."

"Was Wilma even dead when you left her?" I asked horrified at Mick's admission.

Mick shrugged. "I don't know. She wasn't conscious, and in figured if she wasn't dead, she'd die soon enough from shock or exposure.

"I was returning from the pigpens when I saw Scotty leaving his trophy in his little clown car. And suddenly, Poppy was there. They talked. I hid behind a truck and listened to them. Poppy asked Scotty to meet her at the bar. Scotty had a dumb, eager look on his face—like he thought he was going to get lucky. That was when I knew what to do. I stole the trophy and threw it into the pigpen. Do you realize you nearly caught me? You and your fiancé *David* arrived just as I was slipping away."

"And you followed Scotty and Poppy to the bar?" I asked.

Mick nodded.

"I watched them through the window. They had their heads pressed together, talking. Scheming. I knew I had to put a stop to them."

"When I saw you at Namast-Stay, you acted so shocked that Poppy was dead."

"Yeah, and you think that you are an actress! I could have earned an Oscar for my performance. The grieving widower—boohoo! My wife arrived home Friday night—actually, Saturday morning—after she met up with her little friend, I confronted her. I couldn't believe that she was with that little slimeball."

"You thought they were having an affair?" I asked.

"Hardly. Why would Poppy want bologna when she had prime rib?" Mick asked with a smile. Being a vegetarian myself, I refrained from commenting. All meat is repulsive to me.

"I didn't know what that little bitch was up to—until she told me that she needed some space to figure things out. Isn't that always what partners say when they plan to leave? Poppy said that Wilma told her my real name and what I was accused of doing. According to Wilma, I should have been behind bars with Zach Grimes. I don't even know the guy. He's a small-time crook," Mick stopped speaking to let his words sink in.

I shook my head in disbelief. "I still don't understand why you killed Poppy."

"Poppy grabbed a bag and left the house. It didn't take me long to figure out where she went. That damn studio of hers. That's where Poppy always goes—*went*—after one of our disagreements. She usually needed a few hours to cool off, then she would come home. This time, Poppy didn't come home."

"So, you went to the studio, and you killed her?" I asked.

Mick looked off into space, "When I found her, Poppy was in her office, writing a letter to the police. Poppy told me that if I gave her a divorce, she would leave town and not say a word to anyone about who I am. If I didn't let her go, she would mail the letter. I guess Poppy thought I loved her too much to kill her."

"Why didn't you let her go?" I asked. "Why did you have to kill again?"

"Don't you see? I couldn't let her go. Poppy knew about my past, but she hadn't heard about Wilma yet. Poppy never liked the internet and she didn't watch television. She rarely used her cell phone. Poppy was too Zen for all that. I knew that when Poppy heard about Wilma's death through the Spruce Grove grapevine, she'd figure something was up. Poppy would realize that I killed Wilma. Then Poppy would know that the things Wilma told her were true. Poppy would have contacted the authorities whether I let her go or not. I couldn't let that happen. I couldn't go back to prison."

"You'd been in prison before?" I asked. I remembered the ace of spades tattoo on Mick's wrist. I bet that Jack Indigo would tell me the tattoo was prison ink if he'd seen it.

"Yeah."

My head ached. "Why did you go after Scotty? If you didn't think he and Poppy had a romantic relationship."

"I didn't know what Poppy told Scotty at the bar, did I? And after I killed Poppy, I went through her bag. I needed to make sure she didn't pack anything that proved my guilt. What I found was Poppy's phone. She'd been texting with Scotty. He offered to drive Poppy to his cabin. He planned to meet her at the studio on Sunday."

"There wasn't a bag with Poppy when I found her," I remembered aloud. "And I didn't see a letter."

"You're a regular Sherlock Holmes, aren't you? I didn't leave Poppy's bag behind. I'm not stupid, Charlotte. I couldn't let the cops figure out that Poppy was going to leave me. They would eventually figure out why she left. I took her bag with me. As for the letter? I used it to light the fire at the cabin."

"Mick, there is no way you're going to get away with a double homicide. You might think Spruce Grove is full of idiots, but you're wrong. The police will find you."

"Don't you mean triple homicide, Charlotte?" Mick corrected me as he pulled the rope in his hands taut. The noose tightened around my neck and scratched the tender flesh there.

"Isn't it a great coincidence that your millionaire boyfriend decided to put exposed beams in the ceiling? Rustic architecture—you've got to love it. That will make your suicide so much easier." Mick threw his end of the rope over one of the beams with ease and pulled it. I felt my body begin to lift from the bed, The noose grew tighter when I kicked and fought him.

"It's too bad that *David* isn't here to see this. If he were here, you could ask him why I came to Spruce Grove in the first place." He yanked the rope again. "I wonder if *David* will feel guilty when he finds your body."

"Stop!" I tried to scream, but the word fell out of my mouth and landed as a whisper.

Suddenly, the bed covers rustled. I saw a flying blur of white and tan and heard a low, fierce growl. Clouseau was coming to my rescue!

Mick spun around to see what was happening as Clouseau dove into the air and dug his teeth into Mick's arm. Despite Clouseau's small size, he grabbed Mick with all his might, growling, shaking, and refusing to let go. Mick swung his arm trying to fend off my tiny dog. The rope fell from the beam, loosening the noose around my neck and dropping me back to the bed. Clouseau's distraction gave me enough time to draw back my legs, and deliver a swift kick to Mick's groin.

I tore the noose off while Mick screamed angrily. Clouseau held firm to his arm. I wound up and kicked the evil man in the crotch again. This time, Mick staggered and crumpled to the floor, curled in a fetal position.

"You bitch!" Mick screeched.

Clouseau dashed to my side as I grabbed the knife that Mick had dropped. With a quick slice, I released the binding on my ankles.

I took a wide berth as I ran past Mick with Clouseau taking the lead. Mick was still gasping on the bedroom floor as I unlocked the door. On shaking legs, I dashed into the hallway behind Clouseau. I needed to get away from Mick before he recovered and gave chase.

I darted down the stairs and behind me, I heard the sound of Mick getting to his feet and pounding down the hallway in pursuit.

I reached the bottom of the staircase the door was open and a man rushed in. Clouseau scurried through the door to safety.

"Police!" Called the police officer who leveled a gun in my general direction, "Stop and put your hands in the air!"

I realized that I was still clutching Mick's knife in my hand. I dropped the weapon and it landed with a clatter as it hit the hardwood floor.

"Don't shoot! I live here and a killer is after me," I pleaded before I realized that the officer was aiming at the madman behind me. I ran out the door and right into Brian Gold. He was holding Clouseau in the crook of his arm.

"Char!" Brian shouted as he shielded me and my dog with his body and led us to his police cruiser.

"Mick is in there. He was going to… he had a knife and a noose," I babbled as Clouseau squirmed against Brian's tight grasp. Brian released the dog and my furry pup danced at my ankles.

"Char? Did he hurt you?" Brian asked.

My face heated and nausea rose in my throat. I spun away from Brian, and fell to my knees, and vomited on the cool grass.

"I'll kill him if he touched you." Brian mumbled as he knelt beside me and offered me a clean handkerchief.

"He didn't," I gasped as I wiped my mouth with the cloth. It was a little hard to breathe. "He was going to hang me, but Clouseau attacked him. I kicked Mick in the balls as hard as I could—twice—that's how I managed to get away from him."

"Good," Brian said. "When I got the call that someone was in David's house, I jumped in my cruiser. Where's David? I thought you two were flying to Las Vegas."

"We are. Later," I replied in a raspy voice. I ran my hand over my neck. I could feel the skin swelling where the rope burned me. "David was picking up a few things in town. He's probably on his way home right now."

TROUBLE BREWING

"We should call David," Brian suggested. "You need him here right now."

"My phone is in the house, and I won't go back in there," I said.

"I'll call David," Brian offered. "Let's get you in my cruiser. I have the air con on full blast. The cool air will make you feel better."

Brian helped me to my feet, walked me to the cruiser and assisted me into the passenger seat. He surprised me when he climbed into the driver's seat. "I'm so sorry, Char. I wish to God that we found Mick before this happened."

"Me too," I admitted as tears began to slide down my face. "He was going to kill me, and make it look like a suicide. That's what he planned to do with Scotty at the cabin. Mick said he was going to kill David when he got home. Mick said it was David's fault that he moved to Spruce Grove."

"Don't worry. Mick Flint didn't get either of you, and now we have him." Brian nodded toward the windshield. I looked up and saw two burly police officers leading Mick Flint away with his hands cuffed behind his back.

I breathed a sigh of relief. "Mick said that he killed Wilma and Poppy because they found out who he is. Who is Mick—really?"

"It's a long story, Char. And I would be remiss if I didn't tell you that David helped us figure out who Mick Flint is and what happened."

"He did?" I asked, surprised. "My David?"

Brian nodded. "Trust me, Mick Flint was a bad guy before he arrived in Spruce Grove. Flint served time for armed robbery when he was nineteen. That's where he met members of a mob family. Later, Flint was charged with kidnapping, rape, and arson, but a crooked judge and jury let him walk. It's about time that someone brought that man to justice. That guy is pure evil."

I hiccupped and wiped tears from my face with the back of my hand. "Believe me, I know that Mick's a sorry excuse for a human. But what did David tell you that you didn't already know about Mick?"

"Char...you know I can't tell you that," Brian grinned. "I can't risk compromising our case against Mick."

I nodded my head. Brian was right. I didn't need to know how David helped catch Mick Flint, I was just glad that he did.

"Char?" David jogged to the passenger door of the cruiser. "I saw the flashing lights and heard the sirens when I was driving home. They wouldn't let me drive up the road, so I ran. What happened?"

"The police caught Mick Flint," I replied. "They're arresting him."

"Are you alright?" David opened the car's door and pulled me into a hug.

"I will be, when we're in Las Vegas—away from here," I said before I burst into tears again.

THIRTEEN

"Are you sure you don't want to wait?" David asked me as we sat across from each other in the doctor's office. Me, sitting on the examination table clad in a paper gown. David in a chair still dressed in his travel clothes. After the police finished interviewing me, David drove me into town to visit my family doctor. We were waiting for Dr. Flynn to check me over and I guess she was running a bit late. A red and purple bruise was already beginning to show on my neck where the rope had been.

"After what Mick did, or tried to do to you, maybe we should postpone the wedding. I'm not so sure a two-week honeymoon is a good idea right now. You should probably be around family and friends."

I shook my head. "Honestly, David, after everything that happened, I just want to get away from here. I want to get married and disappear with you for a couple of weeks—or forever."

David frowned. I knew he felt awful that I was alone in his house when Mick Flint arrived. I knew about the handgun that David kept hidden in his home office. I imagined that David wished he could go back in time and pull the trigger. "Well, anyway, we're going to miss our flight," David said.

"Can't we catch a later flight?" I pleaded. "David, I can't go back into that house yet. Mick planned to hang me from the rafters in the guest room. Somehow, he got into the house. I don't understand how he did it. I know that I locked the door and set the alarm after Cassie left."

"Mick is a crafty guy. The police found the door pried open. I'm having the door replaced with one made of steel. As for Las Vegas, if you're sure you want to go, we can, but I think we should clear it with the doctor first," David said.

"It is what I want," I said. "I just want to run away with you, David."
Someone knocked on the door.

"Come in," I said.

Dr. Flynn stepped into the room. She wore a white lab coat over a fancy blue dress. Two shiny clips pinned doctor's dark curls back, and she had sparkling diamond studs in her ears. It looked like she left something important to see me.

"Charlotte, I was surprised to hear you needed an appointment. I saw you a few weeks ago for your annual visit and your blood test, but David said this was an emergency."

"Thank you for seeing us," David said.

Dr. Flynn eyed the wound on my neck and took a seat next to the examination table, "Let's have a look. That must be painful."

After I told her everything that happened to me, Dr. Flynn examined and cleaned the wounds on my face and neck. She checked me for a concussion, palpated my belly, and took my blood pressure.

"Your flesh wounds will heal on their own, Charlotte. But it's the wounds in here," Dr. Flynn pointed at my head, "that I'm worried about. I'd like to give you a number for a counselor. You might benefit from talking to someone who has more experience in these matters than I do."

I nodded. It wouldn't hurt to speak to a therapist or counselor.

"Good. Is there anything else you'd like to talk about today?" The doctor asked me.

I shook my head. I was eager to leave. I wanted to forget everything and move on with my life—with David.

"Doctor," David cut in, "Charlotte would like to travel tonight. Before this happened, we were about to go to Las Vegas to get married."

"And you're worried," Dr. Flynn surmised. She knew about our plans to wed. We discussed my wedding plans at my last appointment.

"Yes," David replied. "Char says she still wants to go, but I want to be sure it's the right decision—after everything that's happened."

"I think getting away from here would be good for me," I added.

TROUBLE BREWING

"I can't disagree with you, Charlotte," Dr. Flynn said. "Your wounds aren't bad enough to for me to tell you to stay put. You don't appear to have a concussion or broken bones. If you want to go to Las Vegas, you should. You planned the wedding before this happened. Weddings are happy events. I will ask you to be mindful, however. Be aware of your feelings. If something doesn't feel right, then say so. If you need help, ask for it."

I nodded.

"Have a nice break and relax. Make an appointment with a counselor when you get return home," the doctor added.

I nodded again.

Dr. Flynn stood. "I'll step out so you can change into your clothes. I'll knock when I return, and I'll bring a few phone numbers for counselors with me."

"Thank you, doctor," David said.

"You're uncharacteristically quiet," David observed as he eased ole Blue down the road toward home.

"Sorry. I guess I'm lost in my thoughts."

"Don't apologize, Char. I'm worried, that's all. You're usually such a chatterbox—that's one of the things I love about you."

"I want to get out of town, David, and marry you. Okay? I can stop at the cottage and pack another bag. I don't think I can go into your house yet."

"Okay," David exhaled. "Or I can leave you at your cottage and then drop by my place to pick up our things. You can hang out with Clouseau and your parents until I get back."

"Okay. I guess I do want the bag I packed—it has my wedding dress in it." I wanted to wear the dress for David. I knew he'd love seeing me in it. I wouldn't let Mick Flint ruin our special day.

"I might hang out with Clouseau. I don't think I can face my parents yet. Anyway, Uncle Mark must have spoken to them by now. I have three missed calls from my mom."

"Okay," David agreed, "but we can't avoid your parents forever."

"I know. I'll call them when we get off the plane in Las Vegas—then they can't stop us."

David scratched him chin and appeared to be thinking about something.

"You know, I had a thought. It might be a dumb idea, but hear me out," David said.

"I'm listening." It's rare that David has a dumb idea. He's brilliant.

"What if, and this is just an idea, what if we extended our honeymoon? We could go to Las Vegas, get married, have the honeymoon, and then fly to Italy," David said without taking his eyes off the road. "We could stay in Italy as long as you want. The apartment I rent is available and your passport lets you stay in Italy for ninety days. Once we have all our marital paperwork together, you'll be able to stay longer."

"In Italy?" I asked, *"for three months?"*

"Yeah," David smiled. "This was supposed to be a wedding day surprise for you, but I should tell you now. The construction workers broke ground on our villa last month. Somehow, we were able to get the permits and clearances early. Our new home will be ready by the end of the year. We can spend Christmas in Florence if you want."

"Are you serious?" I asked. I was under the impression that it would take months even years before I'd see our second home.

"Yes. I made a few changes to the blueprints too. I know you gave approval on the original floorplan, but I thought of a few things that would make the house more special."

"What kind of changes?" I asked. We planned a three bedroom, two bath house in the hills. What could be more special than that?

TROUBLE BREWING

"Well, the floorplan is going to be a bit bigger than we originally planned. There'll be five bedrooms and six bathrooms. Two suites on the ground floor, and the other three bedrooms on the second floor. There will be a patio off the first-floor bedrooms that leads to a junior-Olympic-sized saltwater pool," David smiled, "and there will be a hot tub too."

"David! Our house in Italy will be bigger and fancier than our house in Spruce Grove!" I couldn't help but chuckle.

"Not really. The house here has more square footage. The house in Italy is a bit cozier, but it has more rooms—don't worry—they're still plenty big. It's Europe, after all. They do things a bit differently there. You're going to fit in great, by the way."

"But five bedrooms? Isn't that too many?" I asked, skeptical. Five bedrooms felt greedy.

"Well, I started thinking about the house. I realized with you spending more time in Italy, our friends and family are going to want to visit. They'll visit less when they discover how long the flight is." David chuckled.

The flight is long. I might have to bribe my loved ones to visit me. A salt water pool might help.

"Your parents will need a bedroom with a full bath. Joe and Cassie will want to bring Max. We can't have our family staying in a hotel when they visit us. And, when the time comes, we'll have plenty of rooms to grow into."

"With our children," I added as I squeeze his knee.

"Or a bunch of little rescue dogs like Clouseau," David said with a chuckle.

"I don't think there are any other dogs like Clouseau," I said. "I love my dog, but I want human children too."

"I was hoping you'd say that." David chuckled again, "So, what do you think? Do you want to extend our stay? I can make the necessary arrangements when I get back to the house."

"I do," I replied. I had a thought. "Poor Clouseau. I wish we could take him with us. He's not used to being apart from me so long, but he doesn't have a doggy passport."

"Hmm," David looked at me and smiled. "Is Clouseau up to date with his shots? Rabies etcetera?"

"Of course," I replied. Clouseau always gets the best care. In fact, after Clouseau's run-in with Mick, Brian offered to take my dog to the vet while I saw my doctor. Brian had texted me earlier to tell me that Clouseau checked out fine and he'd dropped him off with my parents.

"And Clouseau isn't ill, is he? No kennel cough or viruses? Diarrhea?"

"No, he's in perfect health. You should have seen him go after Mick Flint," I commented. "Clouseau deserves a hero's award—like a medal to wear on this collar."

"Give me a few hours. I'll see what I can do," David said with a mysterious smile.

True to David's words, a few hours later, David, Clouseau, and I pulled into a private airfield outside of Philadelphia. Somehow, David managed to get a puppy passport for my hero dog.

"What is this place? What's going on, David?" I asked.

"I called in a favor when I was at the house," David replied as he parked the car. "My business partner, George, was in New York today. I knew that he took the private jet. I asked if we could borrow it tonight. So, he had the pilot fly it here for us. See the plane over there? That one is for us."

The silver plane was unmistakable with a large MR logo on its side.

"You mean we're flying to Las Vegas in a private jet?" I asked in disbelief. I knew that David used the jet a few times, but he mostly travels using large commercial airlines. I'd never been on a private jet, and I felt my heart skip a beat in anticipation.

"Indeed, we are. It appears that I have friends in high places," David winked at me.

"What I don't understand is how you got Clouseau a passport," I said. "I thought it was much too late to do that."

"I know a guy from college who became a veterinarian. Jeff lives in Pennsylvania too. Your mom sent copies of Clouseau's vaccination certificates to Jeff, and he arranged for Clouseau's emergency passport. But let's be safe, if anyone asks, Clouseau is your support dog."

"That's unbelievable! You amaze me, David. And honestly, Clouseau is my support dog," I remarked. "I don't know what I would have done today without him."

Clouseau wagged his tail in agreement.

Suddenly, the horrible day was falling away from me, and David was the reason why. Marrying David was the right thing to do. Having Clouseau with us was like the silvery-white icing on a ten-tier wedding cake with pink and purple frosting flowers.

"I want you to be happy, Char."

"I am happy, as long as I'm with you," I replied. "I know how mushy that sounds, but I really mean it, David. If I had any doubts before, they are gone."

David parked the car and kissed me. My fiancé didn't ask me about my doubts. I was grateful for that.

"David, before we take off, I have one more question for you," I said as we sat in the car and watched a small plane taxiing down a runway. "Then I want to set the past few weeks behind me and forget about them until I have to appear in court to help convict Mick Flint for his crimes."

"Okay," David nodded.

"Brian told me that you helped with the investigation, but he wouldn't say in what capacity. What did you do?"

David groaned. "Let's get on the plane, and then I'll tell you everything."

"Okay, but I am holding you to it," I said, recalling the conversation we'd had in the hospital. David still hadn't told me whatever his mysterious secret was. I hoped he could tell more one day.

David handed me a glass of Champagne before he poured himself one. He sat next to me in the comfy leather sofa at the back of the plane. Clouseau curled up on a seat along the wall. At first, I worried that the jet would scare my dog, but he seemed unbothered by the sound of the engine or the fact that we were zooming through the air. My dog was a warrior.

"So, tell me," I said to David. "How did you help Brian in his investigation?"

"I'll try to summarize the story, but it's pretty involved," David took a sip of his Champagne.

"Okay," I agreed.

"After what I discovered about Wilma and the beer contestants, I did some extra research on Zach Grimes. He was laundering money for the mob, but I couldn't find any evidence that he'd committed other crimes. I suppose that like many stories, the legend of Zach's criminal past snowballed over time. Gossip is an ugly thing."

That damned Spruce Grove Grapevine!

"Then Poppy died, and I couldn't understand why—who would want to murder her? Poppy was a mild-mannered yogi. I didn't see any connection between Poppy and the other contestants—other than Scotty who went out for a drink with her on the night that Wilma died."

"Exactly," I agreed. I took a sip of the Champagne and told David what I knew. "Mick said something about recognizing Wilma from a federal trial. I know the jury failed to convict him, despite his guilt. Mick had no idea that one of the jurors lived in Spruce Grove until he encountered Wilma after she turned off the heat and water in Poppy's studio."

David nodded. "Right. I didn't discover the connection between Mick and Wilma until the day of the fire—when I was doing research on my own. Mick Flint né Michael Dominick Flinton, was also known in crime circles as *The Ace of Asbury Park*. Mick was a suspect in some pretty violent crimes. Thanks to his friends in the mob, Mick didn't serve time for his worst crimes. When prosecutors tried to bring Mick to trial again, he disappeared. Meanwhile, Zach Grimes was caught and served time in prison."

"Are you saying that Zach Grimes knew Mick?" I asked.

"I don't know. But they worked for the same guys. Zach, it seems, was blackmailed into helping the mob—sorry, I don't know the story behind that. Zach was too scared to tell me much when I spoke to him. Zach is starting his life over. He's in therapy, and he's trying to get a brewery started. He was on his way to a therapist's appointment when you stopped at his home. Zach said that the guys in prison branded him with a heart tattoo. The tattoo was part of Zach's initiation. I understand that Mick has an ace of spades tattoo."

"That's right. The card suits must have something to do with the mob," I offered.

David nodded, then he continued speaking.

"Anyway, fast forward a few years, and Zach returned to Spruce Grove after serving his sentence. Zach tried to start fresh, but people like Wilma Platt recognized him and gave him a hard time. It must be one of those fluky things that both Mick and Zach settled in the same small town," David said with a shrug. "I think Mick was still working for the mob."

I interrupted David.

"Mick said that he recognized Wilma from the trial, and I guess Wilma remembered him too. Mick killed Wilma after she outed him to Poppy. I guess Poppy decided enough was enough and she decided to leave her husband. I inferred that Poppy and Mick had a rocky relationship.

"That's where Scotty Wells comes in," I continued. "All those months ago, Wilma, saw Mick at Poppy's studio, and realized that she needed to tell Poppy who Mick was. Remember, Mick and Poppy weren't married long. Poppy had no idea that Mick had a criminal past—a violent criminal past. To her, he was Mick Flint, maintenance man.

"Poppy started to have second thoughts about Mick—that's the secret that Scotty couldn't tell me. Poppy wanted to leave Mick, and she asked Scotty if she could stay in his cabin until she figured out what she was going to do. That's why Scotty and Poppy met at the bar after the farm show. It was Mick Flint who spied on them that night. He stole Scotty's trophy and planted it at the crime scene making poor Scotty suspect number one. Mick and Poppy argued in the early hours after the farm show. She left him. When Mick found Poppy, she told him she'd keep quiet if he let her go. Poppy wrote a letter to the police as a sort of insurance plan, but her plan didn't work. He killed her. Mick also discovered that Scotty was going to rescue Poppy. That's why he kidnapped Scotty and planned to murder him.

"Mick kept Wilma's cane—I bet it was a trophy—serial killers often take trophies from victims. Mick wasn't a serial killer, but he certainly tried to be one. Mick brought the cane to the cabin and threatened Scotty and me with it. I swear I can still hear him tapping that old cane on the hardwood floors." I shivered at the memory.

David reached for my hand.

"I am so sorry you went through that, Char," David shook his head, "I wish I'd been there for you. There are so many things I would change if I could."

"I wish you were there too. Trying to get Scotty out of the cabin wasn't easy. I didn't know the extent of Scotty's injuries at the time.

Mick beat Scotty nearly to death. I will never comprehend the mind of a killer," I admitted.

"Thank goodness for that," David said.

I smiled.

David spoke again.

"When the police looked for evidence at the studio, they found Mick's fingerprints all over the place. They didn't think much of it. Mick and Poppy were married so it wouldn't have been odd to find traces of Mick's DNA or his prints around. Plus, the police assumed that Mick contaminated the crime scene by going inside to find Poppy when you dialed nine-one-one. He'd trampled through the blood in his work boots. The investigators didn't realize the prints and stuff were from when Mick killed Poppy. It wasn't until later, when the police determined Poppy's time of death, that they realized that the bloody boot prints were older. When you ran into him outside the yoga studio? Mick had already kidnapped Scotty and locked him in the cabin. I think Mick must have grabbed Scotty when you were talking to him on the phone."

"That's right! Scotty didn't hang up on me, Mick attacked him, and we were disconnected!" I exclaimed.

David nodded.

I continued speaking. "Mick returned to Spruce Grove intending to get rid of Poppy's body, but I found her unexpectedly. Mick only pretended to be shocked by her death. He claimed that he's a better actor than I am, and I have to say, I think he's right."

"He's not an actor, Mick's a sociopath—guaranteed. Hopefully, the police will have enough evidence to put him away for a very long time," David said.

"I think Mick was making sure that all the evidence was gone the day that I went to give him my condolences. He needed to make sure there was nothing left if the police noticed something *off* about the evidence they collected," I said.

"I'm sure you're right," David replied.

"Good grief!" I exclaimed. "I almost forgot! Poppy packed a bag early Saturday morning. She planned to leave Mick. He admitted that he took the bag before the police had a chance to find it. I wish I could call the police right now. That bag might contain crucial evidence."

"We can call Spruce Grove after we land," David assured me.

"And now Scotty is trying to recover from serious injuries just because he tried to help a friend," I said, angrily. To think I'd misunderstood the man for so many years. Scotty was a thoughtful, loyal friend.

"Right."

"David, I still don't understand something. When I was in the hospital, you said you wished you could erase your past. I got the feeling that what you said was related to my run-in with Mick Flint. Am I right?"

David's jaw dropped open.

"David, Mick said you were the reason that he came to Spruce Grove. Why would he say that?"

"Char...I promise I will explain everything to you later. I need to tell you something about my first year in college. Something happened to me, but I can't tell you until after Mick Flint's trial. Can you trust me to tell you when the time is right?"

I felt my eyes widen. David wasn't making light of what Mick told me. David went to college in New Jersey—the state where the mob Mick was affiliated with operated. Could that be relevant?

"Okay," I whispered.

My fiancé squeezed my hand.

"David, when we get to Las Vegas, you may have to buy me a very large, expensive drink. Then, I want to go to our room and fall into a coma for about twelve hours," I said. Champagne is great for a celebration, but I'm not a fan of the bubbly stuff. A nice gin and tonic would definitely hit the spot.

TROUBLE BREWING

"Your wish is my command, my darling, but try not to get too tipsy tonight. You don't want to be hungover when we get married tomorrow—unless you want to postpone?"

"No way. We are going to find an Elvis impersonator and we are getting married. You won't believe the gorgeous dress I bought just for our wedding," I said. "I might need to find a scarf to hide the abrasions on my neck though."

"Tomorrow we can go into whatever shop you want. I will buy you the fanciest scarf you can find," David offered.

"Deal," I said as I clinked my Champagne flute to his. "Do you think there are any English-speaking therapists in Tuscany?"

"Um, probably?" David replied. "Why do you ask?"

"I was thinking, if we're staying in Italy until my passport or my luck runs out, I should make an appointment with a therapist while I'm there."

"That's...oddly responsible," David said. I slapped his hand playfully.

"David, I meant what I said earlier. I want to start our lives together. I don't want a dark cloud looming overhead. If a therapist can help me, I'm going to give therapy a try."

"I'm proud of you, Char," David admitted.

"And I know that I'm likely to have many therapy appointments in my future. I want to talk to someone about everything, David."

"Such as?" David's eyebrow lifted.

"I have a history of making bad and impulsive decisions—beginning with marrying Kyle Stalls. Also, I threw myself at Brian Gold shortly after my divorce was final. Maybe I should talk to someone about that."

"I hope I am not one of your bad decisions," David said.

"Definitely not," I replied. "But..."

At that moment, if David's eyebrows had the ability to fly from his forehead, they would have. "But?" He asked.

"I did sort of jump into a relationship with you after Brian broke up with me. And, I worry about the arguments we sometimes have," I admitted, "especially lately."

"All couples argue, Char," David said.

"I know that, but the most common source of our arguments is my impulsive behavior," I said. "I'd like to learn some techniques to control those impulses. I mean, if I want to be a mother—and I do—I should learn impulse control."

"Well, you did take Max into a bar," David recalled.

"Exactly. And there's something else. I considered not telling you this, but I want to tell you now. I don't want you to change your mind about marrying me, David, but if you do, I'll understand."

"Char, haven't we already had this conversation?" David asked with a nervous chuckle. "You know that I'm all in."

"We did talk about this, but I withheld some important information. David," I took a deep breath and released it, "I kissed Brian Gold when I was in the hospital. It wasn't premeditated. Weirdly, the kiss was accidental. But we lingered for second. We both realized our smooch was an embarrassing mistake. It was a pretty chaste kiss, and I haven't kissed Brian or anyone but you since that day. I don't plan to. I thought you should know."

"I saw you two kissing," David admitted, "at the hospital."

"But you didn't say anything," I replied, shocked.

"I realized at the time that the kiss was likely a reaction to stress. I decided to let it go, and I think I was right to do that. Thank you for telling me now, though, Char."

"You aren't angry?" I asked. I wanted to beat myself up over the kiss, but David didn't seem to think that was necessary.

"No. I might be angry if you made a habit of it," David replied with a nervous laugh, "but I have a feeling that you won't."

"I know I've broken some promises to you in the past, David, as long as you and I are alive, I will not kiss Brian Gold again."

TROUBLE BREWING

"I believe you, Char."

"Thank you, David."

FOURTEEN

"This photo is hilarious," Cassie said as she held up the 8x10 snapshot of David, me, and an impersonator of the King of Rock n Roll. "I see you got the seventies Elvis." She took a sip of Champagne and handed the photo to her husband so that he could see it too.

"I wouldn't have had it any other way. Elvis, also known as *Jeremy*, was great as our officiant. He sang *Burning Love* to us," I replied as I sipped my ginger ale.

After three months abroad, David and I returned to my beloved hometown. Some local contractors remodeled the guest bedroom where Mick Flint held me hostage. They also replaced the front door with a heavier steel one.

In our absence, my mother and Cassie planned a welcome home party/wedding reception for us. The party was extravagant by Spruce Grove's standards. Three cater waiters passed platters of canapes while two others passed glasses of bubbling Champagne. Everyone dressed in black-tie attire. My father stood at the open bar at the back of Abby's Bistro and tugged at the collar of his white button-down shirt. He smiled at me when I caught his eye. I winked back at my dad. I didn't wear my wedding dress that night. Instead, I wore a pretty blue Pucci-inspired dress that I picked up in Florence.

"I'm so glad you are home," Cassie confessed as she peered around the room, "Spruce Grove isn't the same without you. I know you plan to split your time between Italy and here, but I hope you stick around a little while now that you are home."

I took Cassie's glass and mine and set them on a table. I grasped my bestie's elbow.

"Come with me," I said as I led her to the kitchen. "We need to talk."

Cassie's kitten heels clicked on the tile floors as I walked her to the back of the room—away from the cooking staff.

"I don't think we're supposed to go into the kitchen. If your mom catches us..." Cassie protested worriedly.

"Don't worry about my mom. She won't catch us. I need to get out of there for a second. I have something to tell you, and I don't want anyone to overhear me," I told her.

"That's mysterious," Cassie replied as she looked at the kitchen staff to check they weren't eavesdropping.

"I won't be flying back to Italy for a while," I whispered to my friend, "David has to go back to Europe periodically, but I'm going to stick around here for the time being."

"Oh my gosh! Is it wrong if that makes me happy? Was Italy awful? Was it the language? I know you think you're lousy at learning foreign languages, but I could help you. There are online classes," Cassie said. Her skin flushed.

"No, I mean, yes, my Italian is *awful*—meanwhile David speaks the language like he was born to it. Despite my monoglot tendencies, I love Italy," I admitted.

"Is it your dad? Is he ill? Does he need your help with the Christmas tree orders?" Cassie guessed. Christmas was only a few weeks away.

"No, Cassie, as far as I know, Dad is fine. He still loves working the farm, and as for me helping him, well, we are going to have to work out a new plan."

"Why? If you're staying here, and your dad is okay, why do you need a new plan?" Cassie asked.

I felt my lips lift into a huge smile. "Cassie, so far only David knows this, but you're my best friend, and I wanted you to be the next to hear. We're having a baby!"

"Char!" Cassie squealed. The startled kitchen staff glanced in our direction briefly before they continued loading food trays.

"It's early—only the first trimester. I am too afraid to tell everyone yet—you know, just in case. But I wanted you to know. You've always been like a sister to me. No. Cassie, you're even better than a sister. You are family that I chose. You are finally going to be an auntie! Max will have a cousin. Will you be my birthing partner when David is out of town?"

Cassie suddenly broke out into laughter.

"What is it?" I asked, "Should I have kept that last part to myself? Was asking you to be my birthing partner too much?"

"No, Char. Of course, I'll be your birthing partner. I'm laughing because I just realized how jealous Sarah Payne will be when she finds out. Sarah got engaged first, but you and David beat her to the altar, and now you're expecting. She will be furious when she finds out! It's like the space race, only smaller."

"Cassie!" I said, laughing, "I can't believe you said that!"

"I bet you'd have thought the same thing after a while," Cassie said, "Now I understand why you aren't drinking Champagne like the rest of us—and why you aren't wearing that fabulous Audrey H dress. I thought something was horribly wrong with you."

I shrugged.

Giving up alcohol was a small sacrifice compared to what I had to gain in about seven months. Champagne wasn't a favorite drink of mine anyway. My wedding dress *was* too tight, but not from the pregnancy. I really loved eating Italian food.

"I have to admit, Uncle Mark is dragging his feet about the whole marriage thing. You would think at his age, Mark would be in a bigger hurry to get hitched."

"Consider who he is marrying," Cassie quipped.

"Cassie, I thought you liked Sarah," I accused.

My friend certainly took Sarah's side a few times in the past when my old high school nemesis and I locked horns.

"She's a bit much, to be honest," Cassie said, "And I can imagine what Sarah will be like when you and David are married with a half-dozen kids, and she and Mark are still engaged."

"A half-dozen!" I said with a gasp, "I was thinking two or three tops."

"Fine," Cassie replied, "My plans to finally organize an ice hockey team in Spruce Grove are ruined."

I shook my head dismissively, "Did I tell you we plan to raise our children in both countries? David wanted me to have this one in Italy so *she or he* would have dual citizenship, but I couldn't stay away from Spruce Grove any longer. I missed this place too much. I won't be able to make the long flight back to Italy soon. I'm going to move into David's house—*our Spruce Grove home*—until after this one is born."

"I hope David spends more time in town," Cassie admitted, "You aren't the only Moore I've missed."

"O'Hara-Moore," I corrected. There were a few things that I failed to tell my best girlfriend while I was away. We needed to schedule a girls' night soon to catch up.

"David and I are each changing our last names. We want to have the same names as our kids. My mom suggested the change when David and I told her we were eloping. She worries that Danny and Kristin will never have children. It's up to me to carry on the O'Hara lineage. David is the last of his clan—his half-sister goes by her husband's last name—we wanted to keep his name too."

"That sounds very modern and diplomatic," Cassie said, "I would expect nothing less from the two of you."

"Would you believe we're already trying to pick out baby names? We haven't agreed on those. I want to name our kids after literary characters, and David thinks we should name them after the founders of modern technology."

"Weirdly, I totally believe that," Cassie said.

"David says that my choices of names from modern mystery novels don't really count as *literary* characters. I'm surprised at how snobbish he can be about books. Oh well, I have several months to turn David to my side."

TROUBLE BREWING

"What's this about turning me?" David slipped in behind me and kissed my neck. I hadn't seen him enter the kitchen.

"I just told Cassie our secret," I whispered.

"Ah," David replied and quietly said, "I thought we were keeping the baby a secret until after the first trimester."

"I promise, I won't say a word—except to Joe. He is my husband. I have to tell him," Cassie said, "And congratulations, David. I remember when you first admitted to me that you had eyes for Charlotte. I guess things worked out exactly as you hoped they would."

"Yes, it took a bit longer than I hoped, but I can't complain," David pulled me into him a bit more tightly and rested his hand on my abdomen.

"Not to ruin this moment, but have you heard? Mick Flint's trial is next year," Cassie said. "I know that in addition to the murder charges Mick is facing, Scotty Wells is suing him too—for assault and many other things."

"Good. I didn't see Scotty here at the party," I said.

I knew my newest friend was invited to the gathering, along with his girlfriend, Penny Collins. I wondered where they were.

"Oh, I forgot to tell you," Cassie said, her face sobered, "Scotty couldn't make it tonight. He had a bit of a setback, but he asked me to say congratulations on the wedding and that he hopes he'll see you soon."

"What kind of setback?" I asked, suddenly concerned.

Cassie shook her head, "an infection, I think. His recovery has been pretty challenging. Scotty was in and out of hospitals these past few months. Luckily, he hasn't been alone. Penny Collins is a godsend, and she's so fun and full of life. You are going to love her."

"I heard that after he left the rehab center, Scotty moved north to be with Penny," I said.

"He did. He gave up his job at the high school, but he has a positive attitude, and that's so important. The last time I saw Scotty, he was using a wheelchair, but Penny called me about a month ago and said that Scotty is walking with the aid of two sticks for a few hours a day. He's definitely making progress."

I shook my head knowing Scotty was lucky to be alive after everything that happened to him.

"I am so glad he's making progress. Can you ask Scotty to call me if you speak to him? I'd love to hear from him. I'd like to see him and meet Penny now that I am back in town. I wonder if he and Penny would welcome a visit."

"Definitely," Cassie replied, "I'm sure Scotty would love to see you."

Joe Binder wandered into the kitchen looking all kinds of cool. His maroon tie was loose and slightly askew, and I noticed he was wearing white, high-top sneakers with his gray suit. Joe grabbed a shrimp puff from one of the prep trays and popped it into his mouth, "I wondered where you three disappeared to." He sidled up to me and kissed my cheek, "Congratulations on the happy news, Char. I can't wait to be an unofficial uncle."

I turned to look up at my husband, "A secret, huh? Who else have you told?"

David's face flushed, and he chuckled. Both of us were guilty of sharing our secrets.

"I may have spilled the beans to Gary. He asked me *what was new*, and I just gushed. Your dad yipped so loud that Brian Gold asked him if he'd hurt himself. Can I help it if your dad told Brian our news? I huddled with the two of them and told them the pregnancy is our secret. They understood."

"Then how did Joe find out?" I asked, skeptical.

Joe smiled, "Brian told me, but I swear, he made me take an oath of silence. I guessed that you'd already told Cassie."

"So, my dad and Brian now know. Joe and Cassie know. What about Momzilla?" I asked David.

TROUBLE BREWING

Sure, my mom would be happy—she desperately wants to be a grandmother while she's still young(ish.) I knew that if I told my mom about the pregnancy, she would insist on giving us baby advice. I wouldn't have a moment's peace. I'm sure I'll eventually appreciate my mother's advice and help, but it was too soon.

"So far, Gary and Brian haven't spilled the beans—except to Joe. We should tell Patty our news by Christmas," David suggested, "She will feel left out if we hold out on her."

I exhaled. *Christmas.* That would buy me a couple of weeks of peace. I laid my hand on my tummy—I wasn't really showing yet. I was nervous about the pregnancy before we told our friends. I was more nervous now that they knew. It was my first pregnancy, and I wasn't a twenty-something anymore. I wasn't old, but I was firmly in my thirties, and David was in his forties. My nerves were going to keep me planted in Spruce Grove until after our baby was born.

FIFTEEN

About Seven Months Later

"The reporter on my favorite news site said that Mick Flint—or whatever his real name is—would serve two back-to-back life sentences without a chance for parole," Cassie said, "It only took a few hours for the jury to reach the verdict."

"Hallelujah!" I said, but the words fell out of my mouth limply. I was exhausted.

"That was my thought." Cassie smiled, but her smile didn't reach her eyes, "How are you feeling?"

I lifted my arm a bit, mindful of the dripline that still clung to my forearm, "I've felt better," I admitted.

"I always knew that births were difficult, but someone should have warned me. I was not prepared for reality. I vaguely remember damning David to Hell in the delivery room. He chuckled as usual. David is used to my moods."

Cassie shook her head, "honestly, having Max was hard enough. Why do you think Joe and I only have one kid? What you went through—eek!" Cassie trembled at the memory.

"I don't think it would have been so bad if I'd stayed out of the courtroom as David suggested. The doctors said that stress may have been a factor in what happened to me. I just wanted to be there for the entire trial. I wish I'd been there to see the jury read their verdict. I wish I'd seen Mick Flint's face."

"You were there when you needed to be, Char. Your testimony and Scotty's were pivotal in the case," Cassie said as she lightly grasped my hand, "I am so proud of both of you."

"Me too, I guess. Is it wrong of me to wish that Mick got the death sentence for what he did?"

Cassie squeezed my hand, "Everyone is entitled to their opinion, Char. After what you went through—and the countless people whom I *believe* Mick Flint hurt—I can't fault you for feeling that way."

Mick Flint would be imprisoned for a long-long time. Knowing that comforted me. Still, I wished that he was no longer alive.

"Where are those adorable babies?" Cassie asked as she jumped out of the chair that she sat in. I was grateful that she changed the subject. The less I thought about Mick Flint and everything that happened, the better.

"The nurses will bring them soon. I have to bottle-feed the twins for now," I replied. "With everything that's happened and the medications I am on, I guess the twins will be on formula for a while. I have to get all of the anesthesia and medications out of my system before I can even consider pumping," I shook my head and grimaced. "That is a word that I never imagined myself saying. *Pumping*."

About a week before, I'd collapsed at Mick Flint's trial—after I'd given my testimony. God or whatever higher power you believe in was merciful because I don't remember much of what happened next. I *do* remember Brian Gold rushing to my side. David clamored to see me. There was a lot of blood too. I was terrified.

I couldn't blame my condition on vasovagal syndrome. A problem with the babies I carried caused me to collapse.

I was rushed to the hospital after I fainted, and the twins, Nick and Nora, were delivered through an emergency Cesarian Section. David was so worried about me that he didn't even argue about their names.

"*For goodness sakes, Charlotte*," my mother had said upon hearing Nicky and Nora's names, "*If you were going to name the twins after a detective duo, couldn't you have chosen Freddie and Flossie after the Bobbsey Twins?*" Then she took one look at the twins and forgot about the origin of her grandchildren's names—a married couple in the Hammett novels.

My mom was smitten with the little pink-faced babies.

TROUBLE BREWING

Had I been strong enough at the time, I would have said, *"Flossie, Mom? Really?"*

"Here we are," a friendly nurse named Mary entered my hospital room. She pushed a cart that carried the twins.

"How are they?" I asked. I lifted myself to have a look.

"Right as rain!" Mary replied with an Irish-sounding lilt. She directed her attention to my best friend, "You must be the famous Cassandra I've heard all about."

"I don't know about *famous*," Cassie replied as she stood to take a peek at her godchildren.

In a somewhat unorthodox move, I'd named Cassie as the godmother of the twins and Brian Gold as their godfather. Joe didn't seem to mind being dissed for the position. If it hadn't been for Brian's quick action and medical training, I might have lost the babies or my own life. Brian seemed to be the right man for the job.

"Hey, you two," Cassie whispered softly to the twins and then turned to look at me, her face beaming like a 1,000-watt bulb, "May I?"

"That's why you're here, right?" I smiled. "You need to get to know your godchildren."

Cassie lifted Nora—who wore pink—and held her gently.

"Oh, new baby smell," she whispered as she sniffed my daughter's head. "When do they get to come home?" Her question directed at Mary.

"Soon," Mary replied, "as I said, they're right as rain. We're keeping an eye on their mam though. She went through a rough patch."

Mary brought Nicky to me along with a tiny bottle so that I could feed him.

I know it's wrong to say this, but the first time I saw my son's face, I *knew* he would be my favorite. Nicky looks so much like David with his chocolate eyes and long, black eyelashes.

I could already imagine my son wearing an ugly sweater at Christmas time like his father.

Poor Nora takes after me. Eek!

I hate saying that I think I have a favorite child, but I know that Nora is the apple of David's eye. I guess it is all even-steven in the end.

I pray that both of our children inherit David's disposition, however. Lord knows that Spruce Grove doesn't need another Charlotte O'Hara-Moore!

"Come here, my Nicky," I snuggled my little boy close and offered him the bottle. I couldn't wait for the three of us to journey home together. I hate staying in hospitals.

David was at the big house making last-minute preparations. He hired a mother's helper for me—a *temporary* mother's helper—to assist us with the transition to parenthood during my recovery. I insisted that Mrs. Beavis only stay with us until I could lift both the babies myself. I didn't want any interlopers around. I know that David and I are wealthy enough to afford full-time childcare, but I want us to raise our children ourselves. I had plenty of family members available to help me too—Mom, Dad, Cassie, Joe, Max, Brian, and of course, David. My husband was staying in Spruce Grove indefinitely. When we learned we were having twins, David said his jet-setting ways were over until the twins were old enough to travel to Europe with us without causing a fuss. We will see if David keeps his promise. I see how David looks when he gets a late-night phone call. It's like Europe calls to him. And now, there's a new Moore Reach satellite office in Lisbon, and David is eager to go there.

"*Eh-hem*," someone in the doorway drew our attention.

It was Brian Gold wearing his policeman's uniform and carrying two stuffed animals—a pink unicorn and a blue dragon. He brought gifts for the twins all week.

"Do you have time for the *Godfather*?" He asked with a phony gangster accent as he rubbed his chin like the guy in the movie.

Brian started making Godfather jokes the minute I'd ask him to be my children's moral guide.

TROUBLE BREWING

"I'll just make myself scarce," Mary told me. She was already used to me breaking the rule about the number of visitors in my room.

"Just press the button if you need assistance, Mrs. O'Hara-Moore." Mary smiled widely at Brian as she floated out of the room. They traded flirty looks every time Brian visited.

Brian set the animals on my tray table and nodded at Cassie.

"She's cute," Cassie said. She handed Nora off to Brian with enviable ease.

I hoped I would be as comfortable picking up and setting down my babies as Cassie was. I treated Nicky and Nora like they were made of thin glass.

"She's adorable," Brian replied. He turned his baseball-style hat backward and smiled down at Nora.

"I meant the nurse," Cassie said, "Is there something between you? I see how Mary eyes you like a sour cream donut."

"Nah." Brian ran a finger down Nora's face, "We're just two public servants being polite to each other."

"I don't know about that," Cassie replied, "There wasn't anything polite in the look Mary gave you. Her eyes were smoldering. I could find out if she's single."

"No thanks; I'm good." Brian's voice was soft and friendly, but I could tell he was more interested in visiting his godchildren than chatting up a pretty nurse.

"Okay." Cassie shrugged and gazed at me, "May I see Nicky now?"

"Sure," I reluctantly replied as Cassie came and scooped up my little boy.

"I can't help it," Cassie said, "I'm a bit jealous that you have a boy and a girl."

"Yeah, now that you have one of each, you're set," Brian said without looking up. He dangled the pink unicorn over Nora. The newborn didn't seem to notice it.

"What's that supposed to mean?" Cassie replied for both of us.

"Huh? Nothing. I meant that you have a boy *and* a girl—one of each; you don't need more kids," Brian shrugged, "You are set."

"Uh, okay," Cassie glanced my way. I could tell she was trying to gauge my level of fury, but it wasn't fury that I felt.

"Honestly?" I said, sitting back, "I'm with Brian on this one. After everything that I went through? I think two kids are enough. Anyway, there's a good chance that I can't have any more babies—at least if Dr. Flynn told me is right. It is unlikely I can carry another pregnancy to term—that's if I can still get pregnant. Ugh! I am sorry; that was too much information."

"Oh my gosh, Char," Cassie's eyes grew larger, "I had no idea; I am so sorry."

"I am sorry too," Brian added, "I shouldn't have said that thing about being set. That was insensitive of me."

I shook my head, "I'm still wrapping my head around the news. It is what it is," I felt tears burning in my eyes, but I was determined not to cry. "I'll have to spoil these two rotten. If David and I decide that we want more kids, there's always adoption."

"Good plan," Brian said as he carried my daughter to me and handed her off, "And anyway, you can't top perfection. These two are perfect. I ought to know; I'm *the Godfather*."

Cassie rolled her eyes, and Brian straightened his police hat.

"Are you leaving already?" I asked, noting his hat.

"Sorry, yeah. I wish I could stay longer, but duty calls." Brian took a deep breath.

I could tell by the expression on his face that there was something Brian was trying to work through. I had the feeling that he was deciding whether he should tell me what he was thinking.

"Char?"

"Yes?" I asked as Brian balanced himself against my hospital bed.

"Mick Flint is being transferred to the Federal prison today. I volunteered to be part of the transport security detail. I want to make sure that Mick Flint is behind bars. I figure it is the least I can do given everything that happened," Brian's eyes met mine.

"I understand, but Brian, you don't have to make amends to me—if that's what you think. You did everything you could, and you saved *my* life—more than once," I said to him.

"I need to do this," Brian replied.

He removed his hat before he leaned forward and kissed my cheek, "I'm *the Godfather* now. I need to keep all of my loved ones safe."

Brian touched Nora's cheek before he placed the policeman's hat back on his head. He nodded to Cassie, smiled at Nicky, and went out the door.

"Stay safe, Brian," Cassie called after him.

When Brian was gone, Cassie turned to me. Her voice was low, "I didn't know that Brian was providing security today. I didn't even know that Mick Flint was being transferred today. If I'd known, I would have told you."

"It's okay, Cass. The earth will keep on spinning."

I pressed the button to call the nurse back. I was tired, and the twins were flailing their tiny arms.

"Now that you know about the transfer," Cassie continued, "I feel I should tell you what I *do* know. There have been threats—against Mick Flint—mostly from a local group who think Flint should get the death penalty. The group started making a fuss when they learned the verdict. They picketed outside the jail and called threats into the DA's office. I guess they are keeping the transfer quiet for safety reasons." Cassie's head turned toward the door, and she stopped speaking.

My bestie's excellent hearing and protective instincts sometimes remind me of a Cocker Spaniel. Cassie is friendly and playful but always alert when looking after her friends and family.

Mary walked into the room and took Nora and Nicky. She placed them back into their carrier and wheeled them from the room. The twins were close to full-term but slightly underweight and got extra attention while in the hospital.

"Anyway, I didn't know that Brian volunteered to help with the transport detail," Cassie said.

"You don't think Brian is in danger, do you?" I asked.

Cassie certainly seemed concerned for our friend.

"I hope not," Cassie replied, "I trust Brian to know what he is doing, but that group I mentioned? They are a local branch of an underground group that claims to act in the interest of victims of violent crimes. I researched the group, Char, and they use violence to end violence."

"Oh, that's awful," I shook my head. I wasn't surprised though. It wasn't the first group to do such things.

"It is." Cassie looked around the room uneasily, "When is David returning?"

"Oh, around dinner time, I think. I asked David to make dumplings for me tonight," I replied.

The hospital food was marginal at best, and David was happy to oblige me by bringing me my favorite foods.

"Honestly, David was making me a bit anxious. I know how bad that sounds, but he was lingering and asking the nurses so many questions. I convinced him to go home and check the new alarm system and help Mrs. Beavis settle. That should take a while."

Cassie laughed and shook her head, "I should get going. I need to cook dinner for my pack." She walked across the room and hugged me, "I am glad you're doing better. I think you might even have some color in your face again."

"It's the potassium supplement they're giving me," I said, "I can't wait to stop taking it. I feel flushed all the time."

"You do what the doctors tell you, okay? I don't want to hear that you collapsed again."

"Aye-aye, Captain," I replied with a salute.

TROUBLE BREWING

Cassie smiled, "And Char, I am sorry about the bad news. David didn't tell me what Dr. Flynn said."

"It's okay, Cass. Right now, I need to focus on Nora and Nicky. As Brian said, they're perfect, and they're enough."

"I'll see you tomorrow," Cassie hugged me again, "and I'll say a prayer tonight that you and the twins can go home soon."

"Thanks, Cass."

I must have napped after Cassie left me. I slept through my usual dinner hour of 6 PM.

When I awakened, I could see the sky outside was inky black, and my tummy was rumbling.

David hadn't arrived earlier—if he had arrived, he hadn't awakened me.

I glanced at my cell phone. It was plugged into its charger since I'd been in the hospital. *No new messages.*

Where was David?

Just as I was about to call the nurse's station to see if they'd seen my husband, someone knocked on the door jam.

David stood on the threshold clutching a bouquet of colorful daisies, smiling at me, "Hey," his chocolate-brown eyes caught mine.

"Hey," I replied. I was a bit disappointed that not only was David late, but aside from the daisies he brought, he was empty-handed.

David walked to me, set the flowers on my tray table, and leaned in to kiss me. His breath smelled of cheap Scotch covered by mouthwash.

"Where have *you* been?" I asked, "Have you been drinking?" I didn't even try to hide the disappointment I felt.

"Char, yeah, I had one drink. I'm sorry." David sat in the chair by my bed. He appeared tired and sullen.

"David, what's going on? Is something the matter?"

"Char, I don't know how to tell you this," David replied.

"What? What happened?"

"Mick Flint was transferred out of the county jail this afternoon," David told me. His face remained stoic.

"I know. Brian Gold came by to tell me."

"Char, the caravan had only crossed the county line," David said as he reached for my hand. His large, tanned hand swallowed my pink one.

"What happened, David? You're scaring me."

"There was a sniper or a group of snipers," David shook his head like he was trying to make sense of his words. "They barricaded the road and opened fire on the bus that carried Flint and some other prisoners." David stopped speaking and swallowed hard. "There were volunteers from Spruce Grove on the transfer van."

Oh my God! Brian volunteered to be part of the transfer.

"Brian?" My voice was a squeak. My heart banged against my ribcage.

David shook his head, "Brian was in a cruiser following the bus. Brian helped to end the shootout. He is okay."

"Thank God!" I replied. I wouldn't hide my relief. Brian was alive!

"Char, there were other police officers and guards on the bus—they anticipated trouble."

"Cassie told me about the threats. Were there many injuries?"

"Three prison guards were shot; one is in bad shape. Mick Flint is dead."

"I'm sorry about the guards, but I won't pretend to cry over Mick Flint," I replied.

"Char, one of the police officers was hurt too. He was hurt badly. I'm sorry I have to tell you this."

"David, who was it?" I asked.

Desperation clutched my heart. I knew several of the Spruce Grove police officers.

TROUBLE BREWING

David's face pinkened. His brow wrinkled, and I noticed the darkness under David's eyes. Then I knew what David was having difficulty saying.

"*Uncle Mark?*" I guessed as tears rolled down my face like rain.

David didn't need to reply. He wrapped me in a tight hug.

When I pulled away, still shaking, I asked David one question. "Is he alive?"

He nodded. "But…"

"David?"

My husband shook his head. Over the past couple of years, David and Mark had grown close. They didn't start as friends, but I knew that friendship and respect now resided where distrust and fear once lived.

"Charlotte!"

My mother slid into the room with Dad close behind her.

David stepped back so that Patty O'Hara could hug her only daughter. Mark is my maternal uncle—my mother's only brother.

"Mom, have you seen Uncle Mark?" I asked her as she pulled away so my dad could hug me too.

"No, Charlotte, he's in surgery now," Mom dabbed the corners of her eyes with a tissue, "Sarah's waiting outside the surgery unit for us. I wanted to check on you before we join her, in case you heard what happened on television or something."

"David told me; just before you arrived," I nodded at David to get his attention.

I used my eyes to guide him to where my bathrobe hung near the small attached bathroom.

"I'm going with you," I told my mom. "To sit vigil with all of you."

If I expected an argument from anyone in my family, I didn't get one. David brought me my robe and a wheelchair.

The four of us proceeded through the maze of chilly hospital corridors until we reached the surgical department.

We arrived to find the place wall to wall with men and women uniformed in blue. Police officers—from Spruce Grove and nearby police departments too—waited to hear about Uncle Mark.

Sarah's two best friends were at her sides, each holding one of her hands.

I felt a warm hand on my shoulder and stared up to see red-rimmed, sea-blue eyes.

"Brian," I whispered, "I'm sorry." Mark was my uncle, but for Brian, Mark Wright was like a father. His own parents never treated Brian very well. Mark filled the gaps.

"Char. Mark will to pull through. He has to," Brian whispered back before he removed his hand from my shoulder and turned to face the wall behind us. His shoulders heaved, and my heart clenched again.

Hours later, a lone surgeon walked through the swinging doors of the surgery. I wondered if the surgeon felt he reached celebrity status when the dozens of cops surrounded him. The first responders sought an update on their fallen comrade.

That was when it hit me, Sarah was Mark's fiancé—not his wife. I wasn't sure how much the doctors could or would tell her about Mark's condition. My mother was Uncle Mark's closest relative. Mom stepped up to hear the surgeon's report.

"He's made it through surgery." I heard the doctor say.

Lost lots of blood. Long recovery. Early retirement? Donate blood.

The cops clapped the doctor on his back like they would if he'd just run a successful Hail Mary. The surgeon left, and everyone quieted down. The solemn wait continued.

I was released from the hospital the following afternoon.

TROUBLE BREWING

Mark remained in the hospital for weeks. He lived, but Mark's recovery would take months.

I didn't return to the house I shared with David—there were too many stairs. Besides, I wanted to be closer to my mother—to offer whatever support to her that I could. David, the babies, and I gave Mrs. Beavis paid time off, and we moved into the cottage next door to my parents. We opened the sleeper sofa in the family room, and the four of us camped out together while I healed and trekked back and forth to the hospital with my family.

We learned that Uncle Mark would live, but he would retire. Brian Gold was the Spruce Grove officer with the most seniority. Brian was named Acting Chief of Police until a new Chief was appointed. I hoped, however, that Brian would get the post—he'd earned it, and it seemed like the right decision.

EPILOGUE

On a dreary afternoon, three months after Nick and Nora were born, my mother and I left the twins in David's care. My husband never refused to look after the twins. He enjoys every single minute he spends with them. Nicky and Nora are growing fast, and David doesn't want to miss a thing.

Mom and I drove to County Hospital to visit Mark at Sarah's request. Over time, my future aunt gained the trust of the hospital staff. Sarah spent many hours at Mark's side, despite the couple's *unmarried* status. It didn't matter that the two were unmarried. The bond between Mark and Sarah was as obvious as the 4mm sapphire stud in my nose.

The antiseptic scents of the hospital cleaning products and chlorine wafted over me as we approached the room where Sarah said she'd meet us. To this day, those odors cause my heart to race.

I knew that the drafty, older wing on the hospital's first floor was where patients completed physical therapy. I hoped that Sarah's mysterious invitation was for us to witness my uncle taking his first steps since the shooting that nearly killed him.

The sign on the door said 2E, "This is it," I said to Mom as I pressed the door handle to let us inside.

The room was huge—like a gymnasium—and it contained various apparatus that I imagined helped patients regain their independence. I saw the source of the chlorine odor—a small swimming pool was at one end of the room with a hot tub next to it.

"Charlotte, over there," my mother said and smiled. She redirected my attention to the opposite side of the room.

I was surprised at what I saw in the far corner.

Stretchy gold streamers hung from every available surface, and colorful balloons clung to the walls.

My dad and Brian Gold stood stiffly in their best dark suits on either side of my uncle.

Mom and I stepped forward to join them.

Mark sat upright in a wheelchair. He wore a dark suit, and a rare smile illuminated my uncle's face.

"What's happening?" I asked my mother, and she pressed her index finger to her smiling lips and shushed me.

Brian pulled his Smartphone from his jacket pocket. He pressed a button on the phone.

Suddenly, *Pachelbel's Cannon in C* played.

Sarah Payne, dressed in a slim, ivory silk gown and sensible ivory heels, entered the room from a door behind me that I hadn't noticed before. Sarah's heels clicked against the hard floor, and she clung to a bouquet of delicate, white roses. She smiled at all of us and approached the men.

Oh my gosh, this was a wedding!

Uncle Mark and Sarah were finally getting married, and they'd invited me to witness it. What surprised me more than the seemingly impromptu wedding was Brian—who I'd *assumed* was there to serve as Uncle Mark's best man. I was wrong.

When Sarah reached the men, Brian turned the music off and faced us.

"If you haven't already guessed, we gathered here to witness the marriage of Mark Robert Wright and Sarah Louise Fellowes-Payne," Brian paused and smiled. "The bride and groom asked me to keep the ceremony short—and I'll honor their wishes. Before the couple starts exchanging vows, I'd like to say *it's about time!*"

We all laughed.

Brian continued, "Mark, do you take Sarah as your *lawfully* wedded wife? To have and to hold from this day forward until death parts you?"

"I do," Mark said, his voice raspy, "And you're right, son, it *is* about time. I am so sorry to have made you wait, Sarah. Death nearly *did* part us, but you've been at my side every day since. I can't think of anyone I'd rather spend the rest of my life with."

TROUBLE BREWING

Sarah wiped a tear from her eye.

"Sorry, Brian, I didn't mean to ramble like that," Mark said as he reached for Sarah's hand and held it.

"No problem, that was better than what I was going to say anyway," Brian replied with a chuckle. He drew a long breath and then exhaled as he turned to face Sarah.

"Sarah, do you take Mark as your *lawfully* wedded husband, to have and to hold, from this day forward until death parts you?"

"I do, and Mark, I promise I won't let you out of my sight," Sarah answered.

"Gary, do you have the rings?" Brian addressed my father.

"Nearly sixty years old, and I'm a ring-bearer," my dad quipped. He reached into his jacket pocket and withdrew two bands of gold. Dad handed the rings to Brian.

Brian cleared his throat.

"There is a passage on the website where I was ordained that speaks to the symbology of the rings. I didn't memorize the passage, but I will give you my take on it. The rings represent a circle—an unbroken line. Infinity. The rings are symbolic for the hope of eternal love and a shared future for the couple. Like the infinite shape of the ring, may your love be never-ending."

"Nicely done, son," my dad said.

Brian handed a ring to Mark and one to Sarah.

"Mark, place the ring on Sarah's finger, and repeat after me: with this ring, I thee wed."

Mark cleared his throat and slipped the ring onto his bride's finger, "With this ring, I thee wed."

"Sarah," Brian said, "Please place the ring..."

Sarah stopped Brian.

"With this ring, I thee wed. Finally!" She laughed, leaned forward, and slipped the ring onto Mark's finger.

We all laughed again, and Brian shook his head.

"Then, through the power vested in me through the internet site *Marry Me Now*, I pronounce you husband and wife. Truthfully, you two have lived together so long that you might already be married in at least a few states," Brian joked.

Sarah leaned down so she could kiss Mark. When they pulled away—after what seemed like an eternity to me (*Mark is my uncle, for cripes sake*)—the couple was beaming.

We all applauded and shouted *congratulations* to the newlyweds.

The wedding party dispersed quickly because Mark had a physical therapy session scheduled in an hour. Mom went home with my dad and left her vehicle with me. Brian and I met up at Magic Beans. We sat in our favorite booth in the back of the cozy coffee shop. Brian had his usual large, black coffee. I had peppermint tea.

"You certainly know how to keep a secret," I said to Brian with a wink. In the past, Brian had always dropped me hints about the criminal cases he was investigating, but he hadn't said a word about the wedding.

"I *do* have some self-control, Char," Brian smiled back at me. He was still wearing his suit, and he looked handsome. I imagined that many of the coffee shop's customers were eyeing him and wondering what he was doing with a dowdy woman with messy hair, jeans, and a rumpled t-shirt. No one told me I was going to a wedding, remember?

"I have plenty of secrets that I haven't shared with you yet," Brian teased.

"Such as?" I leaned in.

"Not this time, Charlotte O'Hara." Brian playfully wagged a finger at me. "Somethings are better when you wait for them."

I didn't correct Brian for leaving the *Moore* out of my name.

"So, do you think the search committee will appoint you as the next Chief of Police?" I asked. Maybe that was the secret Brian was alluding to.

TROUBLE BREWING

"The odds are good. I'm not happy that Chief Wright was forced to retire, but I welcome the appointment if the committee decides to make me Chief."

Brian sipped his coffee before he spoke again.

"There are a few folks on the committee who want to appoint someone new—with more leadership experience. I guess I'll just have to wait and see. In the meantime, Chief Wright promised he will stay as a special consultant to the police force as long as I need him."

"That's if Sarah lets him," I corrected. "For the record, I think you will make an excellent Chief."

"Thanks," Brian took another sip of his coffee, then set the cup down. He shook his head and grinned.

"It's weird, isn't it?" He asked.

"What's weird?"

"All the changes over the past year or two. You are married and have two kids. You have a second home in Italy. Cassie and Joe are talking about opening a second Magic Beans location with a liquor license so they can serve local beers—that's a secret, by the way. Chief Wright and Sarah are married, and he is retiring from the police force. This feels like the end of an era," Brian said. He let out a woeful sigh.

I reached for my second-oldest friend's hand, "Or, it's the beginning of a new era."

The End

FOX PRINTS ICE CREAM

Try Charlotte O'Hara's favorite ice cream at home!
Makes 4 cups
Ingredients:
Ice Cream:
1 ½ cups milk
1 ½ cups heavy cream
¾ cup malted milk powder
3 large egg yolks
½ cup granulated sugar
¼ cup brown sugar
¼ tsp xanthan gum or corn starch
1 Tablespoon pure vanilla extract
Mix-ins:
1 Butterfinger bar, crushed
1/3 cup butterscotch chips
Chocolate syrup, to taste

Instructions:

Freeze the bowl of an ice cream maker according to the manufacturer's instructions.

Place the milk, cream, and malted milk powder in a 2-qt saucepan set over medium heat and bring to a simmer.

While the milk mixture is heating, whisk together the egg yolks, sugars and xanthan gum in a heatproof bowl. Slowly add the heated milk, whisking constantly. Place a strainer over the saucepan and pour the cream mixture through it back into the pan.

Reduce the heat to low and cook the mixture until it thickens slightly and steam begins to come from the top. Remove from the heat, stir in the vanilla, and chill the mixture in the refrigerator. Stir occasionally so that film won't form on top.

To Freeze: Transfer the chilled mixture to the ice cream maker and freeze according to the manufacturer's instructions. Once the mixture begins to set, stir in the chips and candy bar pieces for the last 3-4 churns of the machine to blend.

Transfer the ice cream to an airtight container and freeze for at least 2 hours.

Top with chocolate syrup and serve.

Don't miss out!

Visit the website below and you can sign up to receive emails whenever B. Allison Miller publishes a new book. There's no charge and no obligation.

https://books2read.com/r/B-A-OUKM-VYRCC

BOOKS2READ

Connecting independent readers to independent writers.

Also by B. Allison Miller

Spruce Grove Cozy Mysteries
5 Days 'til Christmas
The Boisterous Bridesmaids
An Open Book
The Vigilante Valentine
Trouble Brewing

Watch for more at sprucegrovearoundthetown.infinityfreeapp.com.

About the Author

B. Allison Miller is the author of the cozy mystery series "Spruce Grove Cozy Mysteries," featuring witty amateur sleuth, Charlotte O'Hara, a blogger/barista/farmer who lives in a guest cottage on her parents' Christmas tree farm. Meet Charlotte and her friends in '5 Days 'til Christmas,' the first book in the in the Spruce Grove Cozy Mystery series.

Allison lives in scenic Colorado. When she isn't plotting a murder, Allison can be found hiking, playing with her dogs, or experimenting with recipes in her cozy kitchen.

Read more at sprucegrovearoundthetown.infinityfreeapp.com.

www.ingramcontent.com/pod-product-compliance
Lightning Source LLC
LaVergne TN
LVHW010237100125
800962LV00023B/323